A War For Love

Legacy of Light Book 3

M. Lynn and Michelle Bryan

Cover by Melissa A Craven
Editing by Melissa Craven

For all those who fight for what they believe in.

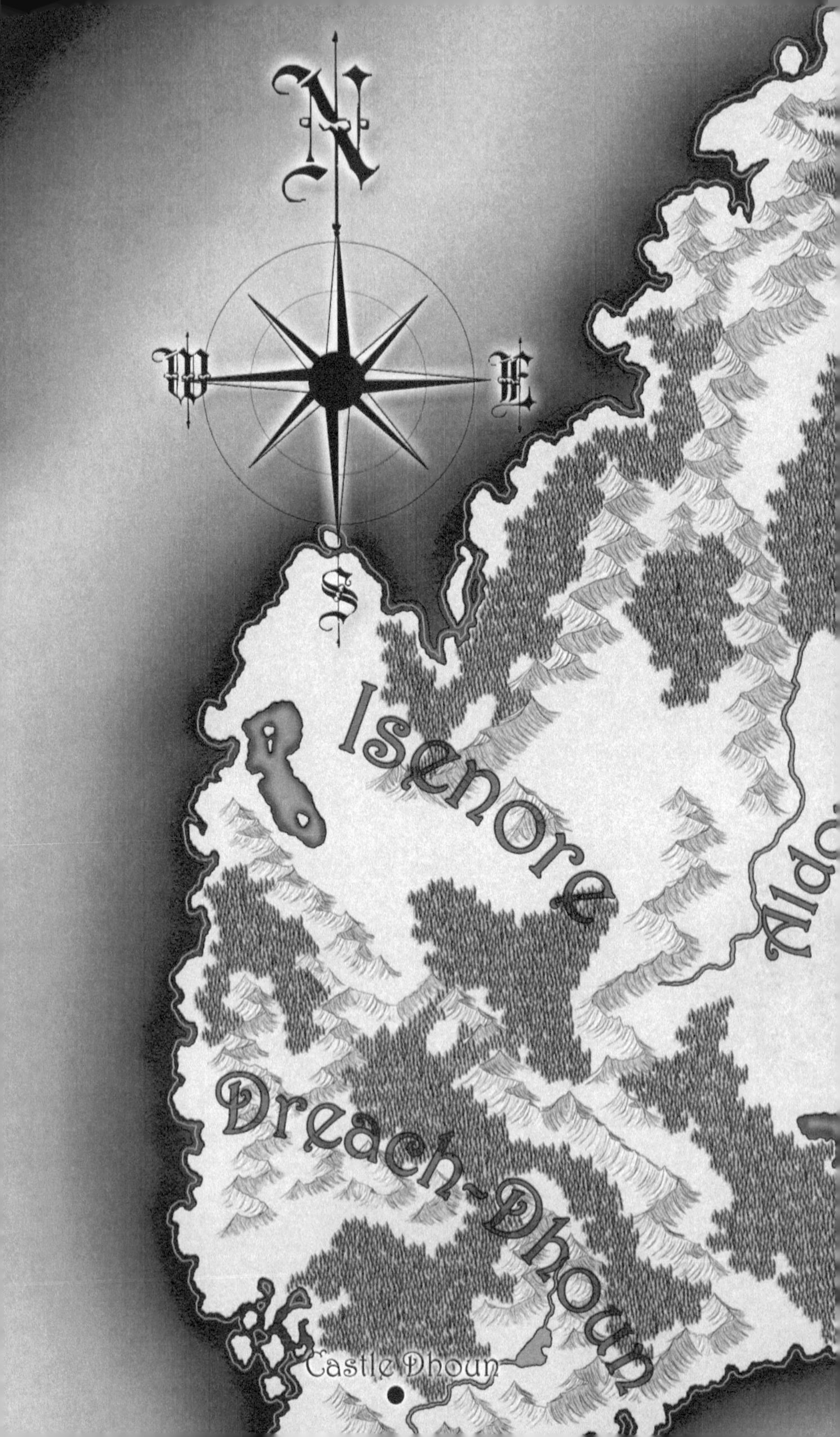
N
W
E
S
Isenore
Dreach-Dhoun
Castle Dhoun

reach-Sciene
Palace of Sciene
The Sea of Uisce
hitecap
Isle of Sona

They were coming.

The only thing louder than the horse's hooves beating into the packed dirt of the forest path was the pounding of Trystan's heart as he ran. A branch whipped him in the face, sending a sting of pain across his cheek. But he didn't slow.

He veered off the path where the horses could no longer follow him and ducked behind the mossy base of a tree, colliding with someone as he came to a stop.

His hands flew out, and he gripped his sister's shoulders, hauling her to the pine-covered ground where they hid from the men on horseback.

"Dammit, Ri." He rolled off her as soon as their pursuers were gone. "I told you to stay with the others."

She set her jaw and jumped to her feet. "Since when do I obey you?"

Never. That was the answer. She'd never listened to him.

He shook his head and ran a trembling hand through his sweat-soaked hair. "You could have been seen."

"So could you."

He let out an irritated breath, turning to walk back into the woods with its canopy of red and gold leaves. He'd left the rest of the group hidden off the main path, Ri included. He should have known she wouldn't listen, but that did little to ease his annoyance. They were so close to home now, but if they were caught, it would have all been for nothing.

Rissa's shoulders dropped. "I was worried about you. It's getting dark and you've been gone a while."

He couldn't fight with his sister any longer, so he swung an arm over her shoulder. "That was the third group of Isenore soldiers we've seen in these woods. We can't be more than half a day's ride from the palace. They've grown bold."

"We'll be safe behind the palace walls by tomorrow."

"Safe." Safety was an illusion. With Calis sitting across the border and Eisner still roaming the mountains, there was no such thing as safe in Dreach-Sciene.

"Stop," Rissa hissed.

Trystan froze, afraid even one crunch of the leaves underneath his feet would give them away. "They're coming back." He looked down at his sister's empty hands. "You followed me and didn't bring your bow?"

"I wasn't thinking about anything other than getting away without Davi seeing me."

"Next time," he said. "Think." He released her. "Come on." He took off, only glancing back once to make sure his sister followed behind. "You're prepared to use your magic?"

His sister hadn't seemed to need training in magic. She knew instinctively what to do, unlike him, but it still wasn't the first mode of protection that came to her mind.

"Yeah," she whispered.

The horses neared and the shouts from their riders grew louder. "Halt!" one ordered. "You are under arrest."

Trystan swerved and jumped over a fallen tree. His eyes flicked back over his shoulder, but Rissa wasn't there.

"Trystan," she yelled.

He reeled around and charged back the way he'd come. Four men on horseback surrounded Rissa. Trystan reached for his sword, but there was no need for his protection.

Rissa dropped to the ground and set her hands upon it. Color rose in her cheeks and a breeze blew her brilliant red hair away from her face. None of the soldiers moved in as she stood and spun, a flash of white light ripping from her hands. It struck each of them, stunning them and sending them flying from their horses.

Trystan's lips quirked up. The magic didn't touch the horses. That was his sister.

"Stop," another voice entered the fray as the rest of their group appeared, pulling up at the sight of Rissa. Eyes flicked from her to the unconscious men until finally finding Trystan.

A young man jumped from his horse and tore his helmet off, throwing it to the ground in haste. He dropped to one knee. "Your Majesty."

Trystan released a breath. "Thank the earth." He laughed as he rubbed his forehead. "Wren."

Rissa lowered her hands, her eyes scanning the green fabric stretched across their chests. "You're wearing Isenore colors." She shook her head and turned away from the men she'd hit with her power.

Wren stood quickly. "Yes, Princess. The woods of Aldorwood have been plagued by bands of Isenore soldiers. It isn't safe for travelers in Dreach-Sciene. These men have been terrorizing the villages at the edge of the forest. Our task is to hunt them." He rubbed the chest of his uniform. "No matter what we have to do to get it done."

"Oh."

Wren nodded to one of his men. "Check the injured."

"They aren't dead." Rissa bit her lip. "Only knocked out."

"I'd ask how you have mastered control of your magic, Princess, but it's the Tenelach, isn't it?" Wren asked.

Rissa nodded.

"We need to get the others." Trystan walked forward. "I'd like to return to the palace as soon as possible. Wren, come with us. Have your men load up the injured and be ready to leave when we return."

Wren jerked his head toward one of his men in silent order before following the king and princess.

There was a beat of silence before Wren spoke again. "I didn't imagine you'd actually do it, your Majesty. Bring us back to magic."

"Thank you for your faith." Trystan pressed his lips together. They'd all had the same notion at some point in their journey. And they'd all been wrong.

A heavy hand landed on Trystan's shoulder and he looked sideways at Wren. As the prince and then now king, he wasn't used to this level of familiarity from anyone besides Davi. He didn't brush him off.

Wren stopped moving and forced Trystan to stand still. "Thank you, your Majesty. You'll be hearing that a lot, but I had to say it. And you, Princess."

Davi's words entered Trystan's mind as they had each night on their trek home. Wren shouldn't be thanking him. He'd done exactly as Calis wanted. He'd opened Dreach-Sciene to a magical war they probably had no chance of winning.

They reached the spot among the vibrant trees where they'd left the others and Davi ran toward them, stopping directly in front of Rissa.

Neither of them spoke. They'd struggled to say much of anything to each other lately. But their eyes held everything they couldn't say. Rissa's shone with defiance and Davi's darkened with anger.

Davi tore his gaze away and turned to Trystan. "What happened? You left to make sure the path was clear and didn't return." He scanned Wren from floppy curls to dirty boots. "And you return with an Isenore man?"

"Davion, this is Wren." Trystan gestured to the man beside him. "He's… well, I guess he is an Isenore man." He rubbed the back of his neck. "But he's a part of my guard. His mother is one of the few loyal nobles in Isenore."

"Davion." Wren pursed his lips, contemplating the name. "Aren't you the guy they're all saying is dead?"

Davi grunted and turned away. "I'll prepare the horses."

Once he was gone, Trystan turned to Wren. "Long story."

"Not so long." Rissa's eyes followed Davi. "He died. Was brought back to life by his evil king father who erased all his memories. Then he tried to kill us. Brood. Brood. Brood. Here we are." She turned a harsh glare on Wren. "Any other questions?"

She turned on her heel and left to join Alixa on the other side of the group. Wren released a chuckle as he watched her stomp off. "Tough crowd."

"She's been through a lot."

"It looks like you all have."

"You have no idea."

Davi's eyes roamed the high walls before him. The palace of Dreach-Sciene hadn't changed at all, yet it was a foreign place to him. The last time he'd been there was before they set out for Sona.

He closed his eyes and sucked in a breath, willing the other images to disappear. The ones he knew were false, implanted to turn him against the place that had been his home. Chains. Prisons. He swore he could still feel the sting of fists beating into him during his captivity.

Trystan's fists.

No. It never happened.

"Davion." Ramsey nudged his horse up beside Davi. "I know this must be hard."

"You know nothing." Davi couldn't keep the resentment he felt for the man out of his voice.

"What Calis forced me to do to you was horrible. I didn't just steal your memories, I changed them. You still feel it, don't you? The anger. The hatred."

"The only person who deserves my anger is you."

"You're right. But there's a difference between someone deserving it and receiving it. Just remember, Dreach-Sciene was not your prison. They are not the ones who kept you prisoner."

"I wasn't a..." What was he going to do? Defend his father? Defend Dreach-Dhoun?

"Prisoner?" Ramsey finished for him. "There are more ways to hold a person than with chains and cages. Love can be a trap. He's your father. And a part of you still sees the Renaulds as the ones who kept you from him."

"Stop speaking as if you know me."

"You forget, young man, I have been in your mind. The only person who knows you better than yourself is me."

Davi opened his mouth to refute that, but Trystan rode up, a frown marring his face.

"A hero's return, can you believe that?" His fingers clenched around the reins. "Wren and the others in the palace want me to return as if I've just saved Dreach-Sciene."

"To them, you have." Lonara shielded her eyes against the bright morning sun. They'd ridden through the night and the palace was just beginning to wake.

Wren came galloping back toward them from the gate, a grin stretched across his face. "We're all set. They're preparing." As he spoke, a bell rang throughout the palace, piercing the air with its shrill song.

Alixa groaned. "I want a hot bath and a soft bed."

"The people need this." Avery straightened in her saddle. "They need to see their king. To thank him."

"Then can we sleep?" Alixa rubbed her eyes. "For a fortnight?"

"Sounds good to me." Ramsey yawned.

Lonara raised an eyebrow. "We have a lot of work ahead of us. Those who were too young or not born twenty years ago will have no knowledge of magic and how to use it. Some will be weak in power, but I suspect we'll have a few who must be trained to use it to fight. We have no idea how long we will have to prepare before the eventual invasion from Dreach-Dhoun, not to mention whatever will come out of Isenore."

Alixa sighed, but the rest sat in quiet resignation.

Lonara's face softened. "But there will be time for a little rest."

They waited for a signal from the gatehouse before lining up in front of the massive stone entryway. Iron gears ground together as the heavy gate lifted, revealing a courtyard packed with people.

A cheer rose into the air, reaching a crescendo as they led their horses into the enclosed square. Some waved their arms, others held flowers.

Davi hung back, letting Trystan and Rissa be the focus. What kind of reception would he receive? He had not only been presumed dead, but he was now known to be the son of their greatest enemy. He'd actively worked against Dreach-Sciene.

The crowd parted. Trystan slid from his horse and the rest followed suit. A host of stable lads appeared to take the beasts.

"Your Majesty," Lord Coille's voice boomed as he pushed through bodies to stop in front of Trystan. He bowed and when he rose, a grin split his face.

"My lord." Trystan clapped him on the shoulder. "It's good to be home."

"You did it, my king. Your father would be proud."

Davi turned away at the mention of Marcus Renauld. The king his cousin had sworn to kill. The one she'd loved instead.

And he'd still ended up dead.

Maybe Ramsey was right. Love was a trap.

"Davion." Lord Coille finally noticed him. "But…"

Davi shook the dark hair out of his eyes and faced him once again. "But I'm supposed to be dead?"

A hush fell over the crowd.

A hand slipped into Davi's and squeezed as Rissa appeared at his side.

"It's a miracle." Lady Destan's soft voice rose above the murmuring of others nearby.

Davi flicked his eyes toward her. She covered her mouth with her hand to stifle a gasp.

"Not a miracle." Bitterness tinged his words. "Magic." He

slipped his hand out of Rissa's grasp and shouldered his way through the stunned throng.

Magic had given him a lot. It brought him back to life, but all he could focus on as he ran up the steps into the palace was how much it had taken from him. He walked the halls as flashes of a different life hit him.

His breaths came heavy as he tried to forget. His feet took him to his old room without his mind telling them to. Proof he'd had a good life here. The room was as he'd left it. He'd never wanted for anything while in the Renauld household.

So why did he feel like he'd had none of it?

He sat on the corner of his bed and hung his head. Why did the false memories still control him? If Ramsey had given him the memories, why couldn't he take them away? He dug his fingers into his hair and pulled while his other hand smacked against the side of his head.

Again, he hit himself.

"You think you can beat them out?" Ramsey asked.

Davi jerked his head up to find the Tri-Gard member leaning in the doorway. Something sparked in his mind. "You. You can do it. Take them. Everything you implanted before, all the memories, they're still here."

Ramsey held his hands in front of his chest. "No. Not going to happen."

"Why not? It's bad enough I'm the dark king's son. I don't need to be questioning my own loyalty."

"Davion." Ramsey walked farther into the room. "Journeying into someone's mind is dangerous."

"You did it before."

"At the orders of someone who didn't care if I scrambled your brains."

Davi met his gaze. "Please."

"Even if there weren't the dangers, I can't. I don't have my crystal anymore."

Davi's chin dropped to his chest, and a breath rattled out of him. "Oh." He barely remembered the ceremony that returned the magic to Dreach-Sciene because he'd been preoccupied fighting Trystan. But he vaguely recalled the crystals exploding into dust seconds before magic entered the earth.

It was hopeless.

"Davion, I'm not going to lie to you."

"That would be a first."

Ramsey narrowed his eyes. "Listen, boy. You belong here, not with your father. My grandchildren need you. It will not be easy. These memories may be false, but to you they're very real. No one can change that but you. You have been freed from your father's control. What happens next is up to you. You're a smart man." He tapped the side of Davi's head. "Fight it. Fight your own mind. For them. For yourself."

Ramsey turned. "Lord Coille has graciously scheduled the welcome home feast for tomorrow. I'm off to find a bed."

When he was gone, Davi kicked off his boots, removed his traveling cloak, and laid back. He tossed and turned for what felt like ages before finally succumbing to his exhaustion. As dreams overtook him, he saw two boys running through the palace side by side with matching grins. A soldier came for them, catching the scrawny dark-haired one around the waist. The grin turn to a look of fear as he was carted away and thrown into a cell where he would be a prisoner for many years.

Davi bolted up, his eyes snapping open. Sweat dotted across his brow and he wiped it away before leaning back again. “Not real. Not real.” He repeated the words to himself until his breathing returned to normal.

Ramsey was right. He had to fight it.

Dreach-Sciene was his home and it would become so once again.

From inside the palace, it seemed to Rissa as if nothing had changed at all. Servants continued to do their duties. Guards stood stone-faced at intervals throughout the hall. None of them had forgotten Drake Renauld and his coup. That rebellion would forever mar the air of comradery that once filled the palace.

Dreach-Sciene castle had always been a busy place. Many people took up residence within those walls alongside the royal family.

And each one of them knew the princess on sight. The villages of Aldorwood, Isenore, and Sona had been different. She'd walked through the streets as anyone else did. Inconsequential. Unknown. Just a girl.

"I can feel you following me, Cor." She stopped moving but didn't turn. It might have been her imagination, but she sensed her father's steward grinning at her back.

A smiled touched her lips. The man had been with her

family since he was a young boy running messages for the king.

When he didn't speak, she blew out a breath and turned. His eyes twinkled as he watched her.

"What?" she demanded, crossing her arms over her chest.

He shook his head. "I still can't quite believe you're home."

"Is that why the staff has been avoiding me?" She quirked a brow. "They think my brother and I are some vision brought on by magic?"

"Magic is why they avoid Davion, but not you. Never you, Princess. We're all kind of worried if we blink, you'll disappear again."

She let her arms fall down to her sides. "Not this time, Cor."

He nodded.

"Trystan is ready to earn his throne and I'm..." What was she now that her brother was king? Now that they'd recovered the magic. Redundant? She didn't fit the mold of just a princess any longer.

Cor's eyes scanned the length of her. "Well, it's nice to see you looking like a princess again rather than a vagabond."

She flattened her palms against the sky-blue lace bodice of her dress. It flared out at the waist elegantly. As much as she'd rather don her travel trousers and tunic, her closet was full of clothes more fit for a princess.

Cor had always chastised her when she'd looked anything less than the perfect image of Marcus Renauld's daughter.

She shot him a scowl, but before any words left her mouth, Davi appeared at the other end of the hall. Rissa's eyes latched onto him, but he hadn't noticed her yet. Cor followed her line of sight and let out a low chuckle.

"Some things never change." His eyes held neither approval or disapproval, only a fond remembrance. He was so very different from the stern, quiet steward who'd always been at her father's side.

Davi lifted his head and his steps slowed. A maid gawked at him, but didn't near. He met Rissa's gaze and scrunched his brow.

Rissa tore her eyes away from him to face Cor once more. "And some things will never be the same." She brushed past him.

Davi had been avoiding her all day. In fact, he hadn't come near Trystan either. Solitude wasn't like him. The man she'd always known had enjoyed being the center of attention. He reveled in it. He still was, she guessed as she scowled at the servants who'd stopped to watch him, but it wasn't the kind of attention anyone wanted.

"Davion." She reached him and stopped. "You've been ducking me all day, and I don't appreciate it."

"I haven't—"

"Don't bother with your lies." She leaned in. "I know you too well for that." She turned toward their audience with ice in her eyes. "Don't you have duties to attend to? The crown doesn't pay you good gold to stand around gawking." When they didn't move, she went on. "You've all heard who Davion truly is. Leave us alone this minute or he'll use his ancestral magic on you."

That set them into motion and before long, the hallway had cleared.

Davi's jaw hung open. "I thought the aim was to let the people of Dreach-Sciene know they didn't have to fear me."

Rissa shrugged. "At least now they won't bother you."

"You know that magic doesn't run in families, right? Just because my father's is dark doesn't mean mine is."

"I know that, and they will too... once they stop wetting their trousers."

His eyes shone with amusement. "Come with me."

"Is that an order or a request?"

"Stop arguing with me for one second." He reached down to take her hand, his palm warm against hers. "It's worth it. I promise."

He tugged her forward, and she allowed him to lead her on a familiar route. It didn't take much for her to realize where they were going.

Davi pushed open the door Rissa used to escape regularly. The garden she'd known as dead and broken stretched out before them, unrecognizable in its beauty. Breath rushed into her lungs as she stepped out onto the stone path that meandered between blooming bushes and healthy trees.

"Davi," she whispered. Life zipped along her skin, the earth's call. She'd felt it in that garden before, but where it had been weak then, it now overwhelmed her.

The earth's song filled her mind and tears stung her eyes.

Davi pulled her toward the center. As a girl, she'd spent much of her time sitting beneath the bare branches of the tree that now stood before her. Instead of dry, cracked bark spanning its limbs, a new smooth, brown skin stretched toward the sky. Green vines wound up the trunk, ending where bunches of white flowers began.

"The magic." Her voice held reverence. "It's beautiful."

"Dreach-Sciene is alive again." Davi released her and stepped forward to set a hand on the base of the tree. He bowed his head and bright yellow flowers shot up the vines.

"You did that?" Rissa's eyes widened.

"No, the earth did it through me." He turned back to face her. "You saved your garden."

"I like to think we saved a lot more than one simple garden." She laughed.

"This garden represents everything you were able to do. Of course, you also brought magic back to the rest of Dreach-Sciene, but the evidence is right here, in this place."

"You speak as if you weren't with us. As if you didn't have a hand in what we accomplished." She bit her lip.

He averted his eyes, raising them toward the crystal blue sky instead. "I didn't." Sadness coated every word. "Unless you count almost destroying everything."

"Look at me, Davion."

When he didn't respond, she lunged forward and punched him in the arm. "Dammit, I said look at me."

He finally obeyed, and it was as if his eyes tore through her instead of seeing her.

"What happened to you?"

He shook his head, unwilling to answer.

"Davi, I get it, I do. I can't imagine everything you've gone through. Everything that's been done to you—"

"You're right. You can't imagine. It's not what's been done, it's what's still…" He stared down at his shaking hands.

Rissa took both of his hands between hers to still them. "I know you think we haven't gone through anything nearly as bad as you, but we lost you. Do you have any idea what…" She released him and spun so he wouldn't see the tears in her eyes. "I thought getting you back would fix it, would fix me."

A gentle hand touched her shoulder, and she covered it with her own.

"We're all so broken, Dav, don't you see that? You aren't alone." She turned, her chest bumping into his as she did. "Let me be there for you. Please. We aren't the same people who last stood beneath this tree. The kids who couldn't say how they felt. Something changed between us before…" She breathed in. "Just before."

He kept one hand on her shoulder while the other played with a curl that had fallen loose from the tail she'd tied her hair in.

"Do you know why my—Calis had to take every memory of you instead of twisting them?" His voice was only a whisper. "I remember it so clearly." He closed his eyes and leaned his forehead against hers. "You were coming back to me. The real you. They couldn't change how I felt about you."

"How you felt about me?"

"Not even Ramsey Kane and his crystal were powerful enough to steal how much I loved you."

His eyes snapped open, and she lost herself in their intensity, drowning in their depths. His hands moved to her cheeks, and she sucked in a breath moments before his lips cut off all oxygen.

Loving Davi was like walking straight through the heart of a battle. You were going to have to fight your way in and might not make it out, but in between, it was exhilarating. And if you won, there was nothing in the world you couldn't have.

As his mouth moved over hers, his words ran through her mind, bringing her back to the present. "Davi," she said against his lips.

"Mm?" He leaned in for another kiss, but she held him back.

"What did you mean?"

"What are you talking about?"

Her hands clasped his upper arms. "You said 'what was still —'" Her eyes widened. "What's going on? What's being done to you?"

Every ounce of heat retreated from his eyes. He dropped

his hands and stepped back. "You don't… no, Rissa. I can't talk about this. Not with the princess of Dreach-Sciene."

"Oh." She crossed her arms. "It's okay for you to kiss the enemy princess but not talk to her?"

"You aren't…" He shook his head. "God, Ri. Do you really think I consider you an enemy?"

"Of course not, you dolt. But, come on. You have some big secret. Even I can tell there's something actually happening in that head of yours for once. Trust me, it rocked me quite a bit to find out who your father was too, so I know it's still on your mind. Is that why you're being weird?"

"Yes… no." He put his hands on his head. "Kind of."

"Well, that clears things up."

"I'm sorry. Being back here is messing with my head."

She studied the high walls around them. "Okay. Why?" When he didn't answer, she dropped to the grass and folded her dress around her legs. Patting the spot beside her, she glanced up.

He took her invitation.

Magic flooded into Rissa's body from the earth and she wanted to sink into its warmth, but she had to focus.

"I still have them," Davi finally said. "The memories Calis twisted."

"You mean—"

"I still see flashes of Trystan and Marcus holding me prisoner? Yeah. Every time Trystan touches me, I have to throw all my power into not flinching. I have the good memories too and I can usually tell which ones are false, but…" He bowed his head. "I'm sorry. I wish I could be the Davion you remember. The one who liked nothing more than annoying you and was quick to smile. You deserve better than the version who can barely stand to be in your home. You said I've been avoiding you, Ri, but I haven't. You haven't seen me because I haven't left my room since we arrived."

"Dav." She closed her eyes briefly, letting the magic calm her. "How can you let me touch you then? If we kept you prisoner."

A tiny smile graced his lips. "It seems my father actually did a good thing when he erased you. My memories of you were never altered because they were gone. So, when I came back to myself, I only remembered you as you truly are."

"Do I have to thank him?" She smirked. "Maybe I'll send him one of my arrows as a thank you gift."

He froze at her joke.

He had to know they were going to kill his father, right? Did he want that? It occurred to her she didn't know how Davi felt about Calis after everything. The man was his father. She imagined her own becoming evil. Would it have made her love him any less?

She didn't have to guess for long because the scene during the Tri-Gard ceremony entered her mind. Both she and Trystan almost killed Davi, yet they'd still loved him.

She reached out and took his hand. "I'm sorry. I'm here, okay? I will always be here for you. Every time you get flashes of your twisted memories, come to me. But, Dav, your father is an evil man and we will stop him. Whatever it takes. If I have to kill him myself, I will. You've known him for less than a year. He is not your family. I am. Trystan is. You're more Renauld than Bearne. I need to know that you see that. Are you with us? No doubts. No second guesses."

A beat of silence passed before Davi rose to his feet and brushed off his pants. He didn't look at Rissa as he turned away. His voice carried down to her on the breeze as if the earth was aiding in Davi's decision. "I'm with you, Ri. I am always with you."

He walked away without another word.

Rissa laid back against the soft grass, the hum growing louder in her mind. As if the conversation with Davi completely drained her, she let the earth fill her up, controlling her, molding her. Strengthening each bone within her body.

When she finally went inside, magic followed her, clinging to every cell. And just like the garden she left behind, she finally knew what it felt like to be alive.

"It's amazing." Lord Coille leaned back in his chair. "We felt it. As soon as the magic returned, we all knew."

Trystan glanced between the men and women he'd assembled around the table. His most trusted advisors along with many of the soldiers he counted on. They all nodded as if they understood what Coille spoke of.

"I was ten-years-old when we lost it," Lady Destan chimed in. "Only a child, but I still remember. I called on the magic to see if I'd still remember, and it was instinctual. My body understood what to do even before my mind caught up. It sensed when to stop drawing in the power and how to release it."

"That's good." Trystan rested his hands on the table.

"Good?" Wren leaned forward. "Trystan, it's brilliant."

"Wren." Coille scowled.

Wren hid his smile behind a cough. "Sorry, your Majesty."

Trystan waved him off. "What about you, Wren? I know you were young, but…"

Color rose in Wren's cheeks. "I… uh. I haven't tried."

"Why not?"

He lowered his gaze to the table. Alixa, seated beside him, place a hand on his arm.

Wren sighed. "My only memories of magic are losing it." His eyes flicked to Lord Coille's. "When it was ripped from the earth, we all felt our connection severed. Every person in Dreach-Sciene had this tie to each other. Magic. The earth. But then we were alone."

The room deflated with his words. Those who'd been old enough to remember nodded in agreement, sadness darkening their eyes.

Wren continued. "I guess I'm afraid giving into the connection once more will bring it all back."

Lord Coille's eyes softened as they remained fixed on Wren. "Son, Dreach-Sciene will need you to be at your strongest. If we fear losing the connection to the earth, to our people again, we will. Give yourself to the magic as we were always meant to."

Trystan needed to get the meeting back on track so he cleared his throat. "It's good to know that anyone who once knew the use of magic can again, but the fact of the matter remains. Every person who was too young or not yet born will have no knowledge of this power. I am one of these people. As is Alixa here. Rissa's Tenelach connection seems to have taught her the earth's ways. And Davion… well, he's already been trained."

The room fell silent at the mention of Davi and unasked questions thickened the air.

"Your Majesty." It was Lord Coille who spoke first. "Are you sure—"

"Adrian." Trystan's jaw hardened. "If you say what I assume you're going to, I'll send you right back to Whitecap without a second thought."

"It needs to be said, sire."

Trystan heaved a breath. "No, it doesn't. Just like it didn't need to be said about Alixa." He gestured to her. "She's since proven her loyalty to Dreach-Sciene despite her lineage. Allow the same for Davi."

"There's a difference between being the runaway daughter of Lord Eisner and actually working for the king of Dreach-Dhoun."

"Where is Davion?" Wren asked. "Shouldn't he be here at your side?" Unlike Coille, Wren had no suspicion in his voice. Only curiosity.

Trystan didn't have an answer for him. Davi had been a ghost since they returned to the palace. Rather than play the role of second in command, he'd been avoiding everyone and everything.

"Be careful, your Majesty." Lord Coille pinned him with a stern look.

"Adrian." Lady Destan gave a delicate shake of her head. "If the king trusts Davi, we should as well."

Lord Coille gave a sigh but didn't say anything further. The Duchess of Sona was not someone people liked to argue with. Trystan smiled at her gratefully. She didn't return the gesture.

"Just be sure, your Majesty."

He nodded. Before anyone spoke another word, the doors to the council chamber burst open. Edric stood panting in the doorway.

"I'm sorry, your Majesty. The guards told me to enter because you'd want to hear the news I bring."

Trystan pushed his chair back and stood. "What is it, Edric?"

"Rion has returned, sire." He sucked in a breath. "And he has prisoners from Dreach-Dhoun with him."

"Prisoners?" Trystan rounded the table as the rest of those present rose as well.

"Rebels. They say they must speak with you."

Without waiting for anyone to catch up with him, Trystan strode from the room. They'd been waiting for Calis to make his move. For something to happen. The border had been too quiet.

Was this finally the beginning?

"YOU'RE TELLING me these men are defectors from Dreach-Dhoun?" Trystan couldn't decide if the men brought before him were more likely to pass out from terror or die from starvation, right in front of his eyes. Sunken cheeks and sharp shoulder bones. When had they last had a decent meal? Fear sparked in them as they stared. What other tortures had they endured along their journey?

"That is correct, your Majesty." Rion ducked his head Trystan's way. "We caught them crossing the border. Actually, we didn't catch them at all. They gave themselves up quite willingly, wanting us to bring them into Dreach-Sciene. They demanded to speak with you, sire, saying they have news of Dreach-Dhoun for your ears only."

Trystan narrowed his eyes and lifted himself out of his father's throne. His throne. He still couldn't bring himself to think of it that way. He paced back and forth across the raised dais, arms crossed, brow puckered in thought. He stopped pacing and stared down at the two men.

"Why now?"

"Sor… sorry, your Majesty?" One stammered as he twisted a dirty wool cap in his hands and stared up at Trystan with red-rimmed eyes. "I don't understand the question."

"Why have you chosen now to switch allegiance? I find the timing to be a little concerning since we've just had a run in with your king."

"This was the perfect time, sire. You've done the impossible. You brought magic back to your lands, something Calis has sworn for years you could not do. He always preached Dreach-Sciene was a dull-witted, backward kingdom that could never stand up to him or his power. That you could never reunite the three who stole your magic. But you proved him wrong. And he's gone mad with his rage. You call him our king, but we in Dreach-Dhoun call him our destroyer."

Trystan stared down at the men in puzzlement. Why would Calis act in rage when bringing magic back to Dreach-Sciene was what he truly wanted? He stopped pacing and lowered himself down to sit on the edge of the dais where his throne rested, face to face with the captors. Raising a hand, he dismissed Avery's worried "sire" at his lack of formality. He needed to sort this out.

"What's happening in Dreach-Dhoun? Tell me all."

The older man on the right wiped a weary hand across his eyes, trying to clear away exhaustion or tears. Maybe both.

"King Bearne was a hard ruler, who brought war to our lands, but he treated his people fairly. If you paid what was owed to the crown you had nothing to worry about. That all changed when his son took over. Calis Bearne is…is different.

He rules with an iron fist. Punishing anyone who dares speak a word against him, and earth help you if you don't have your taxes to pay the crown. They will take it, even in flesh if they have to. There were many of us who hated living this way. Many who wanted to leave Dreach-Dhoun, but we knew we could not seek help from Dreach-Sciene. Your magic was gone, your people starving. So we stayed. Our resentment and hatred of Calis grew. Bands of rebels formed all over the lands, trying to think of some way to oust him from the throne, but he was too powerful and too cruel. We've suffered much under him over the years, but these last few weeks have made the past pale in comparison. His cruelty has only grown. Innocent people, whole villages punished for no reason other than his twisted pleasure. Our lives mean nothing to him and his crusade to wipe out rebellion." The man's voice broke on a sob and the younger captive rested a comforting hand on his shoulder.

He squared his shoulders and continued. "Our village became a target. Although there were a few insurgents amongst us, he convinced himself the whole village was guilty. He sent his men to capture everyone in question, even the children." The man swallowed hard, locking down his tears. "The few of us who escaped made our way here to the border. Not all of us made it, his soldiers took out most. Only me and Sal here survived, but we needed to believe what we heard about you was true, your Majesty. We needed to know that you were as honorable as your father was said to be and that we could ask for your help."

Trystan hid his dismay behind a mask of calm. "My help with what?"

"In rescuing our villagers, your Majesty. Calis is trying to stop this rebellion once and for all. He has announced a mass public execution of the prisoners hoping it will scare everyone into submission. He will kill them all. Women, children, innocents that have nothing to do with any rebellion. Hundreds of people, sire. Anyone in traveling distance of the palace has been ordered to attend or suffer the same consequence. He means to drive this fear deep into our hearts. It's as if he's lost any thread of sanity he had left."

No, he's just lost his son. Trystan did not repeat that thought out loud, but deep down he knew that was the true cause of Calis' insanity.

"When is this public execution planned to take place?"

"In a fortnight." The man fell to his knees. "Please, sire, we need your help. If we do nothing, all of my people will die. My wife and children..." his voice finally broke as sobs racked his thin body, and he dropped his head into his hands. The younger man stepped forward.

"He speaks the truth, your Majesty. So many will die. Not even Calis' own family is exempt from his tyranny."

"What do you mean?"

The voice surprised everyone in the room, but none more than Trystan. Ever since their return, Davi had forgone anything to do with war talk or decision. His refusal to be involved left Trystan no doubt that his childhood friend no longer considered himself second in command. After being absent from all matters concerning Dreach-Dhoun, why was he here right now in the throne room, at this exact moment and advancing on the two captives like they were his worst enemies?

"Answer me. What do you mean not even his own family is exempt?"

The man on the floor cowered while the other stumbled away from Davi's ferociousness. Davi didn't seem to notice.

His glower encompassed both men as he hovered in impatience. "I said answer me."

"Davion," Trystan hissed, waving away the guards at Davi's back as they moved toward him. "Give them time to explain."

"Davion?" The man on the floor whispered as he stared up in dawning horror. "Prince Davion? Here? It can't be." He scrambled back to his feet as he turned to his companion. "I fear we have made a mistake in coming here, Sal. We will not find help from someone who consorts with our enemy's son."

"I assure you Davi is no enemy of mine or yours." Trystan's voice was laced with steel. "Calis has played my friend in his evil plans along with the rest of us."

"But I saw him," Sal pointed a finger Davi's way. "He was with Calis' soldiers when they took the old seer. He was leading them."

"Again, that was not the man you see before you right now. This man standing here is my most trusted friend and loyal follower." Trystan's words were rock solid, but he understood the question in Davi's eyes as their gazes met. Who was Trystan trying to convince, the two men or himself? "You have nothing to fear from him, I promise you. Now explain your earlier statement. What do you mean not even Calis' family is exempt?"

The two prisoners shuffled in uncertainty before the older man spoke up. "The younger seer, Calis' niece. She is to be executed as well, along with the villagers. Calis has announced her a traitor and said that all traitors will hang, royal blood or no."

"No." One simple word spoken so low Trystan had to strain to hear it as it fell from Davi's lips. Yet, the fear and despair echoed around the cavernous room. His shoulders slumped in defeat and Trystan's heart constricted at Davi's clear misery.

"Are you certain?" Trystan snapped at the man, and he nodded in response.

"Where is this public execution to take place?"

"Outside Dreach-Dhoun's castle grounds, sire, in the mountain valley. Already the royal builders are at work constructing the massive hangman's platform. Thousands are ordered to attend to witness the deaths. Will you help us stop it, King Trystan?"

A headache built behind Trystan's eyes as he rubbed the bridge of his nose. He contemplated in silence for a moment, feeling the questioning stares awaiting his decision. Finally, he opened his eyes and settled his gaze on Lieutenant Fields near the door.

"Fields, take these men to the barracks so they may wash and provide them clean clothes. Feed them, let them rest, but keep them under guard until I make my decision. Understand they are not prisoners, but neither are they free to roam around. I will call for them once my decision is made."

"Yes, sir."

Fields led the men away as Trystan launched himself back to his feet. After striding to his throne, he fell into the chair with a sigh. Drumming his fingers on the armrests, he stared at Davi, knowing very well they needed to talk.

"Avery, Rion, Coille, Davi, stay. The rest of you may leave."

The guards did as commanded. Only when the doors closed behind them did Davi finally speak.

"You actually need to think about this, Trystan? There is nothing to think about. We need to save Lorelai." Davi stepped closer to the dais, placing a foot on the lower step as if to join Trystan on the podium.

"How do we know if any of what they've just said is true."

"You think they lie?" Davi asked as he took another step

Trystan's way. Avery moved her body between Trystan and Davi without missing a beat, her hand falling on her sword hilt. Trystan hid his sad smile at her over protectiveness and the fact that she now felt she had to do so with Davi. "I've seen firsthand how he treats his people. Brutality and cruelty are as inherent as breathing to him. I believe him capable of anything."

"And civil unrest in his own country would explain why he has yet to invade." Coille interjected. "If bringing the magic back has given him what he wanted, why would he wait to attack? What those men have told us makes perfect sense. Rion, have any of your men at the border heard any truth behind this?"

"Yes, my lord. We have had spies report back with rumors of Calis attacking his own people. We've had no one to confirm that until now. I think those villagers speak the truth."

"As do I," Trystan agreed.

"Then what do we do about it?" Davi asked.

Trystan stared hard at his friend knowing full well he would not like his answer. "There is nothing I can do."

Davion's disbelief registered for just a moment before the anger took over and he stood taller. "What the hell does that mean? You heard what they said. Hundreds of innocent people will be slaughtered, along with my cousin."

"I heard the same as you. But I cannot leave my country, my people, when I've just returned. There is much to be done, for Calis will attack. Maybe not today or tomorrow, but he will come and I need to be here. What if this multiple execution is all a trick? A ruse to lure me away while he takes our lands?"

"I don't believe you, Trystan Renauld," Davi spat, his struggle to keep his emotions under control obvious in the deep scowl etched on his face. "You would turn your back on these people? On Lorelai who put her own life in danger to help us? The only reason she is to be executed is because of her involvement in your escape, yet you will not go to her in her hour of need?"

"Careful how you speak to our king, boy," Coille growled, but Davi ignored the warning. Trystan sent a slight nod Coille's way, a silent order to stay out of this.

"I understand what you say, friend, and my heart is heavy with this decision, but my place is with my people. I cannot risk the lives of so many for the lives of a few."

"You dare call me friend?" Davi snapped, despair now mixing with the fury. "Lorelai will be executed if we do nothing." He ran his fingers through his hair in desperation. "Trystan, you don't understand. I can't let that happen to her. I can't. I don't expect you to understand because of your father, but she was the only thing that stopped me from losing myself in Dreach-Dhoun. If it weren't for her, I don't think the Davi you all know would still even exist. Do you get that? I would not be here. So I will not abandon her. If you won't go after her, then I will."

"And if I order you not to?" Trystan asked, but he already knew the answer.

"I go anyway. You won't stop me, and you know it. I will save her or die trying."

Silence fell over the room. A silence filled with regret and remorse and lost innocence.

A sad smile lifted the corner of Trystan's mouth. "I expected no less from you. As I said, there is nothing I can do. My place is here with my people, but I will not force you to stay. I will provide you with a contingent to lead into Dreach-Dhoun to save those people and your cousin. I believe you are possibly the only one capable of doing such a thing."

Davi deflated like he expected more opposition and was not prepared for the sudden agreement. Overcoming his surprise, he bowed to Trystan.

"Thank you, your Majesty. You do me a great honor by entrusting me with your men. But if I may so request, can you not include Mistress Payne in that contingent? From the way she is glaring at me right now and gripping her sword, I'm afraid I may wake up some morning a little more acquainted with that sword than I wish to be." A spark gleamed in his eye as he smiled in relief, and for a tiny moment, Trystan thought he saw a glimpse of the old Davi. "No offense, Avery," he added.

"None taken, Davion," Avery answered, her stern facade not cracking a bit. "The truth never offends me. You should know that."

The unexpected laughter it provoked from Davi had Trystan smiling as well. It had been a long time since he'd heard that laugh.

"Please excuse me, Trystan. I have much to attend to before I leave for Dreach-Dhoun."

"Of course. Do what you must. We will meet later to discuss who will accompany you."

At Trystan's nod, Davi took his leave. They watched him walk away in silence. Just before the door shut behind his back, he threw over his shoulder, "As much as my handsomeness dictates discussion, please make sure I'm well out of earshot before you talk about me, Coille."

Trystan swallowed the laughter in his chest because he knew darn well Coille was itching to spill his disapproval of Davi and what Trystan had just promised him.

"Trystan, you can't be serious about this," Coille said as soon as the door clanged shut on Davi's back. "Can we trust him enough to send him back there with some of our men? The boy has been through a lot emotionally and mentally. I don't quite think he's ready for this."

Trystan turned to Coille, all trace of laughter now gone. "I trust Davi with my life, Coille. Always have and always will."

"Yes, well your trust of him may not be the only issue here."

Avery's worried eyes found Trystan's. "Lord Coille is right, your Majesty. You may have to order the men to escort Davion, but you won't be able to stop the one person who will insist on going. You know the princess will follow him into hell and back, with or without your permission."

Trystan sighed to himself. "I know, Avery. I'll cross that bridge with Ri when I come to it."

THE DOOR to his room crashed against the stone wall, shaking Davi's bed and rousing him from a deep sleep. He leapt to his feet and reached for the sword leaning by his bed before his mind even registered who had awakened him so rudely.

"How dare you not tell me of this, Davion?" That tone could only belong to one woman and Davi groaned as Ri marched into his room, the fire in her eyes matching the one burning in the hearth. "I had to hear that you were going back to Dreach-Dhoun from the cook of all people? *From the cook?*" She stopped in front of him, hands on hips and eyes glaring up at him in fury. He hadn't expected her to find out so soon.

He stared down at her, rubbing his chin to hide the grin threatening to erupt at her anger.

"Nice to see you too, Princess. You look lovely this evening, but isn't it long past your bedtime?"

"Don't you try to divert me with platitudes, Davion Bearne.

I hear you're leaving first thing in the morning. When were you planning on telling me?"

"Well as you pointed out, I had until the morning—"

"Don't lie to me." She pointed a slender finger in his face. "You were going to leave without even saying goodbye. Weren't you? You were going to leave me behind...again." The flames of the fire highlighted the shine in her eyes, but whether they were tears of sadness or anger, he wasn't sure. He sighed and ran a hand over his neck. This is exactly what he'd wanted to avoid.

"Ri,"

"Don't 'Ri' me," she snapped as she turned her head and blinked rapidly, trying to suppress the tears. The look on her face ripped at his heart. He reached out and grabbed her hand off her hip, lacing his fingers through hers.

"I was going to come see you to say goodbye, but I needed time to come up with the right words."

She sniffed and yanked her hand away as she spun out of his reach. "How about 'I'm stupid to even think about going back into Dreach-Dhoun, Ri? We barely escaped with our lives last time. So nope, only a moron would do that.' I'm thinking those are the exact words you need to say."

He laughed then. A full on belly-laugh. He couldn't hold it in even as she turned and glared at him once more.

"You know darn well I'm not going to say that, even if I had a choice."

She huffed in frustration as her shoulders sagged in defeat and the anger faded from her eyes. Davi pulled her closer, holding her hands to his chest. They stared at each other, lost in the grip of their swirling emotions, unsure of what to say. Finally, Davi broke the silence.

"I have to go, Ri. I don't expect you or Trystan to understand, but Lorelai saved me. She kept me from losing my sanity and becoming my father. Now I need to go save her. It's that simple."

To his surprise Rissa nodded in agreement. "I understand why you have to go."

"You do?"

She lifted a shoulder. "Nothing about you surprises me, Dav. I know you better than you know yourself. I also know you're not going to like what else I'm about to say."

His stomach knotted as he stared into the face he still could not believe he forgot. "Which is?"

"I'm going with you."

"Like hell," he growled. "I won't allow it. And sure as hell Trystan won't allow it, so get that stupid idea out of your head."

"Too late. You can argue all you want, but Trystan has already agreed. So has Ramsey. You're going to need all the help you can get and with Ramsey's crystal shattered he's no longer the all-powerful Tri-Gard. You need strength and that, my friend, comes with tenelach. Ergo me. I'm the biggest advantage you have against Calis right now. Afraid to say you're stuck with me, like it or not."

With a smug grin she pushed herself out of his grasp. "I'll see you in the morning."

An ache began low in Lorelai's back, traveling up her spine until agony spread out through her limbs. Her eyes slid open to stare into the darkness. How long had she been down there?

Every muscle screamed as she dragged her body toward the wall to sit against it.

Her magic had long since depleted, leaving weakness in its wake. She'd used what little power she had stored up during the first few days of her imprisonment to keep the cold from sinking into her bones.

Now it had taken up root in her very soul.

Did they get out? She still didn't know, but if Davi had caught Ramsey and his grandchildren, they'd be with her in the dungeons.

The only other person she'd spoken to was the pock-ridden man who brought her food twice a day. Her uncle was a man who enjoyed dealing with the prisoners himself. Ramsey had gone through a lot of torture within these walls. Yet, he hadn't come to her.

She wasn't the only prisoner. The cells stretching in each direction were full of people from the villages. Rebels, no doubt. Each time a new group came in, she asked the same question. Was there news coming out of Dreach-Sciene? Did anyone have information on the whereabouts of Ramsey Kane?

The answers never changed. The border remained quiet. Ramsey Kane hadn't appeared.

She leaned her head back against the wall.

"Lorelai." Her name came from the dark and she sat upright.

"Who is that?" she croaked.

"You're the seer?" The voice asked. "The king's niece?"

"Who are you?"

"Is it true?" She could tell it was a man's voice this time. "Has the magic returned to Dreach-Sciene?"

Lorelai closed her eyes. How was she supposed to know? She'd been trying to will a vision to come to her, but she was even too weak for that. The truth was, she had felt no trace of magic in weeks.

"I don't know," she finally said.

"Before I was taken, I met with a rebel spy who'd just come from the border. He told us the power had returned."

Tears pricked the corners of her eyes. They'd done it.

The man continued. "I just… we're probably all going to die down here. I want it to be for something good. Like you. You helped reunite the Tri-Gard."

"We're not going to die." As soon as she said the words, their falseness struck her.

"When they brought us in, we passed a structure they were building for a... a mass execution."

She squeezed her eyes shut again.

Silence stretched between them.

"I joined the rebels because of your mother."

"I'm sorry." Her voice was so quiet she wasn't sure if he'd heard her.

"I don't regret it."

The corner of her mouth tilted up. She knew what he meant. She'd never regret everything she'd done. Not killing Marcus. Trying to save her mother. Helping Ramsey.

The only thing she'd ever get sick over was betraying her cousin. Not when she aided the Renaulds in escaping. No, she'd betrayed him long before that. She'd been betraying him the entire time he'd been in Dreach-Dhoun. Watching as his memories were stolen. Lying to him about everything. Asking Ramsey to take Rissa from his mind completely.

She slid down the wall and curled up on her side.

The door to her cell opened and in walked a man Lorelai would have recognized anywhere. She'd been a young girl the last time she'd seen Briggs Villard, but the Tri-Gard never changed.

"Briggs," she whispered.

"Hello, Lorelai."

She scrambled to sit up. "What are you doing here? Has my uncle captured you as well?" She buried her face in her hands. "The Tri-Gard failed, didn't it?"

A low chuckle escaped from Briggs. "My dear, you have a fanciful imagination. The Tri-Gard fail? No. We have brought magic back to Dreach-Sciene just as your uncle wanted us to do."

"My uncle—"

"He is a masterful planner and much more patient than me. Fifteen years ago he sent you to set his plan in motion and now it's all coming to fruition."

Memories of being a teenage seer in Dreach-Sciene rushed back to her. The prophecy she'd given Marcus Renauld had been Calis' words, but it hadn't been the true purpose of her presence there. She'd been charged with delivering Davion into enemy hands. Her first betrayal.

Briggs walked farther into the cell, not stopping until his boots hit her curled legs. "Stand up," he ordered.

She struggled to get to her feet. He grabbed her arm and yanked her up with more strength than he looked like he had. He released her seconds before a wall of magic slammed into her, forcing her up against the stone face behind her.

A cry left her lips.

"Your uncle has yet to punish you, girl. He seems to think his idea of a public execution is enough. But you chose your side in all of this. Ramsey…" He spat. "Was the wrong man to align yourself with. For so long, I had to watch his grandchildren grow and not do a thing. But your uncle told me he cares about you."

His magic released her, and she slumped forward before a backhand sent her sprawling to the ground. Her lip split, flooding her mouth with the metallic taste of her own blood. She pushed herself up onto her hands and knees. His boot collided with her stomach and she collapsed, gasping for breath.

Briggs looked down on her. "Sometimes it's more satisfying letting my body do what my magic could."

"Briggs!" He froze as Calis' voice surrounded them. "I told you not to come down here."

Briggs opened his mouth to speak, but shut it before he did. Defiance sparked in his eyes.

Calis stepped into the dim light outside her cell and glared at Briggs.

"Sire," Briggs began calmly, as if speaking to a child. "We need to make an example of her."

"And we will. At the executions."

Lorelai shivered. Executions. She'd accepted her fate, but that didn't quell the terror inside her.

Briggs stepped closer to Calis and lowered his voice. "Your Majesty, Lorelai is the reason he didn't give himself over to you fully. You know the truth in my words. She twisted him. It's the only explanation for him turning against you."

Lorelai watched their faces, trying to ignore the pain rocketing through her. What were they talking about?

"Davion—"

Calis cut him off. "Leave. Now."

Briggs sent Lorelai a final glare before disappearing down the long hall.

Calis walked forward and crouched in front of her.

She waited for the blow she knew was coming.

He held his hand out in front of her and she was prepared for his magic to strike. Instead, a cloth appeared in his hand.

She flinched away when he touched the damp end to her lip.

"Lorelai." He sighed. "Let me help you. I'm sorry. Briggs never should have been allowed down here."

He held the cloth to her lip and she let out a yelp of surprise when warmth from his magic struck her skin. The blood dried up and her pain lessened to a dull ache.

"I can't heal it," he said, remorse lacing his words. "But I can help with some of your pain."

This was the uncle she'd known as a young girl. The one she'd loved so deeply her loyalty remained through everything he asked her to do, every change in him she'd witnessed.

But she couldn't let herself be drawn back to him. Not when she knew the kind of man he'd become.

"When are the executions?" she asked.

He reeled back as if she'd struck him and jumped to his feet. "Soon." He tugged at his hair. "I can't stop them."

"I didn't ask you to."

"Dammit, Lorelai." His eyes blazed into her. "When did you turn on me?"

"Not soon enough."

"Haven't I given you everything? A home. A purpose."

She shook her head and pulled her filthy braid over one shoulder. "It's not about what you give, but what you take. I've done so much bad in your name, sacrificed so much. I'm glad I get to die knowing I chose the right path at least once in my life."

He spun and slammed his palm against the wall. "You don't know the meaning of the word sacrifice."

She tilted her head to the side. There's only one sacrifice that would matter to her uncle. "Where's Davion?"

Calis let out a roar that every person in the dungeons must have heard. "Dead if he ever sets foot back in Dreach-Dhoun. I won't hesitate."

Lorelai's mind whirled. The only way Davi would choose the Renauld king over his own father was if he had his memories back. A smile spread across her lips. He was home. That was all she wanted for him. Her death would be worth it knowing that had been made right.

"It's a good thing he's too smart to return here then." She met her uncle's gaze.

"His end will have to wait for a battlefield in Dreach-Sciene." Calis' eyes hardened, but a deep sadness cracked the stone of his expression.

Lorelai pushed herself up and stood on shaky legs. "You don't want to kill him."

"Davion is now the enemy." Calis stepped back away from her.

"Uncle, what are you afraid of? Admitting you love your son?" She narrowed her eyes. "Why didn't you let Briggs rough me up? Is it because you care?"

He shook his head, but she continued.

"I have been by your side since I was young. For my entire life, I have been the only person who did not fear you. Until Davion. We loved you."

"You betrayed me."

"Even now, you can't admit you needed us."

His eyes darkened. "I have a Tri-Gard member at my disposal. The best-trained army in a century. A royal treasury bursting at the seams. And allies in every part of Dreach-Sciene. I don't need you to get what I want."

"What is it you want?"

"I will reunite Dreach-Sciene and Dreach-Dhoun as they once were."

She stumbled as she walked forward and knocked into him. When she righted herself, she looked straight into his eyes. "And you're going to do it alone."

"I just told you—"

"You have armies and allies. But all war does is destroy. It will tear you down. Who will build you back up again? Who will mourn when you lay dead in the middle of a battlefield?"

She pressed her lips into a line and leaned back against the wall to slide down to sit on the floor again.

She rested her arms on her knees and lowered her head.

"I will, uncle. And Davi, I'm assuming. Because you're family. But we won't fight for you. Not anymore." She raised her gaze. "Let me ask you this. When I dangle from your noose, will you shed a tear for me?"

His brow furrowed as he stared at her for a moment. Without answering, he turned and walked away.

She wiped at the tears that had fallen. "Maybe I was wrong. You are the monster you try to be."

He didn't hear her final words because he was already gone.

The signs of life blooming across the land enthralled Trystan. They'd been traveling through Dreach-Sciene for almost a week now, he and a handful of his closest advisors and a large presence of soldiers at their back.

Trees that once reeked of death now stood vibrant and healthy, branches heavy with leaves and acorns reaching to the sky. Weathered grasses now swayed gently in the breeze, a sea of rippling green. Even the air seemed different. Pure and more invigorating. Or maybe it was the magic itself that sweetened the air.

He breathed it in deep, the freshness replaced the usual heavy dread in his chest with a new sense of hope. They'd done this. Him, Rissa, Alixa, Avery. Even Davi. They'd restored Dreach-Sciene's magic. They'd given their people a fighting chance. Their crops would now grow abundant. For some, that was all the magic they'd see. Others would use it to fight the coming army.

Even if Davi believed they'd only accomplished what Calis wanted them to do, bringing Dreach-Sciene back to life for Calis to take it for his own, it was still a chance. Without magic his people would have surely perished. War was inevitable, he knew that, but at least his people would take to arms with full stomachs and clear minds. They'd done the right thing. A tiny smile replaced the usual grim line of his mouth and the constant furrow of his brow smoothed if only for a moment.

"Something amuses you, Trystan? Wanna share the joke with the rest of us?"

Trystan glanced past Avery to Wren, both of their horses flanking his right. His smile widened at Avery's scowl. He knew Wren's familiarity with the use of his name irritated the sword master to no end. Wren, however, didn't seem to notice Avery's displeasure with him. Trystan had realized that Wren didn't let much bother him. And if it did, he let you know. Didn't matter if you were nobility or commoner, the man spoke his mind. He reminded Trystan a lot of the old Davi. It amused and saddened him at the same time.

Trystan's grin encompassed them both.

"Just enjoying the scenery. It's nice to be out in the fresh air, free from all the humdrum of castle life."

"Hmm, nice. Not exactly the word I would use for this foolhardiness, Trys….your Majesty."

Wren's use of Trystan's title was due to the sharp glance from Avery, no doubt. Her gaze of displeasure cut sharp as any knife and could only be ignored for so long. He and Davi had learned that fact well over the years.

Trystan chuckled softly. "And pray tell why would you call our escapade foolhardy, Wren? Do you not enjoy the countryside and meeting the people of Dreach-Sciene? Have the villages not met us with the highest welcome and provided us with the best they have to offer? I've seen more than a handful of fair maidens gush over you in our visits. Do you not enjoy all the attention, Sir Yaro?"

"You know darn well that's caused me more than enough trouble," Wren growled as he glanced back at the light-haired Mira riding a few paces behind. The village girl who had become his constant companion since joining in the fight for the realm, had not been happy with the adoration bestowed on Wren by the other ladies.

"Language, Sir Yaro," Avery admonished, and Wren lifted a hand in mock salute.

"Yes, ma'am. Sorry, ma'am. Don't mean to offend your sensitive ears."

Avery narrowed her eyes as Trystan laughed again.

"And it's not the people of Dreach-Sciene I question. It's the choice to travel the lands when we very well know the whole country is crawling with Isenore soldiers and Dreach-Dhoun spies, while we ride with the sigil of House Renauld displayed for all to see. Forgive me if that makes me a little uneasy, sire."

Trystan's laughter faded away.

"I don't understand what you're saying, boy." Anger strained Avery's words. "You'd rather we travel in pretense? Dressed as Isenore soldiers to creep around what are Renauld lands? We display our Renauld sigil with pride. We will not pretend otherwise."

Wren held both hands palms up at Avery.

"Now, now Mistress Payne, don't get yourself riled up. Trust me, I speak in peace. I am proud to follow House Renauld. Always have and always will. I'm just questioning if it's a good idea to be traveling now of all times, when an attack from Calis is imminent."

Trystan held up a hand to halt Avery's angry response.

"No, Wren, it's not a good idea. Not at all. It is as you said, our enemies surround us. Just being out here in the open puts us in danger, but how will my people come to trust me as their king if I stay hidden behind the safety of my walls and leave them to deal with the fallout? You've seen the response of the villages we've visited. They need to see us. They need to see me. To put their faith in me. How can I expect to recruit their sons and daughters to fight in my name if I can't even forgo the worry of my own safety to check on their wellbeing?"

"The king speaks the truth," Alixa said.

Trystan hadn't even realized she was close enough to overhear their conversation. Her eyes sparkled a greeting at him as she drew her horse alongside his.

"The people need to see their king right now. They need to know he believes in their ability to win this war. He needs to be their symbol of hope, for without hope to bolster them they will give up before the fight even begins."

Wren flashed his teeth. "Nicely said. You're much more than just a pretty face, Alixa Eisner."

Trystan held his breath and winced, waiting for the censure to fall from Alixa's lips. The bright sun must have put her in a forgiving mood this morning since she merely grinned back at Wren.

"Careful. Sir Yaro. Mira still hasn't forgiven you for your flirting behavior at the last village. What she sees in you is beyond me, but I wouldn't piss her off any more than she already is."

Wren leaned over his horse's neck and pointed Alixa's way as his laughter floated on the wind. "Go figure you two would hit it off. Very much alike you are. Avery too. Woe is me if I'm stupid enough to anger *three* stubborn, strong headed women this early in the day. I'll shut up now while I still have a head attached to my shoulders."

Alixa nodded. "Smartest thing you've said all morning."

Trystan couldn't keep his own laughter from escaping. It felt good to laugh. To let loose. Ever since Davi and Rissa had left with Edric and Ramsey for Dreach-Dhoun, he'd been carrying a heavy heart filled with worry and dread. Alixa had decreed the village visits a necessity to earn his people's trust, and it very well was. It was also a way to keep him from worrying too much over his sister and brother. The thought of not being with them, to watch over and protect them, was driving him mad. At least this kept his mind occupied.

They traveled at a slow gait without speaking for the rest of the morning, all of them happy to let the sun's rays warm the tops of their heads and thaw some of the fear from their bones. The sounds all around them were intoxicating, wind rustling through the leaves, birds off in the distance chirping a welcome to the sun, it all confirmed the promise of life once again to Dreach-Sciene. Now if only they could see that promise fulfilled.

As Trystan and his people rounded a bend along the tree covered trail, the morning sounds were accompanied by others. They were met with the sight of a village nestled in the rolling hills below their vantage point. Dozens of small cottages and farms dotted the green landscape. Smoke rose from their chimneys and people scurried about. The echoing of noise soon became distinct sounds. Clanging of metal signified blacksmiths at work, their labors punctuating the din of livestock and dogs and people with the sounds of hammers against iron. This village was alive once again.

Wren halted his horse beside Trystan's, his brow wrinkled in puzzlement.

"This village seems familiar." He glanced back at Mira. "Is this..."

"My village? Yes," Mira confirmed, her face showing little emotion.

Mira's admission came as a surprise since Trystan recognized it as well. It was the village they'd come to on their way to the mountains of Isenore during their quest to find Lonara. The village that had refused to help them and turned them away.

The tiny parish seemed to be in total contrast to the last time they'd been here though. The once dried out pastures Trystan remembered were now green and alive with crops. The cottages that had been falling down around the villager's ears stood fortified. What once seemed broken beyond repair now appeared whole and alive from the return of magic. Their arrival did not go unnoticed. The echoing of the hammers and cries of the people faded away as many sets of eyes turned to the sight of the army contingent lining the ridge above their village. Trystan turned to the blonde girl.

"Mira, would you lead the way? Maybe they need to see a familiar face right about now."

She ducked her head in deference. "As you wish, your Majesty."

She led them down the hill, Trystan and Wren following close behind. Wren's dark eyes never wavered from the long blonde hair hanging down Mira's back, his concern for her written on his face. Trystan was in the dark as to how Mira had left this village, but from Wren's body language it hadn't been on the best of terms.

Memories of how these villagers had treated them with hostility on their first visit came flooding back, and Trystan's hand rested on the sword hanging on his hip. He knew the hostility had been born of desperation. This village along with hundreds of others had suffered over the last twenty years, but the despair and hopelessness he'd witnessed here had haunted him since. He just hoped that bringing back magic was enough for his redemption in their eyes.

As they approached, villagers broke off from the crowd, walking cautiously toward them. Four elders at first, but as Mira got closer, two little ones erupted from the crowd and screamed her name.

"Mira!"

Mira leapt nimbly from her horse. Falling to her knees, she held out her arms as they ran straight to her and she wrapped her arms around them.

"Tara, Toro." Her voice was thick with tears, but none fell as she let go of the children and stood up to face the elders approaching her. Trystan, Wren and Avery dismounted in haste, flanking the girl on either side.

A thin, worn down man stepped Mira's way and Trystan recognized him as the villager who'd asked him to leave them be on their first visit here. His face elicited another memory. Something about losing his daughter to Trystan's war. Could it be Mira he spoke of?

The question was soon answered. Mira's broken 'father' was muffled as the man pulled her into his embrace, his hand rubbing the back of her hair like he couldn't believe it was her.

"Daughter," was all he said, but the word was filled with relief and forgiveness. Mira hugged her father tight before stepping back and studying his face. "Mother?" was all she asked, but the old man's face crumbled, and a single tear trickled down a wrinkled cheek as he shook his head. Trystan felt wetness gathering in his own eyes and he blinked the tears away, staring down at the ground so no one could witness his weakness. He gave them a moment before clearing his throat. The man startled and released Mira, turning his attention on Trystan.

Trystan could see the moment recognition set in. The man's eyes grew wide as he took in the hovering army and the sigil of House Renauld.

"Your Majesty." He spoke clearly and with respect as he went down on one knee. A murmur resonated over the crowd as they all came to the same realization. Their monarch stood before them in their little farm village. As one, they all fell to a knee, heads bowed in respect as the shout of "Long live King Trystan," filled the air.

Trystan shuffled uneasily as he waited for the chanting to subside. No matter how many times he experienced this, it made him uncomfortable.

"Please," he pleaded, raising his voice for all to hear. "Please rise. All of you."

They did as he asked But Trystan focused his attention on Mira's father. He seemed to be the leader.

"You remember who I am, then." It was a statement not a question. But the old man nodded and hung his head in shame.

"Yes. I beg mercy, your Majesty, for all of us. When you were here before....we were not in our right minds. Hunger will do that to a person. We should have helped you instead of turning you away. Please forgive us, sire."

Trystan smiled at him in benevolence. "There is nothing to forgive, good sir. You did what had to be done to provide for you and yours in harsh times, as I would have done in the same circumstances." He looked around the village. "It appears that things have changed since our last visit."

The old man's eyes crinkled in the corners as a smile creased his face. "All thanks to you and the princess, so we've been told. You did the impossible and restored magic. It was a miracle."

Trystan's smile held a tinge of sadness. "I wouldn't call it a miracle, sir. And it wasn't just my sister and I who accomplished this task. There were many others involved. Some who sacrificed much more than they should have." He gestured to the crowd with his chin. "As you all have. But the magic flows and the land lives again. You will suffer no longer."

A cheer rose from the crowd and Trystan felt guilty for raising their hopes, for he knew the next words he had to say would crush that hope again.

"You called me King Trystan. So the news of my father's death has reached you?"

The old man nodded. "Aye. It was a sad day. Your father was a brave and noble man. But we know his son follows in his footsteps. We are not worried. You will not fail us."

Mira's father sounded confident and sure, and Trystan wished he could feel even half of that confidence. "Even at the knowledge that war is imminent? That Calis will try to take what is ours? Are you ready to fight for what is yours, for fight you will need to." His last words came out almost as a whisper, but it only increased the look of determination on the old man's face.

"Aye. We know war is coming. We've known for a while. And we are preparing. The village smitty and farrier have been hard at work ever since the magic returned. We knew what that return meant."

A deep sense of relief filled Trystan at the villager's words. The people of Dreach-Sciene would not let Calis do this the easy way.

"And you are willing to let your young people go? Anyone

able bodied and of age will be needed to train in magic to help fight this war. Are you all prepared to do that?"

The old man straightened his back, staring Trystan in the eye as he raised his voice for all to hear.

"King Trystan asks if we are willing to fight. To protect what is ours and keep it from falling into Dreach-Dhoun's vile grip. I say we tell him yes. I say we let him know that this village will no longer stand back and cower while others do what needs to be done. The king and his sister put their lives on the line to bring magic back to us. Now we return the favor. We will fight. We will contribute. We do this, not just for you, King Trystan, but for us, and for all of Dreach-Sciene."

A roar erupted from the crowd and it took a moment for Trystan to understand what the villagers were screaming as they pumped their fists in the air. But then he understood.

"Dreach-Sciene. Dreach-Sciene. Dreach-Sciene."

His heart filled with pride, he glanced over at Alixa and she smiled at him, her eyes shiny with her own tears of joy. Wren bumped him with his shoulder and Trystan's gaze moved to him. Wren nodded his dark head toward the still chanting crowd, "Well I'd say that's a yes."

The Dreach-Dhoun forest was quiet. It felt different. The tree leaves still glistened with evening dew above their heads and the grass was still supple under the horse's hooves, but something felt wrong. Changed from the forest they had just passed through in their own lands. Rissa glanced around as a chill grazed her neck and a slight shiver ran over her.

For the past week they'd ridden hard, but even through her exhaustion and sore behind from riding all day, Rissa was still aware of the change in their surroundings. Dreach-Sciene's world had reawakened.

Then they crossed over into Dreach-Dhoun. She hadn't noticed the difference at first, but the farther they ventured, the more obvious it became. No one spoke of it. Not Davi or Ramsey, Edric or Rion. She hadn't even heard a mumble from any of the soldiers, yet every single one of them had grown quiet, less talkative. Like they knew something wasn't right, but they couldn't put a finger on it.

Even the lack of enemy soldiers didn't feel right. War was brewing between the two lands, but the only soldier presence they had seen on the border was their own. The border should have been crawling with Calis' men, but they had yet to encounter a single one. Where were they?

She tried to talk it over with Davi earlier, but any fragment of the old Davi she thought she had seen at the palace disappeared the closer they got to Dreach-Dhoun. He retreated more and more into his shell and brushed off every form of conversation Rissa tried to pull him into. He rode ahead of her now, back stiff and exuding an aura that said 'stay away.' She fumed, staring after him riding like he had a stick up his ass. She wanted nothing more to hurl a puff of magic at his back and knock him off his horse, and in the process knock some sense into his head. But she didn't. Instead, she focused her attention on the forest, trying to unlock it's secret. Without physical contact however, she deduced nothing. Sighing in frustration, Rissa turned in her saddle toward the man riding behind her left.

"Where are all of Calis' soldiers?"

Ramsey startled at her question, like he had been lost in thought himself and unaware of her presence. A furrow marred his otherwise smooth brow, and Rissa was struck not for the first time by the incredulity that this man was really her grandfather. He looked no more than ten years Trystan's senior, yet he was their mother's father. The strangeness of the Tri-Gard's appearance was sometimes hard to comprehend.

"I've been wondering the same thing myself," Ramsey answered as he pulled abreast of Rissa's mare. "These woods should be crawling with men, trying to keep us out and his own people in."

Rion pulled alongside her right flank. "The border patrol

told me that the rebellions in Dreach-Dhoun have been steadily getting worse. Maybe he pulled his forces back to quell the uprisings?"

Rissa nodded to herself at Rion's words. "That would make sense. But even that is not the most important question right now. None of us have said anything, but I know you can all feel it. Maybe not as strong as I can, but you feel the unease? Something is wrong with the land. And the closer we get to the castle, the more I feel it. Ramsey, do you know what it is?"

"Without my crystal I cannot say for certain. You have more of a connection with the earth with your tenelach than I do at the moment. But if I were to guess—"

"He's pulling too much power from the earth." Davi's voice floated back at them from his position of point.

"He speaks!" Rissa yelled to no one in particular, but Davi ignored her sarcasm. It frustrated her to no end.

"Calis, you mean?" Rissa shouted out to him. He didn't answer. "Dammit, Davi, stop and talk to us. You've barely spoken a word and we are getting closer to the castle. At least tell me you have a plan."

Her cry must have gotten through since he reined his horse to a halt and dismounted. Rissa and Ramsey followed suit and were soon joined by Edric and Rion. The other soldiers fanned out around them, still on horseback, watching the ever-silent forest for the slightest of movement.

Rissa knelt to the ground and dug her hands into the dirt, like she'd been itching to do all morning. The sweet sounds of harmony and the feelings of peace she had grown accustomed to were inexplicably absent. The magic still flowed, but it was faint and barely detectable. It was scarcely enough for her to draw from. She dug her fingers in deeper, and a dull ache pierced her forehead. She concentrated, reaching out in desperation, trying to locate her connection to the earth, to fill her need for the magic. A faint sound reached her ears, and she tilted her head, trying to comprehend what it was. The sound intensified, rolling toward her as the ground trembled beneath her fingertips. Within moments the slight sound escalated into a piercing shriek, hurtling toward her with the speed of a jungle cat. Pain shot through her ears, so intense she feared they were bleeding. She tried to pull back, to pull away from the ground, but her fingers refused to let go as if they understood the earth was suffering and needed her help. Immobilized, she couldn't move even when her own screams joined with the shrieking in her head.

"Ri!" Davi yanked her up hard by her arms, severing her connection and bringing her blessed relief. "What is it? Why are you screaming?"

He yelled over her fading cry. She shook her head trying to gather her wits, confusion replacing her pain.

"Did... did you not hear that?"

"Hear what?" Davi asked, almost shaking her in frustration. "All we heard was you yelling."

Ri swallowed the fear that still coated her tongue, staring back at the four men who were regarding her as if she'd just grown a second head. "The earth. It was screaming. There was so much pain. So much anger."

Ramsey stepped between his granddaughter and Davi, prying Davi's fingers off Rissa's arms and gently wiping a lock of hair away from her face. "No, we were spared that. You experienced it because of the tenelach. Can't say I'm jealous you possess such a thing at the moment. Are you hurt?"

Rissa ignored Ramsey's question and turned her gaze back to Davi. "You think Calis is behind this? All of this? Why is he draining the earth of magic? And how? How can one man hold so much?"

"It's him all right," Davi muttered as he wiped a weary hand over his face. "And Briggs too, most likely."

"Ah, yes." Ramsey nodded in agreement. "If anyone can find a way to store magic again, it's Briggs Villard."

"But why?" Edric shook off his shock enough to join in. "Why drain his own lands when he wanted magic back into Dreach-Sciene?"

All heads turned to Ramsey as if he held all the answers.

"I see you all expect me to know? Very well then. If I were to guess I'd say it is not only Calis and Briggs draining the magic. They are planning a mass execution to be witnessed by thousands. The condemned will not have access to the land to fill their own magic, but those left outside that care for them will. Calis and his whole slew of soldiers need to be at full power to control the crowd, will they not? If it were your loved ones about to be executed, would you not try everything in your power to save them? Calis is preparing for the barrage of the desperate. That's my theory."

"Or he's finally gone stark raving mad," Rissa whispered.

"I'm afraid he passed that mark a long time ago, my dear." Ramsey replied.

"Be that as it may." Edric's eyes filled with worry. "If Calis and his army are pulling magic, what does that mean for us? Can we go up against such power?"

"No," Davi said bluntly and Edric grimaced at the reply.

"Then what are we doing on this stupid rescue?" Rissa's concern escalated into anger at his candor. "Do you at least have a plan? Or were we just going to march into your father's castle and ask nicely for him to hand Lorelai over?"

"Of course I have a plan," Davi snapped and Rissa's eyes

widened in surprise at his tone. She'd never heard Davi speak that way before. Ever.

"Boy isn't as stupid as he looks," Ramsey interjected, ignoring the glare Davi hurled his way. "Go on then. Tell us how we're to get the girl back?"

A startled "Princess!" echoed through the trees, interrupting whatever Davi was about to say. Rissa glanced in the direction of the voice just in time to see the two soldiers stationed nearby, sail through the air and land in a groaning heap on the ground. Instinct had her tearing her bow from her shoulder even though her gut screamed *magic*.

More soldiers were hurled around as Rissa and the other three stood back-to-back, forming a circle with weapons raised.

"Show yourselves!" Davi demanded, just as a wave of energy shimmered through the air, ripping leaves and branches from trees as it moved toward them. Rissa dropped her bow and fell to her knees. Palms flat on the ground she allowed the magic already stored inside of her to flow free, encapsulating them in a protective barrier. The attack hit, but it was weak, and Rissa's barrier held fast.

"I said show yourselves."

Davi's order was followed by a few moments of silence before figures emerged from the shadows. The large men and women covered in furs and carrying blades was sight enough to make Rion gasp, but recognition set in for Rissa right away and her heart thumped in her chest. This was the same group of border patrol that had captured her and Trystan, Avery and Alixa on their first journey into Dreach-Douhn. The ones that had taken them to the castle. Calis' people.

The two groups stood staring at each other in stony silence. Finally the big brute leading the pack stepped forward and the muscles in Rissa's back tensed in preparation for the attack. The man came closer, headed toward Rissa. Davi moved to flank her side immediately.

"That's close enough." Davion threatened as he pointed his blade. The bear of a man threw his sword to the side as he stepped closer. So close Rissa could see the gray hairs in his scraggly beard and the dirt encrusted wrinkles on his face. All that stood between him and them was her barrier. He pulled a knife from the sheath at his side, and Rissa sucked in a breath, but some instinct made her hold Davi's sword down as he tried to raise it higher.

The stranger studied the barrier in front of Rissa, oblivious of her and the threat of Davi's blade. He tapped the tip of his knife against the magic barrier and the jolt was enough to send the dagger flying out of his hand. Sparks flew and the man shook his hand as if he'd been zapped by the energy as well. His gaze shifted to Rissa and a toothy smile erupted across his face, enhancing the wrinkles already there.

"You are powerful. How are you doing this when the rest of us can barely raise enough magic to wipe our noses?"

"Why do you lie?" she asked. "We just watched you disable all of our soldiers with magic."

He nodded, not denying the accusation. "But they are fine. We just knocked their asses out of their saddles. No harm done."

She looked around finally, to see he was telling the truth. The men and women of their contingent were picking themselves up, with no apparent injuries.

"Why would you do that?" She asked in confusion. "We gave you no reason to attack."

"There is an old saying, better to be safe than sorry. We did not know who you were. Which leads to the question, who are you? You travel with no sigil or house colors. That tells me you are somewhere you shouldn't be and do not wish to be found."

"You don't remember me?" Rissa asked, her eyes narrowing.

The old man raised a brow. "Should I?"

"Well considering you captured me and my brother and delivered us to Calis just a few weeks ago..."

The corner of his mouth lifted again. "Forgive me, Madame, but we've captured so many in the name of King Calis." He studied her a bit more. "Although that red hair does seem familiar."

"It doesn't matter who she is," Davi interrupted the man's perusal. "What matters is that you attacked us unprovoked."

The man spread his hands wide. "But that is what we do. We don't need a reason. And normally we would have robbed you all by now and gotten away with our wares. But the girl's magic intrigues me. I wish to know how she is so powerful when the rest of us are fading." He returned his gaze to Rissa. "You can drop your shield. No need to waste magic. We mean you no harm. I just want an answer to my question."

"You expect us to believe that when the rest of your people look like they want to skewer us on their blades?" Davi growled. "Tell them to drop their weapons."

The man's smiled widened, but he said nothing as he waved a hand and his people obeyed, their weapons tumbling to the ground. The Dreach-Sciene soldiers made haste and moved them out of reach.

The old man studied Davi with his piercing eyes and Rissa knew the moment recognition set in by his sharp intake of breath. "The girl draws a blank, but you I do know. You are the dark king's son. Prince Davion. Some say you're dead. Obviously not true. Others claimed you left Dreach-Dhoun, choosing to pledge your allegiance to the prince...." His gaze switched to Rissa, "...and princess of Dreach-Sciene. Am I correct?"

"Ri, don't answer his questions," Davi said.

"Yes," Rissa ignored Davi's exasperated sigh.

"Princess Renauld." The man gave a mock bow. "I do remember you now, and your capture."

"So you understand our reluctance to face you without my magic barrier?"

"Understandable, yes. But no need to worry. As I'm sure you can tell by our pathetic attempt earlier to penetrate your shield, your magic is much more powerful than ours at the moment."

Ri examined the wrinkled face staring at her. Even though the capture they had experienced at his hands remained fresh in her memory, she saw no deceit in his eyes. She suspected he was telling them the truth. At least she hoped so as she released the pulse of magic still surging from her and the barrier disappeared.

"I'm trusting in your word, Sir...?"

"Bowman," he offered.

"Sir Bowman. Please don't make me regret my decision."

Davi flexed his hand on his sword and pointed the tip Bowman's way. "The Princess may believe you, but I do not. One wrong move and I cut you down."

Instead of taking offense at Davi's threat, the man laughed. "I believe you. If even an ounce of your father's blood runs through your veins, then our fear of your threat is justified."

"Davi, please." Rissa reached out and lowered the blade sticking in the old man's chest. Davi grunted in disapproval but allowed her to do so.

"Tell me, Sir Bowman, what is wrong with Dreach-Dhoun's

magic? When my tenelach connected with the earth earlier all I felt was pain. There's barely any magic left."

The old man arched his bushy brows. "Tenelach? Ah, so that explains why you still have magic while the rest of us can barely squeeze a drop from the earth. Even here in the middle of the forest, Calis and Villard's greedy tentacles have taken root. They've stolen so much, the rest of us are left starving."

"Why?"

"Does Calis need a reason? Because he can. The man does what he desires. Which, being mercenaries such as we are, never bothered us. As long as he paid us in full, we did his bidding."

"So what has changed?"

"You've heard of the mass execution he has planned?"

Ri nodded, ignoring Davi's glare telling her not to say too much.

"That's what has changed. The man has truly earned his title of the mad king. He is prepared to kill hundreds of innocents for the sake of proving a point." Bowman pointed his chin at his motley crew. "Most of my people have family; mothers, fathers, children among the hundreds of prisoners. We, as well as others, aim to put a stop to the madness, but Calis is always one step ahead. He's drained the lands. Him and his sorcerer have figured out a way to keep the rest of us from attaining any decent amount of magic. To stop him, we will have to battle with weapons alone. A battle from which many of us may not return, but we are willing to take the sacrifice."

"The magic still runs strong in Dreach-Sciene." Ramsey stepped forward, deciding on the old man's honesty as well. "We can get you past the border guards so you can fill your power."

Bowman tapped his nose and grinned at Ramsey. "You

think like us, good sir. We had considered that idea. If we are even to stand a chance at saving our families, we need magic. But then a messenger stumbled back to camp this morn with news."

"What news?" Ri asked, even though the cold knot of fear in her belly was telling her she did not want to know the answer.

"Calis' men have finished the gallows ahead of schedule. We don't have time to get to Dreach-Sciene and back since the execution has been moved ahead. As we speak, the people in the surrounding villages are being herded to the castle to stand witness to this atrocity. Everyone will be put to death two days hence."

So many people.

Rissa had never seen so many bodies gathered in the same place all at once. Not even for her father's grand events.

Hidden in the cluster of trees atop the hills overlooking the valley and castle below, they had an unobstructed view of the sea of flesh swarming around the fields. Waves and waves of people all herded shoulder to shoulder around the grand masterpiece of Calis' plan. The massive structure stood out in stark contrast against the pale blue sky. An omen of death. The hangman's platform was fitted with rows of nooses, all awaiting their innocent victims.

Rissa's stomach flip-flopped as she swallowed the bile in the back of her throat. This was crazy. What was Davi thinking? What were they thinking following along with this whole idea? There was no way this plan would succeed. Not with their small contingent. Not even with the addition of the thirty or so forest soldiers would they be able to pull this off. This was a suicide mission, especially with the whole area stripped of any magic. All they had to fight with was what they had stored and come from Dreach-Sciene with. At this point they needed more than magic. They needed a miracle.

"How's your magic level, my dear?" As if Ramsey was reading her mind, he breathed the question into her ear and she jumped in fright.

"Don't sneak up on me like that," she growled but more from hopelessness than anger. The whole situation reeked of desperation. Ramsey picked up on her distress.

"Never fear, Rissa. We must wade through the darkness to get to the light.."

She glared sideways at him. "What the hell does that mean? If it means this is hopeless, then yeah I agree."

He smiled at her. His casual disposition in the face of all this adversity amazed Rissa.

"You have your mother's sense of humor… and sharp tongue, to be sure."

Ri stared at him in disbelief. "Have you completely lost your mind? You do realize the danger we are in, yes? We're about to attempt a rescue of hundreds of people with the saddest excuse for a plan I've ever heard. Between all of us we barely have enough magic to go up against a dozen of magic-saturated soldiers, let alone Calis and Briggs. We're in league with a bunch of mercenaries I wouldn't trust with a bottle of our worst wine, let alone our lives. And to top it all off, I'm doing this to help rescue the woman who had a hand in my father's murder. This is complete madness. Why am I even here?"

Ramsey's smile grew wider as his eyes caressed her face. "Why indeed. Love is a curious thing, is it not?"

Heat flushed Ri's cheeks as her gaze found Davi standing

off to the side and deep in conversation with the forest soldier's leader. She wanted to counter her grandfather's statement, but she couldn't argue the truth. There was no point. She was in the middle of all this because of that dark haired idiot she would do anything for.

"It's something alright," she grumbled as she tore her eyes away and focused once more on the sight below. Ramsey settled by her side, showing no interest in leaving her alone. "In answer to your question, my magic is passable. How about yours?"

"About the same as yours. Functional."

His words did nothing to reassure her.

"Functional? You're a member of the Tri-Gard for crying out loud. Your magic is functional? We need you at your strongest, not functional. Why are you even here if you can't help us do this?"

"I didn't say I couldn't help. I said my magic was functional. Same as yours and Davi's and everyone else with us. I might have a little more control over my magic than you young people, but it was the crystal that allowed me my power. The good news is the same can be said for Calis and Briggs. Without their crystals, we are all on the same level."

"Except we're not. You said yourself Briggs and Calis have learned to store magic, more than we carry. How do we go up against that?"

"With the element of surprise." Davi was the one to answer her question. She hadn't even heard him approach. He squatted beside her, giving her the tiniest of smiles. "Don't worry, Ri. If there is one thing I've learned about my father in our time together, he is much too arrogant. He's aware that some of his people may resist here today and he's taking precaution against that. He's drained the lands so badly, no one will have enough magic to oppose him. Or so he thinks. He won't be prepared for us." He flicked her under her chin. "For you."

She knocked his finger away in irritation. "Explain how this will work again?"

"Ri, we've gone over this-"

"Indulge me," she interrupted and Davi sighed.

"Fine. Bowman and his men will place themselves in position around the platform. We will position ourselves near Calis and Briggs. Since Bowman was kind enough to provide us all with these forest soldier fur cloaks, no one will question our presence or theirs or the kegs of 'wine' they've brought to the execution. The black powder will be placed in a position to take out the platform's base. Once we get sight of the prisoners, Ramsey will disable Briggs while you and I take care of Calis. We must be quick and brutal since we won't be able to control them for long. As soon as they are incapacitated, Bowman will blow the platform. Edric and Rion will grab Lorelai and escape in the confusion, as will we. We will hide in the mass of people and make our escape."

Rissa had heard this twice already. It still elicited as little faith from her as it did the first two times.

"There's so much left to chance. So much that can go wrong."

Ramsey laced Rissa's hand through his. "Yes, as is with any plan. But this is crazy enough to work."

Rissa rolled her eyes and drew her hand back. "No, it's just plain crazy. And what happens after? After we get Lorelai? What happens to everyone else? Where do they escape to? Dreach-Sciene? They won't just up and leave their families... their people. What will become of them?"

"The others are not our problem, Ri." Davi stood and

adjusted his sword, refusing to meet her eyes. "We came for my cousin. The others can fend for themselves. The plan stands."

He sounded so cold. So controlled. Rissa almost didn't recognize him at that moment. She wanted to say something. To ask where the old Davi was, but she already knew the answer. That Davi didn't exist anymore. She may as well get used to it.

"I have a gut feeling this is going to go terribly wrong," she muttered to herself, forgetting about Ramsey. He stood, brushing off his palms before holding a hand out to her. She accepted, and he pulled her up beside him.

"You may be correct. But then again, it could go wonderfully right. The others are waiting for us. Shall we go set this in motion and find out?"

THE HEAT WAS UNBEARABLE. So many bodies squished together under the merciless sun. Ironic that the sun would shine so bright on a day meant for death. These darn heavy fur cloaks they wore didn't help either, but at least it had gotten them and their weapons past the Dreach-Dhoun soldiers without a second glance. The soldiers hadn't even looked their way, too busy joking with Bowman and asking him to save them a drink of his famous forest wine.

But if Rissa thought the heat was bad, the smell as they made their way through the field was ten times worse. Some of these villagers had been here for days already, and the odor of unwashed bodies mixed with sweat and fear and wine all combined into a profusion of stench that nearly took her breath away. Grabbing onto Davi's hand tighter so not to lose him in the crowd, she used her free hand to pull the hood of her cloak over her nose, trying to staunch the smell. Last thing she needed was to pass out before this whole rescue even began.

Once past the guards, they parted ways with Bowman and his men. Edric and Rion walked with them a bit farther until Edric leaned close and whispered in her ear, "Good luck. We'll meet you at the rendezvous point."

Rissa ignored the unease squeezing her innards into knots and kept swallowing the lump in her throat. The plan would work. It had too. She watched the two men disappear into the crowd, heading toward the gallows, while she and Ramsey fell into step behind Davi. She knew where Davi was trying to lead her. The small dais set up next to the gallows was shielded from the sun by a brightly colored canvas and afforded the best seat in the house for the show about to be unleashed on the crowd. Obviously in reserve for Calis. He wanted to make sure he was seen to be in control of this whole fiasco.

The closer they got to the podium, the easier the crowd parted, like they were more than willing to let others take position around their king. Davi and Rissa made their way to the dais and stopped in front of Calis' intended spot. They were soon joined by Ramsey, all of them taking care to stay hidden among the crowd. Ri was thankful that others in the crowd also seeked cover from the hot sun under hoods, making the three of them appear less conspicuous.

"Now what?" Rissa mumbled as she scanned the crowd for any sign of Rion or Edric or any of their men, but they were already swallowed up in the mob. She prayed they were all in position and where they needed to be.

"Now we wait," He replied, but gave her hand a squeeze of reassurance. A small gesture, but Ri took what she could get.

The wait was made worse by the heat, but finally a trump

of a horn pierced the air and the quiet drone of chatter that had filled the valley faded into silence. The horn sounded once again, and Rissa turned in the slight welcoming breeze toward the sound. A fleet headed their way from the castle. An imposing parade of horses and wagons and soldiers marched over the hills, along the dried-up riverbed and toward the valley floor. In the lead was a gilded carriage pulled by two magnificent black beasts, and Rissa's heart constricted in her chest at the sight. No doubt who was arriving with such extravagance. Calis and Briggs were on their way.

The mass of soldiers spilled into the crowd, surrounding the people forced into the valley. So many they almost numbered the villagers themselves. Rissa sucked in a breath of panic. She hadn't expected so many armed forces. How were they to get past them all, but as if Davi could read her mind, he turned to her and the corner of his mouth lifted in a tiny smile as if to say, *Don't worry.*

Don't worry. Yeah, easier said than done. She pulled her hand from Davi's and rubbed her sweaty palms down the side of her cloak.

Keep it together, Ri.

Once the last soldier took position, only then did the gilded carriage settle to a stop behind the tented dais. Rissa couldn't see what was happening, but a loud voice boomed through the air as a tall man took center stage.

"Ladies and gentlemen. His royal majesty, King Calis of Dreach-Dhoun." The herald bowed in respect and backed away as Calis took to the podium. He smiled. He actually smiled and waved at the crowd of hundreds as if it were a pleasant day and he had gathered them all here for a picnic instead of the executions of their friends and families.

Rissa stared in contempt at the hateful man who caused her

family so much pain. Her palms itched, and the magic danced at her fingertips, wanting to rip that disgusting smile right off of his face. A memory of their last meeting flittered in her mind and she shuddered in revulsion at the thought of how he had caressed her cheek. A tug on her arm snapped her out of the memory as Ramsey pulled her down to join the surrounding crowd that were now bowing, not out of respect but out of fear. She complied with the rest, not wanting to draw attention.

An unnatural hush fell over the crowd as Calis walked to the front of the stage, a stern looking Briggs at his back. Briggs' eyes swept the crowd and Rissa, Ramsey, and Davi all dropped their heads in pretend reverence. Calis' voice shattered the stillness.

"My people, it is an honor to see you all here, even as it is a very sad day for all of us." He sighed, and it seemed to sweep out over the crowd. Rissa wondered if he was using magic to project since she swore she could feel his false sadness. "This should have been a time of rejoicing for us. A time of elation and pride. A plan I'd put into motion years ago worked flawlessly. We were this close to claiming our victory over our greatest enemy, Dreach-Sciene." He held two pinched fingers up into the air. "Instead my plan was met with betrayal. I had nothing but the best intentions for the people of Dreach-Dhoun. My people. We would want for nothing. We would have everything. Yet, instead of thankfulness I was given disloyalty. My own subjects plotting against me. Trying to oust me from power. No one was trustworthy, not even those of my own blood."

His head bowed and for a moment Rissa thought he was actually about to cry. Then he raised his head and stared out over the crowd with a look that sent a chill over her body. The blue eyes, so much like Davi's, were solid ice and his mouth formed a grim line. "You thought you would get away with this treachery? Fools! All of you. No one betrays Calis Bearne and gets away with it. You are all here today to observe testament to that."

"Please, sire, I beg you to have mercy!" The voice came from behind Rissa and she turned in surprise, searching for the brave soul—or fool. "These people are naught but women and children. Innocent of all you accuse."

"Innocent?" Calis' eyes narrowed as he searched for the speaker in the crowd. "Step forward."

The man did as Calis requested. He was dressed in peasant garb that hung from his thin frame and his sallow skin reeked of ill health, but his stance stayed strong. He didn't cower under Calis' stare, even as those around him did and distanced themselves from the man brave enough to speak up.

"What is your name, good sir?"

"Giles, your Majesty."

"Giles. And do you, Giles, have family here today?"

The man nodded and wiped angrily at the tears that fell from his eyes and down his cheeks.

"Speak up," Calis growled.

"Yes, sire. My daughter and son are both being held prisoner. They are innocent! They have no affiliation with the rebels. You need to release them. Please, sire."

"Are you telling me that I've made a mistake?" The question was almost a whisper, yet everyone in the crowd heard and an audible gasp filled the silence that followed. The crowd's heads bobbed back and forth as they stared from the king and the man who dared question him. The man's own look was one of total confusion, as if he knew he shouldn't answer, but knew darn well if he didn't the consequences would be the same.

"Ye... yes," he stuttered. It was his last word. The movement of Calis' hand was barely perceptible, but the man was suddenly lifted into the air. His feet kicked out underneath him and his hands fought to tear away the clamp around his neck. Rissa stepped forward as if to help the man, but Davi clamped her arm in a vise grip and shook his head. They couldn't give themselves away. Not yet.

As the crowd watched in horror, the man did the hangman's dance, jerking around wildly like some marionette being controlled by a mad puppeteer. He struggled to breathe, his lips turning blue and his eyes bulging from his head. Rissa couldn't stand to watch anymore. She turned her head and closed her eyes, but she could still hear the man's horrible gurgling. Finally that too stopped and she heard his body hit the ground. It was over. An unnatural silence settled over the valley. Not even a bird or cricket dared break the hush. Then that hated voice slithered along her spine.

"Does anyone else think I've made a mistake?"

No one else spoke. Quiet sobbing whispered through the crowd, but no one dared answer the king's question. Not even Rissa, but her muteness wasn't due to fear. The anger that raged through her heart was the culprit. She raised her eyes to the object of her anger and watched him stride casually to the throne-like chair placed in the middle of the podium. Briggs settled himself off to the right as Calis' waved his hand at the head of his guards. "Bring out the prisoners."

Dozens jumped at his command. Wagon door after wagon door unbolted and the prisoners unceremoniously yanked out. They squinted in the bright sun, tied hands lifted to try to protect their eyes from the harsh light. Dirty, ragged men, women, and children ushered into lines and up the stairs toward their deaths. Some cried quietly as they shuffled up the platform. Some prayed. Some scanned the crowd, desperately searching for the faces of those they loved. But none cried out for mercy, for they all knew it would be a waste of breath.

Rissa tried to count them but lost track after fifty. Fifty faces filled with so much terror and eyes full of fear. Ri knew those faces would haunt her til the end of her days. She tried to block them out and instead focused on finding the face of the seer. Her white hair should have been a dead giveaway in the massive crowd, but her attention was caught instead by movement at the end of the platform. Others in the crowd of watchers had noticed as well, and cries of dismay and sorrow soon saturated the air.

"Davi." Her tone was frantic as the first prisoners on the gallows finally cried out in desperation as nooses were dropped about their necks. "They aren't waiting for all the prisoners to climb the platform. We have to do something now."

"Dammit," he whispered back. "I don't see Lorelai. Where is… there!" Rissa followed his agitated stare. The seer was being escorted up the stairs by a guard, her back held straight and her head held high.

"Do you think Rion and Edric will get to her in time?" Rissa asked, but Davi ignored the question.

"Ramsey, you ready?" he hissed at the other man and Ramsey gave a slight nod. "On the count of three. One…"

Rissa called on her magic. It started as a warm, tingling sensation in her stomach but soon, just like throwing a log onto glowing embers, a flame ignited.

"Two…"

The flame grew brighter, and she struggled with the need to set it free too soon. It leapt eagerly at her fingertips, begging for release. Begging to take its revenge.

"Three!"

The growing fire exploded, aiming straight for Calis. The king's mouth formed a tiny O as if he knew what was coming moments before the chair toppled over and he fell with it. Briggs' overcame his surprise and headed for the king, but was jolted back, locked into place by Ramsey's magic. Dark eyes burned through the crowd, searching for the one who dared do this and settled on them, recognition setting in. He struggled against Ramsey's hold, but Ramsey's magic held even as the strain of fighting Brigg's power soon showed on his face.

"We just need to keep him pinned long enough," Davi grunted and Rissa knew he was feeling the same resistance as her. Calis was fighting back, and he was strong. She felt his push back against her magic and she gritted her teeth. It was like fighting against the wind. A powerful force she couldn't see, but it was there and could crush her at any moment. She had to stay strong. They had to stay strong.

Panic set in on the crowd as they realized something was wrong. Desperation turned to confusion as the soldiers barreled through, pushing people aside in their search for the magic wielders. Ri could feel her power waning and she reached deep, desperately trying to dredge up any remains of stored magic.

"Anytime now, boys," Davi gritted through clenched teeth, glancing over at the soldier narrowing in on them. Almost as if on cue the first explosion rent the air. The ground shifted under their feet and Rissa stumbled, losing control of her magic for just a moment. That moment was all Calis needed. He took advantage. Leaping nimbly to his feet, he countered back with a debilitating strike. The pain tore through Rissa's shoulder and she cried out as her magic shattered around her like broken glass.

"Rissa!" Davi screamed, turning toward her, his hood falling in the process and revealing his face. The sneer of hatred on Calis' face faltered as his eyes fell on his son.

"Davion?"

Davi stiffened but didn't respond. He lunged for Rissa to keep her from falling. His arms tightened around her waist and she sucked in a breath. Her eyes met his. "Dav, it's gone. I've used all the magic I had stored."

His gaze tore into her, darkening as they both felt the looming presence behind them. Davi's eyes flicked to the bow strung across her back in silent communication. She nodded, and he released her. In one swift movement, Davi dropped and Rissa pulled her bow, knocked her arrow, and loosed it toward Calis.

He waved his hand and the arrow hit an invisible wall and clattered to the soft ground. Davi drew his sword and jumped forward to face the one man she hoped they'd never have to see again.

Rissa rested another arrow against the string of her bow but held it there and waited. Davi needed to do this. He needed to face that man. He needed to face the demons that haunted him.

She risked a quick glance at Davi and caught sight of the indecision on his face. Over the past week it seemed as if the boy she knew had returned to them, allowing her to forget what had been done to him. What he'd lost.

She narrowed her eyes and tightened her grip on her bow as she caught the movement of soldiers at her back, but they stopped at Calis' raised hand, even though his eyes never left Davi.

Calis didn't make a move to attack. "Son, you've returned to me."

Davi took a step back and shook his head.

"He'd never return to you," Rissa spat.

Calis finally looked to her. "You're naïve, girl."

Another explosion sounded behind them, bringing all three back to the fray surrounding them. Rissa tried to see through the bodies pushing for freedom, but Rion and Edric were nowhere to be found.

Ramsey continued to struggle against Briggs, but even that couldn't hold much longer.

A man barreled into Davi and almost knocked him over. Davi pushed him aside. "Rissa, now!"

Rissa didn't have to be asked twice. She released the arrow. Calis slammed his hands up, forming a protective wall once again. Davi's eyes followed the arrow. His hand twitched and a loud crack sounded through the air as it burst through the barrier. The explosion knocked Briggs off his feet, but Calis merely ducked out of the way and the steel tip struck a soldier behind him, the shaft protruding from his neck. Blood spurted Calis and he wiped it away without so much as a grimace.

Rissa saw Davi's shoulders slump with the effort it took to break through his father's magic. That was when she knew. They were both without power now and no living earth in sight to regain it.

"Enough of this nonsense, Davion." Calis held out his hand. "Come with me. Together, we can make all of this right."

Davi's sword lowered slightly. He wasn't considering it, was he?

"Davi," she said. "We have to find a way out of this."

Davi shifted his eyes from her to his father.

"Son," Calis pleaded, emotion clouding his words. "Please."

A hand latched onto Rissa's arm. "Time to go," Ramsey said into her ear.

Behind Calis, Briggs lay unconscious on the ground.

"Stop!" Calis' eyes found the prone Briggs. "My son isn't going anywhere."

"If you want him to stay, you're going to have to kill him." Rissa shrugged off Ramsey's grip and stepped forward. She wasn't sure how much truth filled her words. Davi still hadn't moved.

"I am his family." Calis sneered. "You are no more than an enemy princess."

Magic shot from his hands, aimed toward Rissa, and she didn't have a moment to process it before a body bowled her over, throwing her to the ground. Davi jerked on top of her as his father's power struck him.

"Davi!" she screamed. Crawling out from under him, she rolled him over. His chest rose and fell with his labored breath, but he was alive. A tear tracked down her cheek as she raised her head to Calis.

"You would kill your own son?" She shook her head. "What kind of monster are you?"

Davi coughed and reached out to grip Rissa's leg. "He didn't…" He coughed again. "He held back on his magic. I could tell. That was not a death strike." Relief washed over his face. "He doesn't want to kill me."

Calis' mouth opened.

"Let us go, Calis." Ramsey's voice broke through as the chaos of escaping prisoners and attacking soldiers continued around them. "Let us go."

Calis glanced back at Briggs who'd begun to stir.

"We aren't the ones you want," Ramsey said. "Just as you wouldn't have wanted to execute Lorelai. I know you, old friend. You love that girl. Let us leave Dreach-Dhoun. Let us save her life."

Davi pushed himself up. "Please."

Calis raised a hand as if to wield his magic once more.

Davi stepped forward. "Father."

The word broke whatever had been raging inside Calis. "I cannot let you leave me again, Davion." He turned and issued orders to his men. "Capture the prince. Kill the rest."

Rissa heard the words 'capture' and 'kill' but she couldn't worry about the villagers caught in the fray.

Not when her every fear was wrapped up in Davi standing still amid it all.

"Time to run, my Prince." Ramsey jerked his head toward the trees.

He was right. They had to get Davi out of there before the soldiers could get to them. Rissa searched the crowd mingling around them trying to find a soldier-free course of escape, but they were closing in at an alarming speed. She raised her bow and aimed at the nearest soldier. Her arrow found its mark and before the soldier even hit the ground she pointed and yelled above the noise, "That way."

"Davion, stop!" The voice roared, and Rissa felt the magic bind around their ankles like quick sand. It rooted them in place with such force she nearly fell over, stumbling into Ramsey as his body stopped her fall. Reaching deep inside herself, she searched for any last remaining trace of magic to fight back but came up empty.

"No," she cried, her voice thick with frustration. "Ramsey, do something."

The explosion that ripped at their eardrums had nothing to do with magic, but it was just as effective. Rissa knew it was the dais holding Calis that had exploded without even seeing the aftermath. The magic holding them captive loosened and they were able to move again.

"Run!" she screamed at Davi, even as he faltered and looked back where his father had just stood. She grabbed his arm and glanced back as well. The brightly colored canvas fluttered on the wind as it settled down over the pile of debris that had once been the platform.

"He was protected by his magic. Trust me, the bastard is still alive. Don't you even dare think about going back. We need to save our own necks."

Davi shook off his indecision as Rissa's words registered, and he grabbed her hand tight and began to run. Another explosion erupted. People screamed as the gallows listed to the side. Prisoners and soldiers alike toppled off the slippery slope, barreling into anyone unlucky enough to be standing at the bottom. The whole scene was mass confusion. Soldiers and commoners ran in different directions, not quite comprehending what to do next. Orders were shouted out by the captains of the guard, but they were quickly swallowed up by the screams and shouts of the villagers all trying to reach their loved ones. All trying to make the most of this opportune moment to escape.

"Did you see Edric and Rion get to Lorelai?" Davi shouted over his soldier as he dodged a sword that swung his way.

"Uh, I'm a little busy trying to keep us alive here," Rissa yelled back as she aimed an arrow at the soldier blocking their path. "Duck!"

The arrow sailed over Davi's head and struck the soldier in the arm, spiraling him off balance enough for them to run by. Trying to push through the crowd was like fighting against a wicked wind, but finally the crowd thinned out enough for them to break through into a clearing as people ran in all directions, trying to escape the soldiers and get away with their family members.

They stumbled out of the sea of people so abruptly Rissa almost fell to her knees and would have if a strong hand hadn't seized her wrist. She reached for an arrow as the soldier's blade swam into focus, but a voice stopped her movement.

"Head for the spot in the trees," Bowman growled as he steadied Rissa. "My men and I have this. We'll try to keep the soldiers occupied and give anyone we can the chance to escape. We still have one big surprise left. We just need to get as many villagers as we can out of the way."

"Thank you," Rissa said to the big man, staring with gratitude into his eyes. He merely nodded, then whirled with his sword held high. "For the people of Dreach-Dhoun," he yelled at his men as they all ran screaming back into the crowd.

"Move," Ramsey ushered them into movement and they headed for the destination.

The sound of screaming and yelling lessened the farther into the forest they ran, muted by the thick canopy of withered leaves. Rissa gasped for breath as the stitch in her side cut as sharp as any blade. She limped in pain, but still they ran. The surrounding trees all looked the same and she feared they had gone the wrong way. A wave of relief washed over her when she spotted their men waiting in the clearing with the horses.

Coming to a dead stop, she bent over with hands on her knees, and sucked in huge gulps of air, looking around. The couple of soldiers they had left behind ran toward them in concern.

"Princess," one called out, but she shrugged off his hand as she took another deep breath and straightened up, wiping the sweat from her upper lip.

"Edric? Rion?" she asked the soldier, but he shook his head.

"No. You are the first ones back."

"Dammit," Davi breathed hard as he ran a hand through his

dark hair. "We should have looked for them. We should have helped them instead of running off like scared little maidens. What if they didn't make it? What if they didn't get Lorelai?"

"Oh ye of little faith, Davion."

Edric's voice was like a weight lifted from her chest. Rissa whirled as Edric and Rion shuffled out of the trees, a disoriented Lorelai walking between them, her hands still tied. Her panic and puzzlement soon turned to disbelief as she spotted her cousin.

"Davi." She fell into his arms, her sobs mixed with joy. "You came for me. You idiot!"

Davi hugged her back hard, his face softened into a small smile. "Nice to see you too, cousin."

Rissa squashed the twinge of irritation burning in her gut at the sight of the seer. She was Davi's family and supposedly innocent of her father's murder. Rissa tried to rationalize that in her head, but still looking at her only fueled her ire.

"No time for family reunions," she growled as she stepped their way, pulling her knife. Davi raised a concerned brow but Rissa ignored him as Lorelai stepped back and Ri grabbed the girl's tied wrists. Her sharp blade sliced through the ropes and Lorelai let out a small cry of gratitude as the ropes fell from her bloodied wrists.

"Can you ride?" Rissa asked, and Lorelai nodded in answer. "Good. We can't wait for the others. They know to head for the border. We need to move."

"Agreed," Ramsey gave the girl a quick hug as well. "The Princess is correct. We should ride hard while there is still chaos back there."

Rissa turned away from Davi and Lorelai. She didn't want to admit how hard it was watching him show so much concern for the girl who had betrayed her father. Instead she focused her attention on Edric and Rion as Davi fussed with getting Lorelai settled onto a horse.

"You two did well. I will be sure to tell my brother how you did Dreach-Sciene proud today."

Edric's face broke into a wide grin. "How well, Princess? Maybe there will be some talk of reward? Maybe knighthood?"

Rissa laughed at his boldness. "That is not up to me, Edric."

"Too bad," he answered. "Well please make sure you enhance our part of the story. Rion and I would truly appreciate any sort of embellishment you choose to add. Sir Edric does have a nice ring to it, does it not?"

"And Sir Rion," Rion added, grinning at his partner. "The ladies of court will fawn over that."

Rissa lifted her brow. "I think Willow might not be too happy with court ladies 'fawning' over you, Rion."

His grin dropped away. "You may be right, Princess. She does have a wee bit of a temper."

Edric's laughter boomed through the trees. "Well I for one, do not have a quick-tempered lady waiting for me back in Dreach-Sciene, so I'll take whatever title the king decides to throw my way."

Rissa couldn't help but join in with his laughter as she headed toward her own horse. Grabbing the reins, she lifted herself nimbly into the saddle before glancing back Edric's way.

"How about the title of 'pompous idiot' then? I think that suits you well."

Edric's face contorted into a look of mock hurt as he straddled his own horse. "I think—"

His words stopped at the same time an unmistakable *twang* hit Rissa's ears. Rissa stared in horror at the sight, burning into her brain. An arrow erupted from Edric's chest with a splatter of crimson as it tore through his heart. Edric glanced down in disbelief before raising his head once more and stared at Rissa even though he was long past seeing her. Blood bubbled from his lips and he moved them as if to speak one last time before the haze of death covered his eyes and he fell from his horse and hit the ground.

"Cullenspire ahead, sire."

The young guard's announcement was met with a whoop of joy from Wren. Trystan glanced over in amusement as the young man dug his heels into his steed's flanks and shot ahead of the rest of the party, anxious to make the top of the rise. Trystan ignored Avery's headshake of disapproval for he understood Wren's excitement. Cullenspire was his home. His mother and sister awaited him there. The smile on Trystan's face grew bitter as he realized that no longer stood true for him. His father would never again await Trystan's return, and Ri was more absent than not. Things had changed. He pushed the sadness and worry for his sister and Davi deep down. Wren at least deserved his happy homecoming.

Wren crested the rise but drew his horse up short and stared at what lay below him before looking back over his shoulder. Trystan stiffened as Wren's puzzled eyes met his.

"Your Majesty, you need to see this."

The soldiers surrounding them moved aside as Trystan and Avery hurried their mounts through the narrow opening. Trystan was on edge, not quite sure what Wren was seeing, but praying nothing had happened to Lady Yaro and her people in their absence.

He arrived at the top of the hill a mere moment before Avery, but his audible gasp must have raised her hackles since she questioned sharply, "What is it, sire?

He didn't bother to answer for she saw it just as she pulled abreast of him. No words could define the sight.

Cullenspire lay below them tucked away against the fringe of the Isenore forest and caught in the rays of the evening sun. It remained unchanged and the stone wall around it stood intact. That was not what caught the eye. What interested them was the sight of the outlying areas. Cullenspire was like a jewel wrapped inside the sea of blue and gray and brown tents that dotted the fields once covered in dead grasses and crops. Every shape and size imaginable. Patches of green grass peeked out between the tents and shanties. A whole village of hundreds seemed to have sprung up around Cullenspire. Maybe even thousands. A very similar sight to what had waited outside Lord Coille's estate in Whitcap but at least triple in size. Banners of different houses snapped in the wind around sections of the camp. Houses that Trystan recognized well. House Denys, House Godfrey, House Saye, all well-known allies with his father. Trystan couldn't help the smile that lifted the corner of his mouth.

"Seems like your mother has been busy since the last time we were here."

Wren nodded as his eyes shone with laughter. "Seems so. She never was one to sit around idly while there was an army that needed to be raised."

Without waiting for Trystan's approval, Wren started down the slope, his laughter carrying on the breeze. Trystan followed along with Avery. Her muttered "I didn't believe it possible, but this one is even worse than Davion," had him snorting under his breath.

"Sire, let me go first," Avery insisted as she tried to ride ahead, but it fell on deaf ears. While Cullenspire was not Trystan's home, he was as eager to get to it as Wren was.

The sounds and smells of the encampment met them as soon as they hit the valley floor. Laughter echoed in the air, accompanied by mouthwatering aromas of roasting meat and spilled mead. They'd arrived in the midst of mealtime.

"Who goes there?" A voice carried from the encroaching shadows as a couple of guards stepped into the road, blocking their way.

"Wren Yaro. Please let my mother know we are here."

His words were met with silence before disbelieving laughter broke out.

"Wren? Is it really you?"

"Shannos?" Wren leapt nimbly from his horse as he headed for the guard and they embraced, slapping each other soundly on the back. "It's good to see you, old friend."

"You too. I thought for sure you'd never make it back in one piece."

"Nice to see you had confidence in my fighting ability, friend."

Shannos chuckled as he pointed a finger Wren's way. "Had all the confidence in the world in your fighting ability, Yaro. It was your mouth that always landed you in trouble. I figured some jealous husband would have taken you out long ago, just like that time—"

"No need to tell tales, old man," Wren interrupted as he

glanced back at Mira who studied him silently under an arched brow. "Now be a good chap and tell us what is happening. Why are all these people here? Has my mother been recruiting?"

"No need for her to recruit. The talk of King Trystan traveling through the villages looking for anyone of an age to fight has spread like wildfire. These are volunteers who came here willingly. A thousand strong, all ready to pick up a sword and fight for the king that brought magic back to the lands. We even have a few elders teaching the ways of fighting with magic, your mother included."

Trystan glanced at Wren and he smiled up at him. "My mother was a brilliant magic wielder in her day. No need to worry, sire, she will lead them well, just as Lonara will teach all back at the palace."

"Sire?" The guard peered through the dwindling light at Trystan. "Yaro, do you mean to tell me I am in the presence of our king and you said nothing?"

Both guards fell to one knee as the one named Shannos cried out in horror, "I'm sorry, your Majesty. Please forgive me."

Trystan buried the laughter welling in his chest. "Arise, Sir Shannos, and no need to apologize. You've brought me great news. Our armies of Aldorwood and Sona grow every day but Isenore we were unsure of. It is an honor to see so many loyal to the Renaulds."

"Not everyone sided with Eisner, your Majesty." Shannos gripped his sword tight as he spat Eisner's name. "Most of us would gladly lop that traitor's head off if given the opportunity."

"Then pray when the opportunity arises, and it will, you do so with a steady hand."

"It would be an honor to take out that traitorous bastard,"

Shannos agreed and Trystan swore he heard Alixa mumble "Not if I do it first," as she rode up beside him. She'd been unusually quiet the closer they'd gotten to Cullenspire and Trystan watched her now as she observed the manor, a sadness etched in her face. He knew she was reliving Ella's death and he so badly wanted to reach out and take her hand. To offer his support, but he dared not. Not with so many eyes on him expecting him to act like their king. He knew the torment of losing a dear friend and he was glad she still had Edric around to help her deal with Ella's loss.

"As much as I'd love to talk more, Shannos, the thought of a hot meal and a glass of port appeals even more. Please excuse us as I let my mother know her wandering son has returned. We'll have plenty of time to catch up, my friend."

Shannos nodded as he and the other guard stood back to let them pass. By now the arrival of Trystan and his people had caught the attention of others. As Shannos shouted out "Make way for the king!" Trystan groaned deep in his chest. This was exactly what he'd wanted to avoid. Curious eyes and open mouths met their progression down the carriage lane as Shannos' words registered and the whispers of *King Trystan* made its way through the crowd. As they rode, people went to their knees in respect as the whispers grew into a chant.

"Trystan. Trystan. Trystan."

Alixa rode beside him as he stayed silent through it all. "You know they'll want to hear from their king. You can't ignore them."

He ran a weary hand over his neck. "I know. Just not tonight. I'll do my kingly duty tomorrow. As Wren just said, a hot meal and a strong drink sounds mighty nice right about now. Tonight just let me be Trystan. Tomorrow is plenty of time to be king."

Alixa favored him with a sympathetic gaze. "I don't think you're allowed that distinction anymore, your Majesty."

As Trystan watched her snap her reins and ride ahead he had a sinking feeling that she just might be right.

"AND THAT WAS the first time I met the lovely Mira." Wren beamed at the blonde girl sitting beside him and kissed the back of her hand, his love for her shining unabashed in his eyes. Mira's response was a bit more reserved. She cared for Wren, it was easy to see. But sitting here at Lady Yaro's formal dining table made her very uncomfortable, Trystan could tell. The dining hall, with it's ceiling high tapestries and imposing portraits of the Yaro family, would be overwhelming to the best of guests, let alone a village commoner. Ever since Wren had introduced Mira to his family as his betrothed, she'd been made the center of attention, especially by Lady Yaro. Trystan almost felt sorry for the poor girl as the matriarch of the Yaro clan studied Mira with the censure reserved only for the mothers of sons about to be replaced in their hearts by another woman.

"You're a farmer's daughter then?" Lady Yaro asked, not all in innocence, Trystan believed. The question annoyed him to no end.

"Wren left out one important part when he was singing Mira's virtues, Lady Yaro." Trystan couldn't help but intervene. "Mira has Tenelach, just like Princess Rissa. She is very special. She will be a very important addition to our army."

Mira's eyes filled with gratitude as they met Trystan's. "Thank you, your Majesty," she breathed, and Trystan gave a slight nod in response.

Lady Yaro finally smiled for the first time since hearing about her son's impending wedded bliss. "Tenelach? Wren, why didn't you say so?"

"Did I forget to mention that?" Wren's brow furrowed as if he were trying to understand why that was the most impressive thing about the woman he loved.

Trystan hid his smile as he sipped his wine and met Alixa's gaze across the laden table between them. Maybe it was too much of the wine Lady Yaro had supplied them with in celebration of her son's return, but Alixa's cheeks were a rosy red and the sadness that had been her constant companion lately, was absent.

She smiled at Trystan. A pleased, full out smile that brightened her hazel eyes to a golden hue and transformed her face into a vision of beauty. The smile hit him like a punch to the gut, and he sucked in a breath, almost choking on the sip of wine he'd just taken. Coughing to cover his embarrassment, he dragged his eyes away and turned to Lady Yaro.

"The guards told us you have a thousand strong training here, Madame. Quite the impressive feat. You've been busy since we last spoke. I owe you great thanks."

Lady Yaro turned her attention to Trystan, and he saw Mira out of the corner of his eye sag in relief.

"Truth be told, sire, all I did was spread word of the impending war and the need to show loyalty to the king who recovered their magic. These men and women showed up here on their own, demanding to be trained. They all realize they owe you their lives, and the lives of their families as well. We've had our own blacksmiths and bowyers, and those of the surrounding villages working night and day, outfitting them all with weapons and armor. The fletchers have been making arrows and bolts nonstop. Plus the few of us old folk who remember magic have been holding daily lessons, trying to teach them the ways without draining too much magic. It is slow going, but Calis' army will not fight with weapons alone. We must be prepared and able to reciprocate with magic, else they will defeat us. Dreach-Sciene will not go down easily."

"I agree. I appreciate your time and investment. Lonara is also training everyone back at the palace. I have every faith in the Tri-Gard to have them ready by the time we return."

Lady Yaro rested her elbows on the table and placed her chin on her steepled hands, studying the king.

"I have no doubt she will, sire. But truthfully, how much time do we have? To be brutally honest, I thought Calis would have attacked by now. I realize Dreach-Sciene's army outnumbers his, but a quick attack while our wielders are still untrained would have done great damage to us."

Trystan picked up his goblet and took another sip, debating his response.

"I am not sure. Spies from across the border tell us that Calis' army is filled with dissent and his people divided. Civil unrest has broken out. Seems like our returning magic has had consequences in Dreach-Dhoun as well, and it has bought us some time. Calis will not attack until he has his own people in line, we hope. As we speak, my sister and second in command are across the border performing a rescue of the seer who helped us escape. She was sentenced to death along with hundreds of villagers. I hope they are successful in their mission and will have more news for us on their return."

Lady Yaro's brows lifted in surprise. "Calis is holding a seer prisoner and has given her a death penalty? She could prove invaluable to him. Such a move does not make sense."

"I fear his anger outweighs his common sense. The seer I

speak of is his niece and has betrayed the Bearne name. He would rather see her hang then show mercy."

"His niece? But that means..."

Trystan's mouth formed a grim line at Lady Yaro's correct assumption. "Yes. The seer who was sent to the castle to murder my father. I'm sure you've heard a version of that story, although she was not the one to carry out the deed."

Lady Yaro crossed her arms across her chest. "And you believe her? Anyone with the Bearne name would be hard pressed to speak the truth."

Wren interrupted before Trystan could utter the angry retort that sprang to his lips. "You know better than to question our king, Mother. King Trystan's second in command also carries the Bearne name and Trystan trusts him completely, therefore so do I."

"As do I," Alixa added, her tone hard. "If we are to judge a person's character by the name they carry, then I would be found quite wanting, I'm afraid."

Lady Yaro bowed her head in remorse. "I apologize, your Majesty. I do not mean to question your decisions. Forgive me. I am nothing but a silly old woman with a wagging tongue." A wry smile split her lips.

Wren's laughter echoed about the room, breaking the tension. "As I've told you many times over the years to no avail. Trust that it would take a king to make you admit that out loud."

"Why am I cursed with such an impudent child?" Lady Yaro sighed, but it only made Wren laugh harder. The laughter was contagious. Soon they were all joining in. Even Avery cracked a smile, although it looked foreign on her face. The only one who wasn't laughing was Anna, Lady Yaro's daughter and Wren's younger sister. She sat beside her mother, her face grave and her eyes unfocused. Trystan noticed her seriousness a moment before she spoke, interrupting the laughter.

Her voice sounded old, bitter. Not the voice of the child they saw before them. Her eyes burned as if with fever as they landed on Trystan.

"Laugh while we can, for darkness is coming for Dreach-Sciene. I see it. It comes for us all. Death. Sacrifice. Betrayal. That is your curse."

Lady Yaro whirled in shock as she grabbed her daughter's hand. "Anna?"

The young girl seemed beyond hearing. Her eyes rolled back in her head until only the whites showed as she repeated the same words over and over. "It's coming. It's coming. It's coming."

"Anna." Wren yelled in panic and jumped to catch his sister as she slumped in her chair and fell to the floor in a dead faint.

Death. Sacrifice. Betrayal.

Anna's words echoed in Trystan's head as he stared up at the canopy of his bed. The words had mocked him all night, along with a myriad of bad dreams that had awakened him more than once in a cold sweat. Anna's words were an echo of Lorelai's, but he had broken that curse when he'd refused to kill Davi, right? The curse was no more, so why would those words come back to haunt him now?

Anna remembered nothing of her episode. Even when questioned about it she drew a blank. She did not understand where the words came from or why she'd said them, or even what the darkness was that she spoke of. Trystan assumed her prophecy meant the looming war. He hoped that's what it referred to. Any war meant death and he was prepared for that. He just didn't know if his heart could take losing anyone else close to him. He'd felt broken when he thought he'd lost Davi. Devastated at losing his father. He couldn't imagine the pain if he had to cope with losing Ri or Avery or Alixa.

Alixa. Even just saying her name in his head caused warmth to infuse his body. When had the traitorous duke's daughter become so important to him? He had thought her cold and abrasive at their first meeting, but he'd been so wrong. Any relationship with Alixa would be doomed from the start. He knew that. They were too different. The kingdom would never accept her as queen. But that did nothing to quell his heart racing every time she walked into a room. She was the most intelligent, beautiful, and infuriating woman he'd ever met. He couldn't imagine not having her in his life. But with a prophecy and a war looming over them...

Sighing, he ran a hand over his red-rimmed eyes. He might as well get up, He wasn't getting any more sleep. Images from last night's dream came filtering back into his head, replacing thoughts of Alixa. Not a dream. More of a nightmare, brought about no doubt from Anna's dire warning. Every time he broke free and woke up, sleep would claim him again and the images would crawl straight back. Images of fire and death, destruction and pain.

He shook his head, trying to force the memories away. No need to keep focusing on it. It was just a nightmare. He'd had plenty of those before. He had more important worries to fill his mind with now. Like Davi and Rissa's hopeful success on their mission. The safety and wellbeing of his people. How to win a war. How to defeat the coming darkness. Just everyday king stuff.

He got out of bed and walked to the window on the other side of his room. The sun was just rising, and the early rays illuminated the gardens below with streaks of oranges and gold. He smiled to himself as the blooming garden lifted his spirits. It was a nice view. A healing view. The pink orchids of the cherry blossom trees and the colorful carpet of flowers reminded him of life and hope, chasing away the remnants of his nightmare.

As he stood there enjoying the warm rays of the crowning sun on his face, a movement from below caught his eye. Curious, he peered down into the garden, wondering who was out and about this early in the morn. A dark head and a blonde head, close in conversation it appeared, moved below him. Alixa and Anna, he was sure. But what were the two of them doing out in the garden this early when they both should be in their beds asleep?

Curiosity filled him, and he dressed in a hurry, wanting to catch up with them in the garden.

He met no one on his way out, but the smells wafting from the kitchen informed him the staff were already up and preparing for the manor's breakfast. His stomach grumbled, but he ignored it as he stepped into the crisp air of the morning. He breathed in deep, the fragrant scent of the garden renewed him with its freshness and he couldn't help but smile to himself.

It didn't take Trystan long to find the two women. They had rested on a marble bench awash in golden sunlight. They both peered up in surprise as Trystan approached, and he felt the familiar racing of his heart as Alixa smiled at him in greeting.

"Good morning, your Majesty. Looks like we are not the only two early risers."

"Good morning to you both."

Alixa looked as appealing as always, but Anna appeared more perturbed than she had the night before. Her face was drawn and pinched and dark shadows adorned her eyes, evidence to her sleepless night. Trystan felt an overwhelming urge of pity for the young girl. Being a seer was hard enough, but double a curse at such a young age. "Anna, I hope you are not suffering any ill effects from last night."

"I'm used to these... nights," she said, her voice sounding older than her years.

"Then I don't envy you. I believe we all suffered a taste of sleeplessness last night, but possibly worth it since we all get to see this glorious sunrise. May I join you?"

Alixa and Anna shifted over on the bench and Trystan sat with them, all three basking in the comfort of the sun's warmth. After a few moments of silence, Alixa turned her golden eyes from the beauty of the sunrise and studied Trystan in interest.

"Anna and I have been discussing our reasons for our lack of sleep. I think it's beneficial to talk about what bothers the mind, so it doesn't bother the heart. I dreamt of Ella all night. Thankfully it was mostly good memories. Our time together as children. Our conversations and laughter. The bad memories tried as well, but I refused to let them overwhelm me. Anna has told me it's better to focus on the good and the bad will fade." She smiled at the young girl and Trystan realized that Alixa possibly saw a lot of herself in the withdrawn Anna. "Would you like to share your reason for lack of sleep, Trystan? Don't take this the wrong way, but you look terrible. Did you rest at all?"

"Thank you for the compliment on my appearance," Trystan laughed and Alixa joined in. It was nice to hear her laugh.

"Well you know me, never one to stay quiet when something needs to be said."

"Careful, Lady Alixa. That sounds dangerously close to something my mother would say."

Trystan did a double take at Anna's words before realizing the young girl was actually teasing. So, she did possess a sense of humor under all that gloom. Even the slight smile she sent Alixa's way transformed her face, making her look more like the young child she should be. Trystan wanted to make the smile grow.

"Yes we all saw that last night, did we not? I almost felt sorry for Mira and Wren. Your mother is a formidable woman. I must admit, I'm glad she stands with me and not Calis Bearne. You are lucky to have your mother's support."

Alixa caught his gaze over Anna's head and nodded in approval of his words. They had both grown up motherless. They both knew how lucky Anna was to have her mother's love.

"Be that as it may, Trystan, you still haven't told us the reason you've crawled your way out of bed at sunrise. I've told you of my reason. Now it's your turn. Anna says you must talk about your fears or else they will continue to haunt you. She's a smart girl, this one."

Trystan chuckled softly. "Talk about my fears? Where do I begin?" He stared off into the distance for a moment, gathering his thoughts. "I worry for Ri and Davi. It's been weeks now and still no word. I worry about the approaching war. Will we be ready in time? Will we be able to defeat Calis at his own game? I worry for my people. For their safety. I do not wish to lose anyone else. I dreamt it happening last night and…" He glanced down at the girl, rapt at his story. "Never mind. It's not important. What's important is breakfast right now. I'm starving."

"No, please, sire." Anna grabbed his hand imploringly. "You

must continue. To keep your fears hidden will eat at your mind and soul. Tell us what bothers you."

He stared into the young eyes that had seen far too much in their short years. As if he couldn't help himself, his words started up again.

"I dreamt of horrible things. Of loss and death. I dreamt of a village on fire. A village I do not know, yet it was as real to me as this garden is right now. Others were there as well. Ri, Davi, Ramsey, Lorelai, Rion, Edric. They were all there screaming in pain as blue flames swept through the village, incinerating everything in its path and Calis' army looked on."

Anna's tiny gasp stopped his words and he worried he had gone too far. He didn't mean to scare the child.

"A village engulfed in blue flame? Your Majesty, I too have dreamt of this. A horrifying nightmare of people screaming and dying, brought down on them as reprisal from the mad king. Tell me, was there a statue at the head of this village? A statue of King Marcus?"

A cold wave of fear chilled Trystan's blood at the girl's words. The vision of a finely sculpted image of his father at the village's entrance entered his head. He'd seen it in his dream, along with the blue flames.

"Yes." His voice was practically a whisper, scared for what the girl would say next. "But it was just a dream. A nightmare. It wasn't real."

"Sire, the village is very real. I've been there with Wren. It's Briarwood, a village at the Dreach-Dhoun border. That we both share it tells me our dream is no dream at all. I fear it is instead, a prophecy."

"TRYSTAN YOU ARE NOT LISTENING to reason."

Wren gripped the edge of the table and glared Trystan's way. His anger was evident, but so was his concern.

"We do not have time to argue this point." Trystan glared back. "I fear Anna is correct. This event will happen if we don't stop it. Briarwood is three days of hard riding. We must get there as quickly as possible, which means leaving now."

"The king is correct." Avery stared down her nose at Wren, her displeasure with him for all to see. "Speed is of the essence."

Wren raised a hand and rubbed the back of his neck. "I understand your concern. I do. And I believe in my sister's gift, but we cannot walk into this foolishly. If your dream is true, this village's fate lies in the hands of an army of Calis' men. We cannot afford to fall into their grasp. And as much as I believe in the fighting ability of Avery and yourself, you two alone cannot take on a squadron of men. Men armed with magic. We must send an army to deal with an army and that takes time. We need a day to prepare."

"I hate to admit it, Trystan, but I agree with Wren." Alixa's voice severed the stare down between Trystan and Wren. The worst of it was, Trystan did not disagree with Wren's idea. He knew the man was correct. Putting a contingent together took time. Time they could not afford to waste.

"Can you do it in half a day?"

Wren threw his hands up in the air and stepped away from the table. "Mother earth, grant me patience." His gaze flicked Lady Yaro's way. "Mother, help me out here, will you?"

Lady Yaro regarded them both from her position at the head of the table. Anna sat demurely at her side.

"I don't often say this, sire, but my son speaks wisdom. We need time to prepare. If we are to stop this event from happening, we need men, supplies, weapons, horses. We do not have enough horses here to supply an army of one hundred, let alone what you will need to take with you. These people you see outside, they volunteered and have trained well, yes. But they are poor peasant folk, mostly. They walked here on foot or came by wagon. We do not have the horses and wagons needed to transport them. As we speak, my messengers are on their way to the closest outlying villages to gather those things. Packhorses, palfreys, workhorses, anything that can move. We will hurry the best we can but that will take some time." Lady Yaro glanced over at her daughter and grasped her hand tight. "Anna's gifts are a blessing, but they do not always follow a linear timeline. This event may be days away, or it may have already happened. You must brace yourself for that possibility, Trystan."

Trystan granted Lady Yaro a hard stare. "No. I refuse to believe that. This has not occurred yet. Ri and Davi are still very much alive. I know it. I feel it in my heart. There was no way they'd be taken out that easy. Not my sister. Not the woman she's become. She'd take Calis' army out single handedly before she'd let any harm come to that village or her people. Of that I'm certain." He took a deep breath and pushed himself back from the table. Pacing around the room, deep in thought, he whirled back to Lady Yaro and her son. "Fine, I agree. We wait, but we leave at first light with what we have. As of right now, what are our numbers? Avery, we arrived with fifty men and horses, yes?"

"Yes, Sire."

"And what can you provide us with as of this moment, Lady Yaro? Where do we stand?"

"Body wise, we stand strong. Out of the thousand plus soldiers in the fields, over half of them have already been supplied weapons and armor. They are ready to battle. Travel wise, with the horses and wagons we have on hand we can possibly send one hundred and fifty, give or take a few. That gives you two hundred able-bodied men and women, some proficient with magic as well. Some not."

"And what do you expect your villages to be able to supply?"

"With their horses and wagons we should be able to double that number. Will it be enough? You had the dream. You saw Calis' army. Will four hundred bodies be enough?"

Trystan's mind dredged up the memory he had been trying desperately all day to avoid. Closing his eyes he pictured the village. He saw the blue flames dancing from cottage to cottage. He heard the screams of the people as the heat of the flames melted the flesh from their bones. Their desperate attempt to escape the ring of fiery death as Calis' men encircled the village, firing upon anyone lucky enough to make it through the flames alive. A sea of men and women standing deep in shadows that stretched back into the hills surrounding the village. At least double or more of the four hundred they were able to send.

"Yes, it will be enough." He ignored Anna's eyes as they finally lifted and met his. In them he could see her puzzlement. Her disbelief that he had so blatantly lied. She said nothing however, and Trystan was grateful for that. He needed everyone to believe that they could do this. He could not afford to have them give up hope before they even began.

"Lady Yaro, Lady Alixa, I need you both to cull the troops. Check with the commanders of each house and choose their best swordsman, the best archers, the best magic wielders. We need every single body to count. While you are doing that, Avery, Wren and I will be formulating a battle plan. For this to work, we need to act with speed and precision. We can't afford to make any mistakes."

"Understood, your Majesty." Lady Yaro stood and walked out of the room, Anna following close behind. Alixa turned as if to follow, but instead approached Trystan. She placed a hand on his arm, her gold eyes searching his face in concern. "I know you're worried, but Ri is far more resourceful than you give her credit for. Davi too. Even Ramsey. If anyone can save this village before we can get there, it'll be them. Don't worry."

He gave a curt nod, tamping down the need to pull her into his arms for the much needed support he wanted from her touch right now. Instead he made due with lacing her fingers through his and gripped her hand tight. She smiled at him before turning away and he watched her walk out of the room, her words echoing in his head.

Don't worry.

Easier said than done. He was worried. Extremely worried. Worried that four hundred men would prove not enough. Worried that those he loved were awaiting a fiery death. Worried that none of them would make it back alive. Worries his father had faced every day, no doubt. But he was his father's son. He would try his best. For his people. For Ri. For Alixa. He just prayed that they wouldn't be too late.

Son. Please. The words invaded Davi's mind, filling every space, overcoming every other thought. *He is my son.*

They were back to where the worst happened. The mountains of Isenore. It couldn't have been far from where his father's men almost killed him. Where he'd killed himself. His fingers brushed the hilt of his sword sheathed at his waist.

The one memory he wished he'd never gotten back seemed to vibrate through the mountains, blocking out the sun until all he saw was darkness.

He'd plunged a sword straight into his heart. He'd done it to save Trystan. A man he still couldn't quite look in the eye.

Davi rubbed the spot on his chest that had been pierced by the blade. His father saved him. Brought him back to life.

Come with me Davion. Together we can make this right.

But nothing was right and he got the distinct impression it never would be.

The burning inside his chest intensified and he lunged

from his horse, rolling as he hit the ground. Magic flowed from the soil into his limbs and the pain eased as it calmed him.

He'd almost gone. Almost forsaken everything for his father. How could he have even paused? His body jerked as if trying to empty itself, but nothing came up.

"This is as good a place as any to stop," Ramsey's soft voice broke through the silence that had surrounded them for most of the day. It'd been two days since they made it across the Dreach-Dhoun border. Bowman was true to his word in covering their retreat. But what was happening to the rebels of Dreach-Dhoun now?

Since crossing into Dreach-Sciene, they'd been skirting the border, avoiding the heart of Isenore. They would turn in Aldorwood's direction once they reached Cullenspire.

Rion dismounted next to Davi and took the reins of both their horses, leading them farther into the woods toward the stream they'd been following through the mountain pass.

Davi closed his eyes as the images returned to him.

"Edric!" Rissa screamed.

"Get down," Rion yelled as another arrow flew into the clearing.

Ramsey raised his hand as if to send a blast of magic, but even he was depleted.

Rissa dropped to her knees and crawled across the pine covered ground to where Edric lay with blood gushing from his chest. She pressed her fingers to his neck, her blazing hair swinging back and forth as she shook her head.

Davi scanned the trees for their attacker as another arrow sailed through the woods, striking a tree to his left. He jumped back just in time to see a flash of red. Rissa sprinted through branches and underbrush, not stopping as they whipped her in the face.

"Dammit," Davi grunted as he jumped to his feet and took off

after her.

Rissa pulled an arrow free as she ran and set it against the curve of her bow. She didn't slow as she pulled the string back. A scream pierced the air as the arrow struck soft flesh.

Another scream hit him as Rissa loosed a second arrow.

Davi arrived to find their attacker crawling in desperation to get away from Rissa who stood over him with a blank expression on her face. The first arrow protruded from his hand, which had been holding his bow. The second rose from his leg.

Crimson blood stained the dark Dreach-Dhoun uniform.

"Ri, he can't come after us." Davi reached for her, but she jerked away. "We have to go."

She held out her arm for him to take her bow. He looked to her in question but did as she asked.

"Edric was good." Ice entered her voice. She pulled a dagger free from the sheathe of her belt. "Honorable. Brave. He risked his life for his kingdom." Her eyes hardened as she stared down at the man.

Fear shone in his gaze. "Please."

"Ri, let's go." Adrenaline still coursed through Davi's veins from the fight and their escape, but he knew they needed to move quickly.

Rissa acted as if she didn't hear him. Instead, she bent to look Edric's killer in the eyes. "I am not good." With a swift movement, she sliced the dagger across his throat.

Davi pulled his hands away from the earth so quickly he almost fell back. He'd never seen Rissa so cold. So emotionless. When he'd left her, she'd still been a princess who knew how to shoot.

Now she was a… killer? Not just a warrior, but something else. That man hadn't needed to die. Marcus Renauld always taught his children—including Davi—it didn't matter what another person did, but what you did in return. That was what defined your character. That man had killed Edric. Was Rissa just as guilty of evil as him?

As Davi's father?

That was what it came down to. Davi wanted to make some sense of his father's actions. To find reason among the chaos. Good mixed with the bad.

If he couldn't, that would make what he felt for the man a betrayal of everything he was.

A hand landed on Davi's shoulder and he jumped.

"Just me, kid." Ramsey lowered himself to the ground.

"Kid," Davi scoffed. "You don't look a day older than me."

Ramsey smiled kindly. "There have to be benefits to this Tri-Gard business. It certainly isn't the lack of danger."

"If you and Lonara can appear young, why not Briggs?"

Ramsey sighed. "Out of the three of us, who did you trust the most?"

Davi nodded. He understood finally. Briggs spent years pretending to be an ally. Just a crazy old man. He wasn't the Tri-Gard member one had to worry about. Ramsey had been thought of as the betrayer by all of Dreach-Sciene for two decades. And people feared Lonara.

"He isn't crazy, is he?" Davi asked.

"No. Briggs Villard is many things, but his mind works better than just about anyone else's. Those 'voices' he always speaks too… that's your father. They were in constant communication."

So much made sense now. He looked up, hoping to see Rissa, needing to tell her. To talk to her. To touch her and remind himself she was there with him. She wasn't a memory that had been implanted.

"I'm going to sit here a while longer and let the earth's power soothe away everything from the past few days. You should go to the river."

He sat there in confusion for a moment before Ramsey nudged him. "My granddaughter went that way."

"Right." Davi climbed to his feet and followed the path set by the horse's hooves. Their weight left imprints on the mossy floor. Before long, a sheer rock face rose up on his right, forming a wall to the river.

Familiarity struck him. This same river wound down out of the mountains all the way to the forests of Aldorwood. They'd followed it when they first set out on their quest what seemed like a lifetime ago.

His feet stopped when he caught sight of Rissa. She sat in her underclothes on the edge of the river. A trickle of water ran down the rock wall, dropping into the current. She stuck her head under it, letting it lace through the thick strands of her hair.

He should have turned away. Given her the privacy she deserved. But his entire body froze to the spot as she stretched her arms out and scrubbed at the dirt caking onto her skin. She flung her hair back over her shoulder and rivulets of water streamed down her face.

She was beautiful.

Her cold eyes flashed through his mind, but that wasn't the girl who was before him now. She'd turned into someone else.

I am not good.

The Rissa he knew represented everything good in this world.

And she'd slit the soldier's throat without a second thought. They hadn't been in battle. He was no longer a threat.

She only wanted revenge.

He remembered the feeling well. He'd burned with a need for revenge before his memories returned to him. And now he hated himself for it.

Did she feel the same way?

As if sensing his question, she looked up, her eyes widening at his presence.

Her shirt and trousers lay on the rock beside her but she didn't reach for them. Her underclothes revealed a sliver of creamy stomach and his fingers itched to touch her. To make her see she didn't have to be that other person anymore. He was back. It was time for her to return as well.

"Dav," she breathed, heat swirling in her eyes.

His body moved of its own accord as he jumped down to the riverbank and stood inches from her.

Tears hung in her lashes but she didn't let them fall. Not his Rissa. The strong, resilient fighter. What she didn't realize was choosing not to feel didn't make you strong. Bravery was facing that which we did not wish to face.

Davi didn't hesitate any longer as he leaned in and pressed his lips to hers. Her hands gripped his biceps as if afraid she would fall.

They'd faced the hell of Dreach-Dhoun and returned alive. Again. They'd lost a dear friend. Rissa had taken a life with her own hands.

As he kissed her, Davi gave it all back to her. The emotions. The grief. He wanted to make her brave, just for a moment.

One arm circled her back while his free hand rubbed circles on the exposed skin of her stomach. There were always events or people stopping them from being in this together. From becoming a team.

Rissa pulled away and sucked in a shuddering breath. "You wanted to stay with him." She rested her forehead against his.

Davi couldn't take back his indecision. He couldn't erase those memories from Rissa's mind. "I won't leave you again."

In that moment, he knew it was true. His father didn't hold half the power over him that Rissa did.

She stepped back and hugged her arms over her chest. "I want to believe that, Davi. I do. But what if it comes down to him or us?"

"I wouldn't—"

"I saw the way you looked at him!" She breathed deeply. "He's your father, Dav. And he's the enemy. I know that. But do you know what I…" She turned away. "I'd do anything to have my father back."

He stepped toward her, pressing up against her back, and wrapped his arms around her. "I'd give the world to have your father with us again."

She sighed. "Really?"

"I won't lie to you, Ri. My head is a mess. I'm still sorting through real and false memories. My father will always have some weird pull on me. But your family has always been my family. Marcus Renauld raised me. He trained me. He made me into the man I am." He rested his chin on her shoulder. "Without him, I might be just like Calis Bearne."

"Or like me." A third voice joined their conversation.

Lorelai stood behind them, her watchful eyes studying them. "I'm sorry. I just came to bathe. This is the first time since… Well, the first time in a while. I didn't mean to interrupt."

This was the most his cousin had said to him since her rescue. He released Rissa who quickly gathered her clothes and ran off without even slipping her shoes on first.

Davi let her go as he examined his cousin. Ramsey said she'd barely slept since the night they broke her free and the stress was clear in the rings around her eyes. Her beautiful white-blonde hair was matted with the same grime that streaked her face.

She stepped by him and bent to unlace her boots. Without straightening, she looked back at him. "Do you plan on giving me some time alone before I lose the last bit of sun?"

He ignored her annoyance. "What did you mean when you said 'or like me?'"

She stood up and faced away from him as her voice took on the sad note he'd heard too often. "I was raised by Calis, Davion. Or at least in his household. And you know what I've spent more than a decade doing?"

He didn't make a move.

"Lying. Cheating." She paused. "Killing." A sigh pushed past her lips. "I did it all in the name of the uncle I still love. Even after he tried to execute me. If there's anyone who understands you, it's me. But you were lucky. Yes, you still served as your father's unwitting pawn, but it meant a different path forward for you. Marcus..." Her voice shook and trailed off.

"Lorelai—"

"Let me have some peace, Davion." Her voice hardened. "I know you don't understand the consequences of your stunt in Dreach-Dhoun, but that doesn't mean they don't exist."

"What consequences?"

"Exactly. You saw someone you love in danger and wanted to save them, but what other dangers did you cause? I won't lie, I am happy to be standing here before you. But that is a selfish joy. Sometimes you shouldn't risk everything for the ones you love. You have to know when it's time to let go."

She turned to face him. “I’m sure Ramsey and Rion would like help setting up camp.”

She began undressing and Davi walked back the way he’d come. A wolf howled in the distance, but he didn’t worry about Lorelai. If anyone could take care of themselves, it was her.

They were so well trained. It was the first thought that entered Rissa's mind the moment they came across a patrol in Isenore.

But not just any patrol. These soldiers didn't belong to the lecherous duke. Eisner would no doubt send troops of his own to cut them off soon enough.

This unit once pledged their loyalty to Marcus Renauld and now followed his son. Rissa smiled for what seemed the first time in ages as she took in the Renauld colors. A red and gold banner flapped in the wind as if singing of their arrival.

Rissa jumped from her horse. Trystan would have rolled his eyes at this move in front of their soldiers as it wasn't very princess-like. She didn't care.

"Captain," she greeted, taking note of the rank emblazoned on his worn uniform.

"Princess." His weathered face relaxed in relief. "It sure is good to see you, my lady."

"It's quite a shock to see Dreach-Sciene troops this far

South. Are we pushing into Isenore? We are still dangerously close to Duke Eisner's land."

He scratched his face. "We are making our way to the border."

She nodded, a smile returning to her lips. "Good."

Davi slid from his horse and stepped up beside her as his eyes scanned the sea of soldiers.

"About time we caught a break." He ran a hand over the top of his head and shielded his eyes from the sun. "Have you run into any trouble."

"Yes, sir."

Davi grimaced at the title. He was no leader. Not anymore. The captain went on. "We had a minor skirmish when we first crossed from Aldorwood into Isenore. We sent a liter of injured back to the palace and lost a few good men."

"I'm sorry about your losses, captain." Rissa reached out and gripped his arm.

The soldier's eyes widened in surprise at the informality of the gesture, but Rissa didn't remove her hand. "Do you have messengers with you?"

"Yes, Princess."

"I will need one of them brought to me. I must send a message to my brother to let him know of our victory in Dreach-Dhoun and our return trek."

"But Princess…" The captain glanced from Rissa to Davi. "When we saw the king last, he was headed to Isenore."

Rissa dropped her hand and glanced over her shoulder to Ramsey. "Why would my brother come here when we're preparing for war?"

Ramsey shrugged, but Rion nudged his horse forward before sliding down. "May I speak, Princess?"

She nodded.

"If we are to battle the great army across the border, the king must call on all loyal people. There are still those in Isenore who will answer that call."

"Cullenspire," she whispered. "That's where he went."

"Cullenspire?" Davi asked.

She looked from Ramsey to Davi to Rion to Lorelai. None of them had been there. Edric had and now he was gone. Would she be able to find the way herself?

That was a question for tomorrow. Exhaustion weighed down on her and she sighed. "Captain, we camp with you tonight and part ways tomorrow."

"Of course, Princess. We will have a tent prepared for you. I'm sorry, we're lacking certain luxuries."

Rissa waved his worry away. "If you knew what the last few months have been like for us..." She shook her head. "No, Captain. We will be more than happy with anything you can provide."

Two soldiers came forward to retrieve the horses and Rissa followed the captain through the camp with Davi and the others close behind. Tents rose on either side of them. Every soldier was very aware of their presence, but they only watched them go by. Never approaching. Never speaking.

Rissa recognized the curiosity in their stares, but also the fear. It had been the same inside the palace.

Stories of Davi's death and resurrection had spread throughout Dreach-Sciene, but not only that. His father's name sat on the tip of every tongue. Calis Bearne. They knew Davion wasn't one of them.

Rissa lifted her chin, hardening her features. Davi belonged there as much as any of them.

"Forgive my men," the captain said, turning to Davi. "They only know what they've been told. Who your father is. But I trained as a guard inside the palace before being assigned to this patrol. I watched you fight King Trystan repeatedly. Always with honor. Always with mercy. And I was in the hall the day he broke tradition and chose a boy with no family name as his second." He dipped his head. "I believed in his choice that day and still do."

Davi stopped walking, his feet frozen to the spot and his breathing ragged. He shook his head. "I can't… it was a joke. A humiliation."

The captain's eyes pleaded with Rissa for an explanation, but she ignored him and took Davi's hand. Leaning close, she dropped her voice. "Dav, it was real. Pull the memories apart. Separate the false from the true. You've been doing well. You are Davion, second in command to the toha of Dreach-Sciene. It was a great honor, given of love." He closed his eyes and his chest expanded as he sucked in a breath.

When he opened his eyes again, clarity had returned. He gave a short nod and pushed past them into the tent they'd arrived at.

Rion followed him in, but Lorelai walked by them, taking a path to the trees at the edge of the camp.

Ramsey put a hand on Rissa's back. "Captain, can we count on your discretion as to Davion's… troubles?"

The captain nodded. "Alert my men if you have need of anything. I'll send my best messenger your way."

When Ramsey and Rissa stood alone, she turned to look at him. "What are we going to do? Davion sits on the edge of a cliff. It'll only take one strong false memory to push him over it."

"We can't trust him," he agreed. "But we can watch him." He took off into the sea of tents. "Come."

Rissa ran to catch up, taking two small steps for every one of his larger ones. He followed the same way Lorelai had gone.

"Where are we going?" she asked, avoiding the eyes of a few passing soldiers.

"Lorelai always seeks peace. Something I'm sure she hasn't had in her mind since we recovered her."

She grabbed his arm and forced him to stop. "But why are we going after Lorelai? You just said we need to watch Davi and then we left him."

"Rion is with him. Not that he'll do much good." Ramsey shrugged her hand off and started moving again, even faster this time. "In order to protect Davi—mostly from himself—you must have at least a basic understanding of magic."

"I use magic just fine."

He stopped at the edge of the trees and turned to her. "You think being able to do a few tricks, use a little power, means you understand? The tenelach gives you an advantage, I admit. Without training, you are able to control the flow of power and shape it. But, my dear, that is only the surface. This power the earth allows us to have is so much more than flashes of light and emboldened strength."

They walked past the first row of branches to find a clearing surrounded by a circle of trees. The sky had long since grown dark and away from the torches of camp, the night was black.

Ramsey stepped forward and found a stick on the ground. Nestling it among the grass, he snapped his fingers and a flame burst free. The light illuminated the pale-haired Lorelai in the center of the space.

She lifted her face, the fire reflected in her eyes. "What do you want, Ramsey?"

Her harsh tone didn't deter him. He lowered himself to the

ground in front of her. "Lorelai, it's time." His eyes flicked to Rissa. "You cannot continue to hate us for a choice that was no choice at all."

"Still the same man, I see." She shook her head. "Take your riddles somewhere else."

"No."

"No?"

Ramsey rocked in agitation and Rissa couldn't remember ever seeing him so worked up.

"Listen to me, Lorelai. We had to come for you. Davion and I couldn't have allowed you to die."

"Of course you could have. Ramsey, you are the one person in your little band of..." She looked to Rissa dismissively. "Rebels, who should understand what your actions have unleashed. Hundreds will now be dead. Calis will send his army through the villages, wiping away any trace of rebellion. He'll station his best men along the border now. No longer ones you have a chance of bringing to your side. It will be impassable. You gave my uncle reason to turn on his own earth darned people. I am not worth their lives."

"You're right." Rissa sat down hard, splaying her hands on her knees. "You're not. If I'd had it my way, we wouldn't have come after you at all. We'd have let you hang."

"Rissa Renauld." Ramsey's eyes burned into her.

Lorelai leaned forward. "No, let the girl speak."

Anger rose up in Rissa, swirling through her mind. The woman before her was the reason her father was dead. She may not have slit his throat herself, but that didn't matter.

"I don't like you," Rissa stated. "I didn't agree with letting you escape Dreach-Dhoun with us the first time and frankly, I was secretly relieved when you were caught. You got my father killed."

"I did."

"He was a good man."

"He was."

Rissa jerked back. "Don't agree with me, dammit!"

"What do you want from me, Princess?"

What did she want? Rissa wasn't sure of anything anymore. Before she could stop them, words tumbled from her lips. "How was he? In the end?"

No explanation was necessary and Lorelai met her gaze, the ice melting away. "Kind." Her voice grew quieter. "Brave."

"Did you love him?"

Was there a right answer to the question? If she said no, then she really had just been a traitor who'd lost her nerve.

But if she said yes… had her father held any love for the seer?

Lorelai's shallow breaths were the only sound in Rissa's ears.

Finally, the seer nodded. "I did."

A fist clenched around Rissa's heart.

Lorelai wasn't finished. "You have to understand… I've spent my life catering to the whims of powerful men. Being what they wanted me to be. Obeying them. Never challenging. To my uncle and those he deemed worthy, I was something to be used." A small smile tilted her lips. "Marcus respected me. You don't know how powerful that is."

"And you tried to kill him for it." The accusation faded from Rissa's voice as sad truths smacked her in the face. Lorelai really hadn't had any other choice.

She'd forgiven Davi for the things he'd done when under his father's control, but she would never forget the look in his eye as he tried to kill them.

Just like his cousin, he'd been trapped in a sequence of events he couldn't escape.

Rissa swallowed. "Teach me."

Lorelai's eyes flicked to Ramsey. "What?"

"That's why my grandfather brought me to you, yes? Teach me. I want to learn. Push aside your anger and regret and I'll rid myself of mine. The past cannot be undone." Rissa rose up on her knees and scooted closer. "I want to help Davion. Save my people. Keep Dreach-Sciene from disappearing into darkness. Teach me."

"I don't think—"

Rissa reached forward and gripped Lorelai's wrist in desperation. "Please."

Images of the injured soldier in Dreach-Dhoun flashed through her mind. She could almost feel the feathers of her arrow against her fingers. It changed to her uncle's vacant eyes staring up at her.

She shook her head as the months crashed in on her. None of the hatred or the darkness went away when Davi returned. It was still there, wrapped around her beating heart, threading through her chest.

"Please," she whispered. Magic was the only thing that could spark the light inside her. But only if she gave everything she had to it. Her grip on Lorelai tightened as the words she'd said in Dreach-Dhoun echoed through her skull, filling the spaces of her mind. *I am not good.*

Finally, she released Lorelai and sat back. Her voice was barely audible. "I want to be good." Her words carried on the breeze that wrapped around Isenore like a cloak. *I want to be good.*

Ramsey reached out to take Rissa's hand, but thought better of it and pulled away.

Lorelai watched them with burning intensity. Moonlight caught in her hair, giving the pale strands a silver glow. The orange flicker of the fire danced across her skin.

She placed her palms on the ground as if seeking strength from the earth's magic for her next words.

"I do too."

"Don't use your strength, your body," Lorelai barked. "Use your mind."

Rissa could see it so clearly, what she wanted to accomplish. She closed her eyes, feeling the hum of the earth's power vibrate underneath her skin.

It was difficult fighting instinct. The magic wanted to be released in big explosive bursts of power. Holding it in, shaping it into something else, was beyond the ability of most sorcerers.

"Now." Lorelai's voice echoed across the space.

Rissa let the power trickle from her, controlled, slow. It struck the ground, spreading out like a cloak. She opened her eyes as the last of it left her and found white flowers spanning the clearing. Vines that hadn't been there before hung from branches.

A grin split Rissa's face.

Lorelai stared at her in wonder. "How did you do this?"

Rissa shrugged. "I just imagined it and here it is. Are flowers hard to create?"

"Pick one of the flowers."

Rissa stepped forward and bent to pull one from the earth, reeling back when her fingers closed around a blade of grass instead. She reached for a different flower, once again only coming away with a handful of grass.

"The first rule of magic," Lorelai began. "Is you can't create something from nothing." She waved a hand and the flowers disappeared. "You're adept. I've never worked with someone who had the tenelach. It's as if the earth itself is aiding in your magic use."

She pursed her lips. "Second rule of magic. You cannot change something into something else."

"Then what did I do?" Rissa asked. "How were the flowers here?"

"They weren't. One of the most necessary tools of magic is the ability to trick the eye. You made us both see flowers where there was only grass. Once you know the first two rules, your magic is only limited to the amount your body allows you to hold at once, and your imagination." She nodded. "Try something else."

Rissa didn't know how long they'd been working. It was still dark when they rose and they hadn't killed each other yet. She saw that as a victory.

By the time the sun broke through the treetops, sweat dripped down her face, but she couldn't remember the last time she'd felt so good. So strong. So… ready.

She twisted on her heel, pulling on her magic as if it were a rope tied to the nearby tree. The tree leaned and she grit her teeth to keep her hold. Lorelai watched, arms crossed over her chest.

"Gah!" A cloud of dust erupted as the tree fell to the earth with a loud boom. Rissa finally let go of her magic, letting it snap away from her and send her flying back onto her butt.

A slow clap sounded nearby and she turned to where Davi, Ramsey, and Rion stood watching them. Ramsey continued to clap.

Davi stared in awe. "You…" He pointed to the tree.

She wiped her face and jumped to her feet. Each muscle ached and she enjoyed every bit of pain.

"I was going to ask how Rissa was doing," Ramsey started, "but I think we can all see for ourselves."

"She's okay," Lorelai said, her voice emotionless.

Rissa spun to face her. "Okay? I was awesome!"

"And so modest." Davi chuckled and it was the best sound she'd ever heard.

The after-effects of the magic still pumping through her, she jogged toward him. "You okay after last night?"

His smile dropped and he sighed. "Yeah. Still just have some things to sort out. I think I need to talk to Trystan."

Ramsey clapped him on the back. "Then it's a good thing we're ready to leave. With Rissa as our guide, we can make it to Cullenspire in a few days' time."

"About that." Rissa faced her grandfather. "I don't know if I can find it."

He only smiled and turned to walk back to the camp.

Lorelai stepped up beside her. "Remember, Rissa, only your imagination limits you." She followed Ramsey with Rion close behind.

Rissa took Davi's hand.

"She still isn't speaking to me," he said. "I risked everything to save her."

"I think that's the problem, Dav. She doesn't think she was worth it."

He pulled her against him. "She told me that sometimes you have to know when to let go, but how was I supposed to do that? How did you let go of me?"

She sighed. "If I'd had any idea you were still in there, I'd have fought evil Davi to get you back. But this isn't just about us. It never has been. A lot of people will die if we make the wrong decisions. I'm not sure rescuing Lorelai was the right choice." She breathed him in. "But it's done now. We paid the price. Soon, we'll be with Trystan and Alixa again."

She raised her face to look at him. "How am I supposed to tell Alixa about Edric?"

Davi smoothed her hair back. "Edric knew the risks of coming with us."

"If I said that to Alixa, I'd probably get punched in the face. Edric and his sister meant a great deal to her. I was there when Ella died. And now I'm the one who has to destroy her once again."

He kissed her forehead and released her. "Alixa is stronger than any of us. She'll be okay." He tugged her hand. "But we have to get to Cullenspire. Any idea how you'll find the path?"

She focused on the clearing and the flowers that had been there. "A few."

THEY LEFT the unit of Dreach-Sciene soldiers with well-wishes and earth-speeds. Once their horses took them out of the pass and into the rolling hills on the front side of the mountains, they stopped and looked to Rissa for instruction.

She slid from her horse and walked a fair distance to be

alone with the earth. Its hum rang in her ears. She kneeled and placed both palms on the ground, echoing the hum in the back of her throat.

"Show me how to get to Cullenspire," she whispered. Magic flooded her body, but no clear path laid out before her. "Please don't let me down."

Still nothing.

Your limit is your imagination.

The earth wasn't showing her the way to Cullenspire. What was she missing?

A connection.

The answer sang softly in her mind. She had no connection to Cullenspire. What was she supposed to do now?

Her hair hung forward, shielding her face from the sun.

Trystan. The answer seemed so obvious now, as if the earth had spoken his name.

"Show me the way to my brother. Lead me to Trystan."

The tug began in her heart and worked its way out through every cell in her body. She jerked forward, almost falling. "Thank you."

Her chest ached as she walked back to the others as if screaming "wrong way!"

Ramsey eyed her, a question in his gaze. She only nodded in response. She'd get them there.

The last time she'd made the journey, the world had been covered in a blanket of snow. Since the magic returned, warmth threaded through every part of Dreach-Sciene. Summer. She'd heard of it in stories, but never experienced the stable weather.

Throughout the day, Rissa rode at the front of the group with Davi never far from her side. She let the pull on her magic dictate their path.

But something wasn't sitting right with her. "Ramsey," she called. "Get up here."

He rode up next to her. "Everything okay?"

"No." She contemplated her words, not wanting to cause offense but needing answers. "You could have led us to Cullenspire."

When he didn't respond, she grunted. "Thought so."

"Rissa, if I had volunteered to get us there, you wouldn't have learned to find a way yourself."

She opened her mouth to refute that, but then snapped it shut.

"What use are the Tri-Gard?" Davi asked. "You seem no more powerful now than a normal man. Your magic is finite just as ours is. Why do you exist if you cannot change the fate of this war?"

Rissa met Davi's stare in silent communication. She'd wondered the same thing.

Ramsey scratched his chin and peered into the distance. "We no longer have our crystals. That much is true. Without them, we are normal beings. But you're wrong about the last thing. We can change the fate of war. We did that very thing twenty years ago when we drained the magic." He paused. "Our power comes from working in harmony with one another. The triad. But we don't exist to change fates. We exist to protect the earth. Just being alive keeps the balance of the magic. There must always be three, each channeling a different side to the earth."

"So, you're saying we're on our own," Rissa said. "You and Lonara don't have the kind of power we need."

"Child, power comes from many places. Lonara and I will fight *with* you, but we cannot win *for* you. That is up to more than just us."

His words deflated her and she fell into silence. They stopped to rest the horses and eat, but then decided to push on into the night. Rissa could feel them getting closer and didn't want to delay any longer.

She didn't know how she recognized the landscape, but she knew exactly what they'd find nearby. "There's a village just over the ridge."

As soon as the words left her mouth, a cry rose up into the night.

"Is that smoke?" Davi pointed to the hazy columns spiraling up into the sky.

Rissa kicked her heels against the sides of her horse, not caring if the rest of them followed. She crested the hill and stopped, staring in horror at the sight below.

Blue flames threaded through the village, catching on the thatched roofs as if they were nothing more than kindling.

Villagers raced through the streets, some dragging children with them.

"Magic," Ramsey said.

There was no doubt magic could create the flames, but who was powerful enough to send them over an entire village.

Lorelai gasped when she joined them, her head shaking rapidly. "It's happening."

Davi set his jaw. "He followed us." His words were so sure. "This is punishment for coming into Dreach-Dhoun."

"Calis," Ramsey bit out.

"You don't understand." Lorelai's words were almost lost to the night. "I saw this come to pass."

They rode hard, stopping only long enough to eat and rest their horses. There was no sign of any forces. No Isenore or Dreach-Dhoun soldiers waiting to ambush them or impede their progress. Alixa was thankful for that. Ever since finding out that Trystan and Anna shared the same dream, he had been acting like a feral dog with a thorn in its paw. She knew his irritability was due to his worry for his sister and best friend. She understood that. She worried for them as well. Edric too.

They had made camp at sundown. They were close, Wren had told them that, but traveling in the dark was not a good decision. The troops were weary. The horses worn out from the unforgiving ride. They had no choice but to make camp.

The decision only seemed to raise Trystan's ire. If it were up to him he'd probably continue on in the dark by himself. While the rest of the camp was settling in and looking forward to something hot in their bellies and a few hours rest, Trystan prowled restlessly about the camp. She watched him now as he paced back and forth in front of the soldiers waiting in line for their chance to grab a bowl of rabbit stew.

One of them caught his eye, and he leaned into the young man's face. "I remember you from earlier. Your horse was hobbling and slowing us down," Trystan snapped at the soldier and Alixa could see the young man's face flush even in the moonlight. He glanced around in unease as the surrounding soldiers moved slowly away, not wanting to be the next to garner Trystan's attention. The soldier ducked his head in apology.

"I'm sorry, your Majesty. My horse has a broken shoe I think."

"You think?" Trystan snapped. "Then why are you standing here doing nothing? Find the farrier and get it fixed, boy!"

"Yes, your Majesty." The boy slunk away, looking back over his shoulder at the two crudely erected fire pits and their steaming pots of stew. He was hungry, but too terrified to defy the king. Alixa looked down at her own bowl of stew and sighed. Trotting after the boy, she caught up to him.

"Hey," she called softly, and he glanced back at her. "Here, take this with you. Last time I saw the farrier he was working on a horse at the west side of the camp."

She handed the boy her bowl and an awkward smile lit up his face. "Thank you, milady. Are you sure?"

She patted his arm in reassurance, then turned back to go after Trystan. That man needed a talking to.

It was easy to find where he'd stomped off to. All she had to do was look for the spot the soldiers were avoiding. She passed Avery on the way. The sword master had kept enough distance between her and the king to give him his privacy, but still keep him in sight. Always the loyal watchdog.

"Is he sulking like a child?" Alixa asked.

Avery stared back with her stoic look. "The king has much on his mind, my lady. Perhaps you should give him some time."

"Thanks for the warning, Avery, but the only thing I aim to give him is a piece of my mind."

Alixa swore the moonlight played a trick on her for she thought Avery's lips twitched in amusement. "I don't think that wise, Lady Alixa."

"Yes, well, I'm not known as a wise decision maker, now am I, Avery?"

The sword master chose not to respond, and Alixa passed on by without another word.

He was standing at the edge of the forest, peering into the darkness like he could see straight through to the other side. He didn't hear her approach. As if a sudden weight settled onto his shoulders, he leaned over and rested a palm against the nearest tree. At the precise moment he looked more like an overwhelmed boy than a powerful king, and her heart ached for him. She swallowed the angry reprisal sitting on her tongue for his earlier action. This wasn't the time for anger.

"Trystan." She said his name softly so as not to startle him and laid a comforting hand on his shoulder. He stiffened for a moment, then relaxed again and covered her hand with his own.

"I know. You don't have to say anything."

"So you mean I don't have to tell you what a jackass you're being? Good."

He snorted. "I'm sure you'll tell me anyway."

"If you insist."

She stepped around to face him and he lifted his head, so she was staring straight into his eyes. "You are being a jackass. You're distancing yourself from your people. You cannot afford to do that. Now is the time when you need their support the most. You are asking them to go to battle for you, yet you criticize them with your surliness and coldness. I don't recognize this Trystan from these past two days. It is not the Trystan I've come to know. Everyone is trying their hardest, but you can't push them. They need to rest. They need to eat. They need to have the support and care of their king behind them, else you are no better than Calis."

He sucked in a breath at her words and Alixa feared for a slight moment she had gone too far. She was talking to her king after all.

He closed his eyes and released a deep breath. The air tickled along Alixa's cheek. "You're right. I know that. I know I need to rally them. It's just..."

She waited for him to continue, but when nothing else was forthcoming, she urged him on. "It's just what?"

"I can't do this again." His face twisted in pain.

She softened her voice. "Do what? Come on, talk to me, Trystan."

He closed his eyes as if trying to hide from her. What he didn't realize was that no matter what he did, she saw him, every broken piece of him that matched her own.

He didn't answer her, but he didn't need to.

"This isn't like before. We aren't going to lose them."

He snapped his eyes open. "How do you know that? I couldn't stop it when Davi plunged that blade into his chest. When the dreams showed me their presence at the village, I saw it again. My own helplessness. I am a king." He bit off the last word and ripped his hand from the tree.

He lowered his voice and repeated himself. "I am a king. This feeling... this clenching in my chest... it won't do the kingdom any good and yet I can't escape it. I had to be strong when Davi died because if I broke, Rissa wouldn't have had anyone to hold her together." He shook his head. "I have an entire kingdom on my shoulders and the only thing I can think of is losing one of them. Because if I break this time, I'll take the entire kingdom with me, and I won't allow that."

"Trystan—"

He released a loud breath. "And you know what was missing from all of that? What I didn't mention? The villagers who will be slaughtered or homeless. They weren't the first concern in my mind. My father would be ashamed of me."

Alixa closed the distance between them and grabbed his shaking hand. "No. Trystan. No. Even a king is human. Just look, we're almost there and not delayed thanks to your worry for Rissa. It was tight, but we managed to gather the supplies and men we needed. That's the kind of leadership we need in this war."

She glanced over her shoulder to where the others settled in for the night. "We aren't going to beat Calis by strong organization and waiting for the right moment. There is no right moment. We're going to beat him because we're fighting for something, for each other. We need to push beyond our limits whether it be time or abilities."

He was quiet for a moment. "I thought you said I was being an ass?"

She shrugged. "I said jackass actually, and I stand by that statement. Your decision to override advisors and make haste was a good one. Your decision to yell at unsuspecting people who've done nothing wrong was not."

He wrinkled his nose. "I need to apologize, don't I."

She laughed. "No. That boy will never delay care of his horse again." She wrapped an arm around his waist. "Just remember, you're not the only one who's scared. We have no idea what we will find. We may be too late, or we may have a battle on our hands. If it is battle, then for some here it will be their first taste of war. But even with not knowing what awaits us, they do this because they believe in you Trystan. You brought magic back to their lands. You gave them back hope. They do this not because you order them too, but out of gratitude and loyalty. Show them you're worthy of it."

He reached out and gripped her forearms, as if he could gain strength just from her touch. They stayed that way for a bit, neither of them saying a word. Then the corners of his mouth lifted a little. It was the first time she'd seen him smile in two days. "Have I ever told you how happy I am you're on our side." He kissed the corner of her mouth.

"Yes, but I never tire of hearing it." She smiled against his lips.

"What would I do without you?"

"Not sure but let's hope we don't have to find out. Your head would probably swell and burst like an infected wound."

His nose bunched in disgust. "Charming."

"I try. Now are you ready to go back and act like the king you are?"

He nodded and released her. He took a few steps and stopped to turn back to her. "Thanks, Alixa, for… just thanks."

THEY SET out long before sunrise. Alixa had not slept a wink. She was positive none of them had. At least the horses were rested.

She rode alongside Avery and Mira. Trystan and Wren led the way, but no one spoke. Even listening to Wren's incessant chatter would have been better than the deathly quiet that accompanied them.

Just as the sun painted the sky in beautiful shades of coral, screams rent the air, carried on the slight breeze from the east. Off in the distance, atop the ridge and highlighted against the glowing sky, were rising columns of smoke.

"No," she heard Trystan whisper before he yelled back over his shoulder. "Ride out!"

They rode through the valley at breakneck speed and crested the rise. The fear churning in Alixa's gut turned to lead and she felt as if she would vomit. Were they already too late?

She topped the rise directly behind Trystan, and almost went head first over her horse as he pulled up short, causing her mare to do the same. His expression suddenly changed. She drew abreast of him and finally saw what he saw. The large village spread below them was awash in blue flame, just as expected. As they watched, it leapt from cottage to cottage as if it had a mind of its own. People and livestock alike screamed as they jammed the tiny pathways trying desperately to get away from the intense heat. Even atop the rise Alixa could swear she felt the heat searing her face. An almost perfect circle of blue surrounded the village, encasing it in a ring of flame. But that wasn't the worst of it. What was worst was the vast army of foot soldiers surrounding the village on all sides. Rows upon rows. Soldiers led into more soldiers. They had to be two thousand strong at least.

And there at the head of the road was the statue of Marcus Renauld encased in flame, just as Anna and Trystan had seen.

"Mother earth help them," Mira prayed as she too caught sight of the slaughter below. "It is the blue flame, Wren, just as Trystan foretold. Extremely powerful magic," she called out louder to Wren and he turned back to her, eyes filled with fear.

"Only the most powerful can exert this much magic. Calis must be near."

Trystan turned in his saddle to look at Wren and Mira, their fear mirrored in his eyes. "Can you both do this? You are our strongest wielders."

Wren's grip tightened on his reins, but a look of determination replaced the fear. "Just get us through the soldiers to the flame. We can do the rest."

That seemed to be what Trystan needed to hear. He maneuvered his horse to survey his troops.

"Men," he yelled, his voice bold and strong and echoing down the rise. "Our plan will not play out. We are too late to evacuate the villagers, but we will not allow them to die. Not when we still have breath in our bodies. It takes a lot of magic to fuel that circle of flame. They outnumber us greatly, but their magic consumption will make them weak. Those of you that have been trained, attach magic to every strike. We will fight well and win, for today we not only fight for Briarwood. We fight for every other village that Calis will attack in reprisal. We will not let anyone else suffer this same fate. This stops here today!"

As one they let out a huge battle cry. Alixa joined in, the screams ripping at her throat like claws. She was still screaming as they charged over the rise, rushing at their enemy. Their intent was simple; get Wren and Mira close enough to the ring of fire so they could quell it and allow the villagers a chance to escape the circle of flames holding them hostage.

Even as she raced down the hill with the others, Alixa knew most of them rode to their deaths. There was no way four hundred could defeat two thousand, even with magic. They wouldn't stand a chance. And everyone knew it. But that did not stop their attack. For as Trystan said, they were not fighting for just the villagers. This village meant nothing to Calis. It was under attack for one simple reason: it was closest to the border of Dreach-Dhoun. But Calis would not stop here. There would be another village. And another. They were not just fighting for their own lives, but the lives of their families.

By now Calis' men were aware of their presence and prepared for the attack. Soldiers clamored together, tightening the circle. Shields were raised and spears stuck out at every angle. But still they advanced. The war cry became a roar, deafening Alixa to any other sound. It thrummed through her head and vibrated in her bones. A flash of energy coursed through her as she called on her magic. It jolted through her arm and into her blade as she leaned low in her saddle, still screaming, and sliced through the first wave of soldiers. Warm blood splattered her face and the taste of copper filled her mouth. Her blade turned from dull gray to bright crimson. She kept slashing, for as much as the killing appalled her, she knew it was an instance of us or them.

Trystan was right and although the array of men slowed them down, they were weak and no match for the magic of Dreach-Sciene troops. They plowed into Calis men, both with blades and magic, clearing a path. Alixa leapt nimbly from her horse, following suit as Trystan and Wren and Mira did the same.

"Alixa, Avery, protect the wielders and get them close to the flame. We will keep Calis' men off your back." Trystan screamed above the roar of shrieks of anger and wails of pain.

"Trystan, no," Alixa tried to argue but the king had already disappeared into his throng of troops, helping to cut a pathway covered in blood. She turned toward Wren and Mira. "Go!" she yelled.

They ran. Alixa tried not looking at the carnage, but it was unavoidable. Bodies blocked them at every step. Soldier or villager, it did not matter. Every mutilated body made her heart wither a bit more. Life was a gift and it was needlessly being taken away by both sides.

She didn't even realize she was crying until she felt the heat scorching the wet tracks down her cheeks. The blue flame rose up in protest as they approached, as if it wanted to deny them access.

"Close enough," Wren called to Mira and they both fell to their knees. He looked over his shoulder long enough to yell to Avery, "Mistress Payne, I know I'm not your favorite person, but please do all in your power to keep us safe."

Avery did not get a chance to reply. A barrage of Calis' men pushed through the Dreach-Sciene troops. They knew what Wren and Mira were attempting to do and were determined to do everything in their power to stop them. As Avery took on three soldiers, two more charged Alixa, swords swinging for her head. Alixa turned her blade sideways, grabbing the tip with her free hand and blocked one blade, sparks flying at the impact. Pulling magic to help her, she pushed the soldier back and pivoted on her heel to block the other blade coming her way. Back and forth she wove, blocking the blows and trying to keep the soldiers away from Mira and Wren.

The soldier on the right attacked again, but he swung too high and Alixa saw her opening. Raising her sword, she stabbed into his exposed armpit. The soldier screamed and dropped his sword as he toppled sideways.

Whirling before the next soldier's blade found its own mark, she sidestepped the attack and kicked at him, sweeping his feet out from under him. He fell hard on his back and Alixa leapt high in the air and brought her blade down across his neck.

Gasping for air, she closed her eyes to block the sight of what she'd just done. She swallowed the bile in the back of her throat and whirled, blade ready, as a hand gripped her shoulder.

"Trystan," she breathed in relief as familiar brown eyes scrutinized her face, checking for injury. His gaze averted over her shoulder and his lips tightened into a thin line as he took a stance against the new wave of Calis' troops about to overwhelm them.

And then time and the universe froze. That's the only way Alixa could describe it. As she turned to face the new wave of attacking soldiers with Trystan, she felt the ground shake under her feet. All sound ceased to exist. The screaming of thousands of people suddenly stopped. The noise of the marching soldiers disappeared. Alixa had never truly understood the meaning behind deafening silence, but it truly was deafening.

The shaking under her feet intensified and she stared in disbelief as Ramsey ran toward them, arms held out to his sides and exuding waves of magic that had the soldiers toppling like dominoes. He cleared a path through the troops as Rissa ran behind him. The soldiers were picking themselves back up and trying to attack, only to bounce off and back into the crowd. Alixa finally understood. She wasn't deaf after all. Ramsey had them encased in some sort of protective shield.

"Ri!" Trystan yelled in disbelief, but Rissa ran straight past him without acknowledgement. Falling to her knees, she joined Mira and Wren, planting her hands deep into the soil.

"Pull it back into the earth as soon as the barrier goes

down," she yelled at them and Wren nodded in understanding. "Ramsey, on my signal drop the shield."

"Get ready to fight," Trystan growled Alixa's way as he raised his sword once again.

Strain creased Rissa's face as the wielders struggled to control and bind their magic as one.

Alixa wiped the sweat out of her eyes. The soldiers bared teeth at them outside the barrier, awaiting their chance. She raised her sword and prayed once more.

"Now!" Rissa shrieked.

The noise stuck them like a slap to the face. Soldiers that had been battling to break the barrier fell over with their momentum. One slammed into Alixa and she stumbled back with him toward the wall of flame. Both screamed as they braced, expecting to feel the excruciating pain of being burnt to a crisp. But nothing happened. They both hit the ground, the soldier on top of Alixa and staring into each other's eyes with incredulity.

"They did it!" Alixa yelled and the soldier actually grinned at her, animosity forgotten as they reveled in still being alive. A sword came out of nowhere, the hilt plowing into the young soldier's temple. His eyes glazed and rolled back into his head as he fell over. Avery stuck a hand down to Alixa and pulled her to her feet.

Alixa glanced around. The blue flame was gone. Extinguished. Villagers stumbled around as if dazed, calling out to loved ones. Crying and shrieking as if they didn't even realize they were no longer in danger from the flames. Silver smoke hung heavy in the air and Alixa coughed as her eyes watered. Pulling her cloak over her face, she ran through the smoke toward the three still kneeling on the ground.

She held her hand out to Ri, pulling her to her feet.

"You did it," she beamed at Ri as she crushed her to her chest. "I am so happy to see you, you beautiful creature."

"No time for hugs, Alixa," Ri snapped as she pushed Alixa away.

"It's not over yet," Avery interrupted, pointing over Alixa's shoulder with her blade. She turned in fear. Now what?

Avery was right. Their army may have disposed of the first wave of Calis' men but there were plenty more to take their place. There was no way they could take on the throng headed their way.

"Come on, Lorelai and Davi. Let's hope this works," Ri muttered as she raised her muddy hands to the air. She closed her eyes, her wild red hair hanging over her shoulders, making her appear more madwoman than princess. Alixa could feel the power emanating from her. It had heat, almost like the blue flame. A horn blasted through the air, startling Alixa. As she watched, soldiers crested the hills all around them. Soldiers carrying Dreach-Sciene banners. There had to be hundreds. Thousands maybe. They kept coming in waves, running down the hill toward the Dreach-Dhoun troops.

Another bugle call joined the first, only this one was followed by a command. "Retreat!"

The Dreach-Dhoun soldiers wasted no time. One look at the attacking army sent them scurrying in the opposite direction. It didn't seem possible that so many men could disappear into the hills and forest so quickly, but they did. Amidst the cheers and whoops and jeering from the Dreach-Sciene troops, Calis' men ran with their tails between their legs. And then a more peculiar thing happened. As Calis' men disappeared, so did the advancing Dreach-Sciene soldiers. The hillside appeared covered with troops but as soon as they hit the bottom, they faded into nothingness.

"Magic," Alixa whispered as she finally understood. Ri was doing this. She had created those soldiers. They weren't real. It was all an illusion.

Alixa ripped her gaze away from the unbelievable sight back to their three saviors just in time to watch Ri tilt and fall to the ground.

It was a strange phenomenon: magic. One moment, unchained power ripped through Rissa's body and every possibility spread out before her.

The next, her knees buckled and she fell to the earth without the strength to even stand.

She toppled to the side and rolled onto her back. As she watched the strange silver smoke curl into the atmosphere, her lungs struggled for breath.

Was this what it meant to be all-powerful? To experience weakness as intense as any strength? Adrenaline buzzed in her mind. They'd done it. When they'd first arrived at the village, she'd thought it was lost to them.

But maybe that was the point.

Nothing was lost to them anymore.

Nothing was impossible.

Even Calis Bearne was beatable.

Her eyes found Davion as he ran through smoke and rubble to reach her. *And anyone can be saved,* she thought.

Davi stumbled to his knees at her side. His mouth moved, but she couldn't hear the words that escaped his lips. Someone on the other side of her shook her shoulder.

Wren and Mira sat nearby, as spent as her. Mira waved a hand her way and pointed toward the ground.

Rissa hadn't realized she'd been closing herself off rather than letting the earth's power flow freely into her. As she slowly dropped her walls, a torrent of magic flooded her. With it came a world in chaos as the silence broke away, yanking her back to the matter at hand.

Davi ran his hands over her, checking for any sign of injury. "Ri. Rissa! Can you hear me?"

She winced. "Can you stop yelling? I'm developing a wicked headache."

He pulled her to him. "Thank the earth. I thought you'd taken in too much magic and…"

She leaned her head back to stare up at him and raised a brow. "Doesn't feel good when people make you think they're dead, does it?"

A slow smile spread across his lips moments before he pressed them to hers. "You aren't allowed to get hurt."

"Is that an order from the king's second-in-command?" she asked against his lips.

Trystan's voice intruded on their moment. "What if it was an order from the king himself?"

She climbed to her feet to face her brother. "Calis will keep coming."

"We'll be prepared."

She crossed her arms. "Without us, you'd be dead. I wouldn't exactly call that prepared."

He ran a hand over the top of his head. "Rissa." His voice broke on her name.

She couldn't hold back any longer, not caring if others saw her informality, as she lunged at Trystan and buried her face in his chest.

He wrapped his arms around her and squeezed so tight she wasn't sure she'd ever breathe again.

When he finally released her, she smacked his shoulder. "Don't you dare do that again, Trystan Renauld."

"Hug you?" he asked. "Because I think you're the one who started it."

"No, you ass. How many men do you have with you? Two hundred? Three? You sent them riding against Calis' force. The village was already lost."

He pushed out a breath. "Ri, this was important. We saw it."

"What do you mean you saw it?"

"Anna, the young seer, has been dreaming of a village surrounded by blue fire. I had the same dream last night."

She opened her mouth to speak but closed it when she realized she didn't know what to say to that.

Trystan continued. "We knew you'd be here."

She pursed her lips. "Okay… so you were worried about me?"

He didn't answer, instead his shoulders lifted in a shrug.

"I see. Okay, brother, in case you haven't noticed, I can take care of myself." She gestured to the destruction surrounding them. "If we are going to do this—fight Calis—I can't hold you back. What am I saying 'if' for? We're in this. There's no going back, only forward. You're the earth darn king. You don't get to be a concerned brother. Not now. Dreach-Sciene needs better than that."

"Ri." Davi joined them. He gestured toward one of the roads

leading into the village. Villagers streamed toward them, but one person walked in the opposite direction. Lorelai's white-blonde hair was unmistakable among the crowd.

Rissa pushed her way through to catch up with the seer. "Where are you going?"

Lorelai's voice seemed to be in a far off place. "I saw this. All of it. For months whenever I closed my eyes, the screams echoed in my mind. People burned." As she spoke the words, the acrid smell of smoldering flesh reached them.

Lorelai stepped over a body.

Rissa pulled her shirt up over her mouth and averted her eyes. They'd been too late to save many people. Most died in their homes. The lucky escaped into the streets where they risked being run over by the stampede of scared folk trying to flee.

Lorelai continued. "I never saw how it ended." She led Rissa past the smoky remains of row after row of crude huts. When they reached the center of the village, Lorelai lowered herself to the ground and closed her eyes. "I think I understand now."

"What do you understand?" Rissa wasn't sure if Lorelai was speaking to her or the earth.

"The sight. The visions. These events. I only see part of the whole because there is no whole. No end." She glanced up, her eyes shining. "I thought it was a prophecy of darkness the first time the village appeared to me. But it wasn't a prophecy at all. It needed to happen to show us the way."

"Now you lost me. The way to what?"

"I know how we're going to win this war."

RISSA HAD ALMOST REACHED the others by the time Lorelai caught up to her.

"You have to see the possibilities."

"You're insane." Rissa sped up.

"No. I want to beat my uncle."

Rissa turned and found herself face to face with the seer. "And you think I don't?"

"I think you're not willing to do everything that might be necessary."

"Don't speak of necessity. I have given up everything. My father..." She shook her head. "I am prepared to sacrifice anything." She glanced over her shoulder at the people gathering for the ride back to Cullenspire. "But if your idea doesn't work, my people will be sacrificing everything as well. I won't do it. We'll find another way."

"Just talk to Trystan."

"If you're so hell bent on this, you can do it."

"You know as well as I he'll never listen to me."

Rissa scowled. "Because he has more sense than I do." She caught sight of Alixa searching the surrounding crowd and her heart squeezed. "Excuse me. I have to go tell my friend that one of the few people she loves is dead because of you."

She knew it was harsh. Lorelai had as much guilt, if not more, about Edric's death. But what the seer wanted to do... Rissa wished a small part of her didn't believe it was an option.

She brushed by a stunned Lorelai. Alixa ran toward her, a smile stretching her lips. "I'm so glad you're okay, Ri. And you did it! You got out of Dreach-Dhoun. I was so worried." She glanced over her shoulder. "Have you seen Edric? I'm sure he's helping the villagers, but I just wanted to tell him I'm glad he's back." She faced Rissa again, her smile dropping slowly as she took in the broken expression on the princess's face.

"Rissa?" Alixa stepped toward her. "Where is Edric?"

Rissa's lip quivered.

Alixa shook her head. She clenched her jaw to keep it from shaking. "I'm going to need you to say the words, Ri."

"Our rescue of Lorelai went off as planned. We evaded Calis and got to the tree cover."

Alixa stepped forward again and lowered her voice. "I'm not asking for a step-by-step account."

Rissa wiped an errant tear. "There was a Dreach-Dhoun soldier hidden in the trees."

"How did he go?"

"An arrow to the heart."

Alixa sucked in a breath. "Quick at least." She twisted to hide her face. "Earth darn it, Edric."

"I'm so sorry, Alixa."

Alixa peered over her shoulder. "Did you take care of it?"

Rissa didn't have to ask what she meant. The two women understood each other on a level few others did. "The soldier is dead."

Alixa sniffed and straightened her spine. "We must prepare to move out." She walked away without a backward glance.

Rissa didn't need to tell the others about Edric. The news traveled among their party quickly. No one spoke of it as they mounted up. Trystan left a sizable force behind to get the villagers to safety. Some would be taken to Cullenspire village for refuge, others would join the force at the manor.

Her eyes flicked between the faces in their group, knowing for the first time this was it. These were the people she was going to battle with. There were no more rescue missions or lost friends to be found.

All quests were finished, and they didn't know what would happen next.

Would Calis march across the border? Where would his next strike be? When?

She lifted her eyes to her brother who rode in front of her. “We need to pull the people in from the villages.”

Trystan glanced back at her. “I know.”

Her shoulders sagged under the weight of the realization. Calis could come for any village and they couldn’t protect them. The people of Dreach-Sciene just got their magic back, but it seemed they were about to lose their freedom now.

For they were all still playing the game. The one that started in a Dreach-Sciene tavern more than fifteen years before when a king met with a seer. Maybe it was time Trystan and Rissa played their own game.

She glanced toward Lorelai.

If Calis Bearne was willing to sacrifice his own family to win, what could Rissa and Trystan put on the line?

Cullenspire manor loomed behind Trystan, ripe with more activity than it had seen in years. Every day, citizens poured into the stronghold from the surrounding villages. Fighting men and women set up a camp that stretched as far as their king could see.

Twenty years ago there'd been a war of such a size none of them had seen before. Was this the sight that struck his father? Had he walked among the tents wondering how many of these good people would make it out of this?

Had his mother seen women piecing together armor from any material they could find and then fitting it to their daughters?

Had they seen the fire in the people's eyes?

It wasn't the blue fire of magic that had consumed the village, this was a pure burning will. A readiness. Had they known it would come to this?

Trystan hadn't. Not until his father set him on the quest to recover their magic. He hadn't seen first-hand how the crops withered and died. How the children starved.

In Isenore, they'd been subject to the tyrannical rampages of their duke.

For the royal family, the war stopped when the magic left and along with it the Dreach-Dhoun forces. For the people, it had never ended.

Avery walked a few steps behind Trystan, never far. They were still in Isenore after all. A few people bowed and muttered formalities, but most were too busy to notice his presence.

A familiar voice came from behind him. "What's the punishment if I decide not to bow?"

A smile grew on Trystan's face. He didn't turn as he spoke. "The king will have you whipped for insolence."

"The king doesn't allow whipping."

"We could always start."

It was a familiar conversation. One they'd had many times, always in jest whenever Davi did something Trystan's father wouldn't have approved of.

"So," Davi went on. "I guess that's one memory that's real then."

Trystan finally turned to the perplexed Davi. "You didn't know if it really happened?"

Davi shrugged. "I—" He sighed. "I just needed to be sure. It seemed like something either real or fake Trystan could say."

"Fake Trystan?" Trystan raised an eyebrow.

"The one tied to the memories my father created in my mind."

Trystan grimaced at Davi's use of the term father. Was that still how he thought of Calis? The man just burned an entire village. Trystan saw Davi very little since his return and he always felt as if his old friend avoided him. Was this why? The memories?

"Dav," he started. "You can ask me about any of them. The memories, I mean."

"I'm not..." He shook his head. "I'm not sure I'm ready for that."

Trystan nodded.

Davi scratched his neck. "Look, I don't think I can do it. Not anymore."

"Do what?"

"Be your second. People keep calling me that, but..."

"Davi—"

"No! Let me get this out. Every time someone calls me the second in command or 'sir', I can't breathe. You gave me the title back when you and I were partners. Best friends. Brothers. We trusted each other with our lives. Truwa Brathair."

"Trust—"

"Stop. Don't repeat it." Davi squeezed his eyes shut as if the words hurt to say. "That's not us anymore. You need someone to lead in battle who you can trust one hundred percent."

Trystan set his jaw. "I don't want anyone else, Dav. It's still you and me. I trust you."

"You shouldn't!"

Trystan took a step back as Davi fixed him with a dark gaze. *My father.* That was what he'd called Calis. "Are you trying to tell me you're a traitor?" His hand drifted to the hilt of his sword. Would he be able to do it? He'd fought Davi before, but this was different. This time he had his memories. Trystan could look into his eyes and see the boy he'd called his brother.

"No." Davi shook his head vigorously. "That's not what I... Argh!"

Avery stepped forward, but Davi held up a hand. He lifted his eyes to meet Trystan's. "When I'm not consciously picking apart the memories, everything in me still thinks you're the man who imprisoned me for most of my life. And I know it's wrong. I know what we were, Trystan. I would give every bit of magical ability I have to get that back, but I don't know if we can." He clenched his fists. "Years. My father spied on Dreach-Sciene for years. Through me."

He ran a hand through his hair. "How can you still…?" He swallowed his words. "I'm sorry, Trystan. You can't plan battle without a second and it can't be me."

WHEN TRYSTAN WAS A CHILD, his least favorite game was imagining himself as king. He'd picture ornate clothing, decadent balls, and the people's eyes on him.

He never wanted any of it. The only part he looked forward to was declaring desert to be the first course in the dining hall. Well, surprise, kid, the palace cook was a stubborn woman.

He didn't need adorations. He wanted his people to be loyal to Dreach-Sciene, not to any one king. He'd never been good at inspiring people.

What he had wanted was his father to be there to guide him and Davi as his general.

He tried to drown out the people behind him. Did they ever stop arguing? He couldn't think.

"Cullenspire is the only stronghold in Isenore that can withstand a full assault." Wren slammed his fist on the table.

Trystan flicked his eyes to the window and the surrounding land beyond while they argued.

"We need to consolidate our power." Rissa's voice sounded

calm, but Trystan could pick out the undercurrent of venom in it. "Isenore is not worth us losing this fight."

"How can you say that?" Wren pointed toward the door. "Those people outside have come to defend Dreach-Sciene because Isenore is a part of this kingdom."

"Easy." Rissa leaned back. "We move them to Aldorwood. Combine them with the force at Whitecap."

"And leave Isenore for Eisner and Calis to pick off? Not everyone from the villages have come. What about the ones who stayed behind?"

She crossed her arms. "Their loyalty is obviously not with us."

Wren threw his hands up in the air. Before he came up with a retort, his mother laid a hand on his arm.

"If we leave Cullenspire," she began, "Calis will have a straight road to Aldorwood. And you'll have nothing. No way to delay. No warning."

Trystan's gaze lingered at the window for a moment longer before he turned his attention back to the council. "Lady Yaro is right." He crossed the room and dropped into a seat. They were all scared, Alixa had told him. It was time to see that. To lead them through it. He folded his hands on the table. "We cannot leave Isenore undefended or all of Dreach-Sciene will fall with it." His eyes flicked to his sister. "Rissa is also right. We must get those who can't or won't fight to Whitecap. There, they can take ship to Sona. As for us…" He scanned the faces around the room. "I must return to the palace to prepare the army. Riders have been sent to every village. We must expect continued arrivals and be ready. Those numbers will bolster my force as well as Lord Coille's."

He shifted his eyes to Wren's. "In another life, I'd appoint you to a position at my side. But this life is all we get and I need someone I trust to stay here."

Wren nodded and opened his mouth, but Trystan held up a hand.

"I won't order you to do this. Or anyone. We don't know what is going to happen, but Cullenspire will stand between Calis and what he really wants—all of Dreach-Sciene, me. Do you understand what I'm telling you?"

Mira reached forward and gripped Wren's hand as he swallowed and nodded. A wry smile tilted his lips. "If I have to die, I'm going to go down fighting for my home."

Trystan hadn't known Wren long, but he'd grown to like the man. Now he respected him as well. He stood and circled the table to get to Wren's side. He held out his hand. "Me too."

Wren clasped the offered hand and nodded.

Trystan walked from the room. Avery followed him.

"Make preparations," he said. "We're going home."

PREPARATIONS ONLY TOOK A DAY. Trystan left orders for the force camped nearby to be moved, leaving some of his best officers behind to lead them.

Forty-eight men and thirty-two women volunteered to stay at Cullenspire. Eight people left on horseback at dawn. Nine-hundred-eleven would begin the long march toward Aldorwood soon.

Lady Yaro insisted on staying with her son and Anna refused to leave her mother. But Wren would keep them safe. He would safeguard Isenore while training the men and women under his command for the battle to come.

Trystan had never met a man whose destiny was written so

plainly for all to see. He was meant for this fight. Wren was a boy when he fought alongside Trystan's father, now as a man, he'd be giving orders instead of following them. It fit him.

As Cullenspire disappeared from view, Ramsey hummed a tune and the sound surrounded them, tying them together.

Rissa picked up the song, glancing sideways at Davi. He blew her a kiss, and the moment was so like a million others they'd had before… well, before the world fell apart.

Trystan focused on the feel of the horse beneath him, the sun on his face. If he concentrated, he could erase Davi's words from his mind.

Because his friend had been wrong. They could get it back. Davi could still be trusted.

And he'd prove it to him.

Ramsey stopped his song and kicked his horse to walk up next to Trystan. "Feels strange to be going home when it may not be your home much longer, doesn't it?"

Trystan shook his head and suppressed a grin. "That's not what I was thinking at all. We aren't going to lose it."

Ramsey shrugged. "We might."

"If you're just going to speak nonsense, I suggest shutting your mouth."

"Don't speak to your grandfather that way."

Trystan leveled him with a stare. "I will when he looks not a day older than myself."

Ramsey laughed. "I'm just joking with you, boy. You're too serious."

"We're in the middle of a war."

"Is it a war on smiling?"

Trystan grunted in response.

Ramsey grinned. "If I'm going to die soon, I'm not going to spend every moment all doom and gloom. Your Majesty…

Grandson, don't let this fight or this crown strip everything else away from you."

Davi chuckled. "He's always had that gilded stick up his ass, Ramsey."

Trystan froze and Davi looked away as if he was embarrassed to show any kind of comradery with Trystan.

Trystan pushed out a breath. "Well, when you have someone constantly getting you into trouble, you have to develop a calm demeanor to get out of it."

"He's blaming me," Davi scoffed. "My thirteenth birthday, whose idea was it to go into the village disguised as palace servants—maids—so as not to be seen as we went to beg sweets off Lady Maisel."

"You were just mad that Lady Maisel recognized me instantly but really thought you were a girl because—as she put it—'You had such a pretty face.'"

Davi's cheeks reddened, but his smile widened. Trystan laughed at the memory.

Rissa's eyes filled with hope as they flicked between the two boys. Trystan met her gaze and winked. They'd get back what they were.

As soon as the thought entered his mind, the moment snapped and Davi's smile fell.

"What is it?" Rissa asked him.

"It's wrong." Davi ran a weary hand over his chin. "So wrong. I have a second memory of that day. I disguised myself as a woman to escape the palace. You found me and I was… punished."

"But that's not true." Trystan's voice broke.

"I know." Davi sighed. "I always know when it's false but it doesn't erase it from my mind."

The group descended into silence. Each moment it seemed,

carried a weight none of them had been prepared for. Every smile could quickly turn.

The darkness was inside all of them, trying to tear them away from each other. Davi's confusion and guilt. Rissa's anger. Alixa's sadness. Trystan's fear.

It drove them all.

Pushing them. Torturing them.

If they didn't escape it, they were going to lose.

Every time Rissa opened her eyes, a feeling of foreboding washed over her. Another day dawned and another chance for Calis to come for them.

Why hadn't he?

The roads throughout Aldorwood held a haunting stillness, only interrupted by messengers to and from Cullenspire and the villagers still scrambling to get to the safety promised by their king.

Each day their numbers grew. They trained and prepared with bated breath.

Rissa pulled a heavy robe on over her sleeping gown and let her curls hang loose down her back. She couldn't stand this feeling of anticipation anymore.

Not bothering to put shoes on her bare feet, she crept from her room. The stone floor of the corridor sent chills up her legs. What had Lonara told her? Now that magic had returned, the seasons would be more even. Summer was ending and she called the new season... autumn. Yes, apparently it would soon be autumn. A time marked by the colorful leaves scattered along the ground and a chill in the air.

The torches had not yet been lit for the day and shadows danced in front of her. How early was it?

They'd returned to the palace weeks ago much to the relief of Lord Coille. He was able to return home to Whitecap where he'd aid the Duchess in getting the refugees to Sona all while preparing the forces camped at his estate.

As a girl, Rissa had never had any interest in the running of the kingdom. She hadn't yearned to sit in with the council. Yet, she now found such things as battle plans and grain stores filling her mind.

It was better than the other items she could think of.

She reached her intended destination. A room she'd been to a million times before. She didn't knock, assuming he'd be sleeping. Placing her palm against the door, she twisted the handle with her other hand as she pushed slowly.

A low creak came from the door and she froze. Peering inside, she saw the unmoving form on the bed.

Davion laid sprawled on his stomach, one arm tucked underneath his head. A linen sheet tangled in his legs, but his torso had not a stitch of clothing. Her cheeks heated and she couldn't look away.

Everything about that man was beautiful. Not only his dark hair, mesmerizing eyes, or lithe frame—but *him.* His courage. His heart.

She'd always seen it. Even back when all he did was chase the palace women and ignore her attentions. He'd thought he couldn't possibly be enough for her because all he saw was a boy with no family name. But she'd seen what he could be.

She pushed the door shut with a soft click and padded

toward the bed. If they were waiting for the worst to happen, she wasn't going to do it alone. She shrugged off her robe, lifted the sheet, and slid beneath it, turning on her side to stare at his profile.

Her hand inched forward, needing to touch him. To make sure he was real. Her fingertips trailed down his cheek, over his strong jaw, and down the curve of his neck.

A hum sounded from the back of his throat. Without opening his eyes, Davi wrapped his free arm around her waist and dragged her against him. He rested his head on her shoulder.

"I didn't mean to wake you." Her fingers drifted to his hair.

"Then you shouldn't touch me." His breath warmed her neck. "I never want to be asleep when you're touching me."

"Are you okay?"

"Shouldn't I be the one asking you that? You're the one who showed up in my room for snuggles."

She snorted. "Don't say snuggles."

"Why not?"

"We aren't snuggly people."

He opened his eyes and lifted his head to gaze up at her. His lips formed a pout. "I'm snuggly."

She bit back a laugh. "I'm more likely to shoot an arrow into someone than hug them."

"True."

She smacked his arm.

"Hey! What was that for?"

She stared down at him. "You weren't supposed to agree."

He pulled her tighter against him. "It's not like you to show up here before the sun. I'm not complaining, but…"

She ran her hand along his arm until she reached his hand and intertwined their fingers. "Sometimes I wake up and there's this moment where I forget we have you back. I just needed to see you, to feel you and make sure you're real. You're here."

"I'm real," he whispered. "I'm here. Maybe a bit busted up, but definitely here."

She touched his chin and tilted his head moments before kissing him. Rissa had been in love with Davion for as long as she could remember. He kept her moving forward. She could have drowned in everything he was, everything he had to give.

His kiss consumed her, swallowing up every thought of the battles to come, overcoming every bit of grief she held in her heart. For her father. For Edric. Even for Davi himself.

His arms wound around her back and he rolled them so she gazed up at him. His dark eyes lightened as he scanned her face.

"I love you," he said. "No matter what happens, no matter what has happened, you have to know that."

Tears stood in her eyes, refusing to fall. Was it possible to love him more than ever? Even after the things he'd done? She knew exactly who he was now. The son of Calis Bearne. She'd seen his hesitation with his father.

But as her eyes traced the contours of his familiar face, she only saw the boy who'd stood under the dying tree on the night of the ball unable to say the words he was saying now.

She thought of her mother, who'd by all accounts loved her father more than anything. Had that loved stopped with her death?

Rissa hoped not. How could it? The earth remembered everything.

DAVI REFUSED to leave Rissa's side when she decided she needed to visit the forest behind the palace. The valley of kings had always been beautiful, even without magic, but now it was magnificent.

Flowers had sprouted up as if marking where each former monarch or others of royal blood were buried. The farthest had a small statue commemorating Trystan the Bold. He wasn't buried there because his death was centuries before, but his story was told throughout Dreach-Sciene.

He'd sacrificed himself by taking in too much magic, letting it break his body down, while he waited for the opportunity to strike. Davi didn't know if he'd truly been bold or just desperate.

After their early morning 'snuggling'—he chuckled at the term—Rissa returned to her rooms to dress for the day.

She'd arrived in the courtyard as he sparred with a young recruit, using only magic. After watching for a few minutes, she'd had a boy fetch her riding cloak and horse. That was when Davi stepped in. She was crazy if she thought she could go anywhere alone.

Rissa kneeled on the ground in front of a stone that had been carved with her mother's name. Davi squeezed her shoulder as he passed her. There was one man he needed to see.

He stopped and stared at the place where Marcus Renauld had been interred into the earth. Was he watching them now?

A drop of water landed on Davi's cheek but he didn't bother to pull up his hood. Marcus Renauld had been a father to him. He knew that. But he didn't feel it.

"I'm sorry," he whispered. "Earth, I'm sorry." He felt as if he was betraying Marcus with every ill thought. He'd done enough damage just with his presence in his life. "Dammit,

Marcus, if you hadn't taken me in, if you hadn't been kind, we might not be in this mess."

As soon as he said the words, he knew they were false. His father would've found another way to have eyes inside that palace.

He glanced back at Rissa who was lost in her own conversation with her mother. "I'm going to fight for them. I promise you that. Rissa would probably tell me to shut up because she can take care of herself, but I'm going to take care of her. And Trystan… I'm going to try." He bent to place his hand on the stone. "Thank you." He squeezed his eyes shut. "Thank you."

If it hadn't been for Marcus, would he have ended up like Lorelai? Living with memories filled with torment and regret? He understood now—what she'd said by the river after the rescue. He'd been saved her fate.

He hadn't noticed Rissa beside him until he stood. They both peered toward the sky as raindrops fell with a steady rhythm. Rissa pulled up her hood and held out her hand to him.

He took it and let her lead him back to the horses.

"I don't want to go back there yet," he said.

Things seemed so much more complicated behind those walls.

Rissa nodded as if she knew exactly what he meant. "There's a cave nearby with a big enough opening for the horses."

By the time they reached the cave, they were both sopping wet. Once the horses were under cover, Davi shook the wet hair from his face and unclasped his cloak.

Rissa searched the cave, finding a single stick. She set it on the ground and flicked her hand. A flame broke free.

He laughed. "It took Lorelai a lot longer to teach me the things she's taught you in only a few weeks."

She shrugged. "That's because you were probably so annoying she could only stand to teach you in small doses."

He raised an eyebrow and advanced toward her. "You think I'm annoying?"

She backed away from him, nodding and biting her lip. Her back hit the wall of the cave and he continued closing the distance.

"Am I annoying now?" He dipped his head so his lips brushed her ear as he spoke.

"Yeah." She swallowed.

He grinned as he pressed a kiss just below her ear. "Still annoying?"

"Mmhmm," she sighed. "So annoying."

He ripped his lips away. "Okay then. I'll just go to my side of the cave."

A groan rumbled low in her throat. "You don't play fair."

"Never did, sweetheart." He flashed another grin and sat along the opposite wall.

She slid down until her butt hit the dirt. "Fine, I'll listen to someone who wants to talk to me."

He scooted across toward her. "What's it feel like? The tenelach?"

She closed her eyes, giving in to the music of the earth as she opened herself to it. "Power," she answered. "It feels like power." The magic flowed along her skin, creating a barrier between her and the rest of the world. "I think anyone can hear it. Most have just closed themselves off. But if you try, really try, the earth will speak to you as well. You only have to be ready to hear it." She held out her hand, palm up. "Come here."

He got to his knees and slid to kneel beside her. She took one of his hands and placed it against the dusty ground.

"You feel the magic, yes?" she asked.

He nodded.

"I see the concentration in your eyes. You're putting up walls to restrict the flow of power. The tenelach is unrestricted, unrestrained. Loosen your hold on the control."

Davi sat in silence for a long moment as if speaking to his magic. His eyes widened.

"Do you feel it?" she asked.

"The current." He shook his head in wonder. "It's effortless. I don't have to pull it free. The magic wants to live in me."

Rissa smiled. "Welcome to my world, Davion."

She let it fill every empty part of her until she was buzzing. It wasn't until the current slowed that she noticed Davi had fallen back and stopped moving.

She slammed up her walls, blocking the earth's call as the real world struggled for breath. "Davion." She lunged for him and gripped his shoulders, shaking hard. "Wake up. Davion!" She slapped his face and a cough burst out of him. He gasped for breath and his eyes flew open.

She collapsed on top of him. "You're okay."

A giggle escaped his lips. An honest to earth giggle. She raised her head to study his stupidly grinning face.

"Hi." He burst into laughter.

She sat up. "What's so funny?"

"Have I told you today how beautiful you are? My beautiful little princess."

She narrowed her eyes.

He sat up suddenly and then climbed to his feet. His hand shot out and a burst of wind tunneled into the cave, bringing the rain in bucketfuls.

Rissa screamed as the water struck her in the face. "What are you doing?" She released her own magic to counteract his and the wind stopped.

He shrugged. "There was fire."

"That was keeping us warm, you idiot."

"I'm not an idiot, you're an idiot."

"Oh my earth." She got to her feet and put her hands on her head. "Are we ten years old?"

"Were you in love with me at ten?"

She scowled.

He went on. "You didn't have the nice girl bits then."

She choked. "What is happening?"

"We're standing in a cave," he said proudly as he stood up straighter.

She buried her face in her hands. "I've broken Davi. Oh my earth."

She looked back up, but he was no longer in front of her. A tap on her shoulder made her jump.

Davi cackled as she twisted to glare at him. Did the magic do this?

She grabbed his sleeve and pulled.

"Where are we going?" he asked.

"To find someone who can fix this."

"Fix what? Did something happen?" He drew his sword so suddenly she jumped back. "Who do I need to fight." He made a jabbing motion. "I'm ready."

He touched the blade with his other hand and yelped. The blade dropped to the ground with a clatter.

"What just happened?" Rissa asked.

Davi stuck his finger in his mouth and glared at the discarded sword. "It's sharp."

Rissa groaned and pointed to Davi's horse. "Get on."

It was still raining when they reached the palace, but a stable lad ran out to take both their horses. Davi cradled his arm against his chest as they hurried across the room. Rissa rolled her eyes.

Ramsey and Lonara were in the hall with Trystan for lunch and both stood as Rissa rushed in. She ignored her brother and went straight toward the Tri-Gard members. She pointed back at Davi. "Fix him before I lose my mind."

"What's wrong with Davi?" Trystan asked.

Davi ran forward, stopping at the end of the high table. "Lonara, Ramsey it is so good you're here. You as well, your Majesty."

Trystan shot a questioning look at Rissa.

Davi held up his hand. The blood on his finger was barely visible. "I have been injured in battle. I must be tended to."

Rissa closed her eyes and groaned.

"Battle?" The worry in Trystan's voice was unmistakable.

Rissa held up a hand for the now panicked hall to quiet. She flicked her eyes toward Davi. "He nicked himself on his own sword." A tittering of laughter surrounded them and Davi grinned, eating up the attention.

Rissa met Ramsey's eyes and jerked her head toward the door. He followed her and Lonara tagged along. Davi trailed behind them.

"Something is wrong with him," Rissa whispered. "It's like… Well, years ago, Trystan and Davi got ahold of this rare herb with hallucinogenic properties. I ended up having to hide the two of them in my bed chamber to keep my father from finding out. Davi was exactly as he is now."

Ramsey looked to Lonara and she nodded. "Has Davion been pulling magic?"

"No more than me. I was teaching him how to put fewer restrictions on his power."

Lonara's hand shot out and gripped her arm. "You must never do that. Our body's restrictions exist for a reason."

"She's right, dear." Ramsey rubbed his chin. "You have the tenelach and can hold untold amounts of magic. Davion cannot. He has been poisoned by magic."

Rissa sucked in a breath.

Lonara glanced back at Davi. "It will fade soon. But next time, Rissa… Magic poisoning happens when we take more than we can handle. If we push past that point, past the high feeling, the next step is death."

"You mean I could have killed him?"

"Yes," Ramsey answered. Lonara elbowed him and he only shrugged.

Rissa came to an abrupt stop, her feet freezing in place. He almost died because of her? A body slammed into her from behind and she went sprawling to the ground. Davi landed heavily on top of her and a laugh burst free of him as he rolled off and offered her a hand.

"Many sorries, my dear." He grinned.

She followed the line of his arm up over his shoulder until her eyes met his. The darkness that had been such a thick presence had vanished, replaced by a twinkling mirth.

When she took his hand, he yanked her to her feet and pulled her against him. "Mmm you smell good. You say you've loved me most of our lives. That you've been mine long before I knew. But you're wrong, Ri Ri, I've always been yours."

He pecked her lips and then spun away from her. He clapped his hands. "I feel it. All of it. The power. The magic is calling to me. I need more."

"No," Ramsey barked. "That's a lie, Davion. It may feel like it isn't enough, but any more will kill you."

"I don't feel weak." He cocked his head. "I won't die."

"He needs to release some magic." Lonara directed this to Rissa.

Ramsey nodded in agreement. "But we can't allow him outside the palace grounds where he can draw more from the earth."

"The training yard." Rissa didn't wait for them as she grabbed Davi's arm and practically dragged him in the opposite direction.

The rain hadn't let up, but there was no helping it.

Lorelai appeared behind them. "I heard. Is he okay?"

"Hi, cousin." Davi leaned forward and gave her a sloppy kiss on the cheek.

Lorelai peered around him to shoot Rissa a look. "How did he take in this much magic? I taught him how to control the current."

And Rissa taught him how to destroy his control. She couldn't say the words so instead, she stepped out into the rain.

"Rissa." Lorelai looked to the sky. "You can do something about this. I'm not powerful enough, but I don't particularly like the thought of stepping into the freezing rain. Channel what I've taught you."

Water streamed down Rissa's face. She blew out a breath. Ramsey and Lonara could have helped her, but they waited.

Rissa retreated into herself, communicating silently with the magic held in her body. It writhed in time with her thoughts. *Envision what you want to do. Listen to the rules.* Rissa couldn't control the weather. She couldn't stop the rain.

But she could alter its path. She raised her face to the

coming torrent and directed a slow stream of power into the air. The water bent around her until raindrops no longer struck her face. She sent more power out and expanded the radius of her protection until half the courtyard was saved from the pounding of the rain.

Others had stopped to watch their princess perform a task that seemed so simple to her. Their eyes widened.

Ramsey grinned.

Lonara even smiled.

Lorelai only nodded in approval before stepping into the training yard.

A rapid clapping sounded behind them. "Bravo," Davi yelled. "Bloody brilliant."

Pride bloomed in Rissa's chest. "Do I have to let his high fade? I kind of like him like this."

Lorelai laughed and for a second, Rissa wondered if she imagined the sound. The seer had been solemn since the day they rescued her.

"Trystan!" Davi yelled as the king appeared. "Everyone! The king has graced us with his noble presence." Davi bowed.

Rissa snorted. She couldn't remember Davi ever even bowing to her father.

Trystan tried to contain a grin. He straightened his jacket. "This isn't funny." It was as if he was telling himself not to laugh. "Davi could have been hurt."

Davi walked toward Trystan and stopped only inches away, dropping his voice into a whisper. "I didn't die." He wrapped his arms around Trystan's shoulders. "Davi needs a hug."

Rissa brought her hand to her mouth and bit her knuckles to stifle a laugh. Ramsey didn't bother to hide his as it boomed free of him.

Trystan pushed Davi away and looked to Rissa helplessly. "I think I like evil Davi better."

"Not me." Her eyes watered from her contained laughter. She reached for Davi and guided him out into the training yard, her concentration torn between him and protecting them from the rain above. She couldn't hold it for much longer.

Davi just stood there.

"Do something." She shoved him.

He shrugged and lifted his face to the sky.

Her hold on the rain burst as Davi shot his magic straight through hers.

Her shoulders hunched forward and her breath left her in a whoosh. Davi didn't seem to notice.

"Oh my earth," Trystan gasped.

The water hitting Rissa had turned red, leaving streaks down her skin.

"Is that blood?" Trystan asked, the horror plain in his voice. He made a move to stop Davi, but Rissa shook her head.

It wasn't blood. She cupped her hands to catch the rain. Wine?

"Davi," she yelled. "You're a proper drunkard, aren't you?" She shot Trystan a grin. "It's wine. The toss pot."

But what had Lorelai told her? One rule of magic was that you couldn't turn one thing into another.

Rissa brought her hands to her lips and tilted them so the wine ran into her mouth. Not wine. Still water.

He hadn't changed its properties, only their perception of them.

Davi put his hands on his hips as if he was the smartest man in the world. Maybe he was.

As each moment ticked by, his hold on the magic loosened, until red no longer fell from the sky.

Rissa wiped raindrops out of her face and ran a hand over her sopping dress. She glanced toward the others who were still in the dry alcove at the entrance of the training yard.

Davi stumbled and she ran to him. When she met his gaze, the light from before was gone, but maybe that was okay. The darkness was a part of Davi. It made him who he was.

"I'm so sorry," she yelled over the thunderous rain. "This is all my fault."

He shook his head and stumbled back again.

She caught him around the waist and pressed a kiss to his lips.

"I didn't know." Those words were for her more than him.

"I know." He fell backward and she wasn't strong enough to catch him as he crumpled to the dirt.

Davi's pulse pounded in his head and there was no respite from the pain.

Bang. Bang. Bang.

A cool cloth touched his chest. Where had his clothes gone?

"He's burning up," a voice said. It was a sweet voice that sent warmth through Davi's chilled limbs.

"Rissa." Someone else must be in the room with her. This voice was deeper.

Davi moved his lips, but no sound came out.

He put all his energy into opening his eyes. Rissa hovered over him, her blazing hair hanging over one shoulder. If he could only lift his arm, he could run his fingers through the silky strands.

She smiled slowly. "Trystan, he's awake."

The king in question appeared.

Davi's chest inflated painfully. "What happened?"

"You don't remember?" A third voice asked.

He hadn't seen Lorelai at the end of the bed but he was glad she was there.

Rissa bit her lip. "It's probably good he doesn't remember, yeah?"

Panic clawed at Davi's chest when the thought struck him. More memories gone. Lost. Was he lost again? No. He was home. His pounding heart slowed as relief washed through him. Home. Not Dreach-Dhoun.

Trystan reached across and swatted Rissa's arm. "The man could have been hurt and you're making fun."

"I don't understand what's happening here." Davi's eyes flicked from brother to sister.

Rissa's eyes challenged Trystan. "But he didn't die, did he? Not this time and dammit, brother, if I have to laugh to recover from how scared I was, then I will."

Confusion clouded Davi's mind. He lifted the sheet and peered down at his body. "Why am I naked?" He twisted his head. "So help me, Trystan, if the king of Dreach-Sciene stripped me down…"

"You'd enjoy it?" Trystan smirked.

Rissa laughed, her cheeks growing almost as red as her hair. "Relax. It was me."

"You…" Davi shook his head. "How did I stay unconscious for that?"

"Oh earth." Trystan put a hand to his forehead. "I definitely didn't need to hear that."

Davi flashed him a grin.

Just then, the door burst open and Ramsey ran into the room. He held his hand out in front of them. "Help. Help. I've been wounded in battle."

Rissa brought both hands to her mouth. Trystan turned away to hide his grin.

"What is so funny?" Davi yelled.

Lorelai's glare swept the room. "They're assholes, cousin. That's what's going on." She rounded the bed and picked up the cloth Rissa had discarded before dipping it into a bowl of water near the bed. She dabbed it across his brow. "You took in too much magic earlier today and you were not yourself."

That explained it. The pounding head. The aching muscles.

"But wait… That doesn't explain my current state of dress." He settled his accusing eyes on Rissa. "Did you take advantage of me?" At her gasp, he smirked. "I knew it."

"You were soaking wet," she said matter-of-factly.

Trystan chuckled. "I'm glad you're okay, Davi. Thanks for the entertainment earlier, but now I must attend to a few things this evening. I am king after all."

"Show off."

Trystan flashed him a grin before shutting the door behind him. It felt good to joke with his old friend even if he currently felt the need to vomit.

"Alright, boy." Ramsey patted the bed. "Up up."

Davi groaned. "If you think I'm moving from this bed, you've lost all sense."

"No time for rest. We have to get you outside."

Davi's entire body recoiled at the thought of being in such close proximity to magic.

"Are you crazy?" Rissa asked her grandfather. "He was almost killed by magic and now you want him to take more?"

Ramsey tapped his chin and studied them. "Davi's current state has nothing to do with taking in too much power earlier and everything to do with releasing it all at once. He depleted his body of every bit of magic. The earth breaks us, yes, but it can also heal us. Give him a minute in the forest and he'll be good as new." He cocked his head. "Well, as good as Davi gets anyway."

"I feel like I should be offended." Davi groaned as he sat up and slid his feet over the edge of the bed. "Are you all going to stand there watching me dress or give me a bit of privacy?"

Rissa stepped to him and wrapped her arms around his shoulders, dropping a kiss onto the curve of his neck.

He squeezed her arms.

A moment later, she released him and followed Ramsey and Lorelai from the room.

Once he'd clothed himself, he joined them. The stones of the courtyard were slick with water underneath his feet. He gripped Rissa's arm to steady her.

"We're just going right outside the gates," Ramsey said. "It's getting dark and I think it's better if no one strays far."

The guards at the gate nodded as they passed and as soon as his feet left the stone path, Davi felt the power all around him.

Ramsey had been right. As each ache faded away, he remembered more of the day. He rubbed a hand over his eyes. "I made a fool of myself today."

Rissa shrugged. "As opposed to other days?"

He shook his head, a grin spreading slowly. It didn't matter to him. He'd walk back into that palace and hold his head high.

He cut off the flow of magic into his body just as a horse thundered up the road to the palace.

He froze beside Rissa as a man in Dreach-Sciene livery rode as if his life depended on it, aiming for the gates. He yelled as he got near.

"They're coming!"

The evening loomed dark and cold outside. Trystan stepped onto his private balcony, the cold air biting through his clothes and his breath lingering in front of his face.

He shivered as he took in the brooding clouds moving off to the south, allowing the stars behind them to come alive. The storm was finally moving out. About time. Not that they hadn't needed the rains, but he was glad it had finally passed on. The only bright spot in the last few days had been the quick flash of the old Davi. Even knowing he'd almost died, it had been worth it to see the return of his brother. He smiled into the growing dusk, the memory of Davi's behavior causing the laughter to build up in his chest. It felt good to laugh. It felt good to not be in constant worry. He'd forgotten the pressure of being king, if only for a moment.

He walked to the edge of the balcony and spread his hands wide on the stone wall, taking in a deep gulp of night air. He had always enjoyed the view from the king's chambers. His chambers now. From up here he could see the open valley south of the castle that lead to the dense forest stretching farther into Aldorwood. His lands. His kingdom. He'd do everything in his power to protect it and its people.

Commotion from below caught his attention, breaking his moment of peace. He was too far up to hear what was being said, but shouting and raised voices lifted from the courtyard below, along with the sounds of the portcullis clanging as it rose. It didn't worry him too much. He knew Ramsey was planning on taking Davi out to the copse of trees beyond the gateway. They wouldn't go far, not with night almost upon them.

The banging of the opened gate faded away only to be followed by more yelling. Trystan felt a tingle of unease nipping at the back of his neck. There were no alarms being raised, yet something did not feel right. He returned to his room and strapped on his sword and sheath just as a rapid knocking started on his door. In quick strides he crossed the room and yanked it open to find Alixa standing there, her brow furrowed and her golden eyes shadowed in worry.

"What is it?" He asked immediately.

"A messenger has arrived, Trystan. A young man from one of the border patrols. He says Eisner and a Dreach-Dhoun army march toward the castle as we speak."

Trystan's heart dropped into his stomach, even though he had been expecting some move on Eisner's part. He didn't show Alixa his fear at her words. A king never showed his fear. His father didn't even though he had admitted to Trystan many times of being afraid. Instead Trystan pulled his shoulders back and stood taller.

"Where is this messenger?"

"In the council chambers, along with Lonara and Ramsey and the others. They all await you, Trystan."

Trystan swallowed his dread. "Then let's not make them wait any longer." He stepped into the hall but Alixa laid a hand on his shoulder, stopping his stride. He glanced at her in surprise as she flashed him a tight smile.

"You've got this," she said, squeezing his shoulder in reassurance. "I believe in your ability to keep us all safe."

He dropped his eyes, not wanting her to see the wetness gathering there at her unwavering faith in him. Instead he laughed. A laugh devoid of any humor. "I hope you're right, Alixa. I guess we shall see."

It was as Alixa said. The council chamber held everyone Trystan needed to see. Ramsey and Lonara sat at one end of the long table. Rissa, Davi, and Avery sat at the other, replacing the faces that had once sat there. His father, Lord Coille, Lady Sona, and so many others. What he wouldn't give to have them all there now, making the decisions that he would soon have to make.

Captains Brown and Fields stood off to the side, in deep conversation with a travel weary young man who looked as if he hadn't slept in a week. The two guards standing at the doors bowed their heads at the king's entrance and one announced to the rest of the room, "King Trystan."

They all stood at his approach, but Trystan waved their formality aside. His eyes stopped on Brown and the man at his side.

"So is it true? Eisner and an army are on their way here?"

The young soldier gave a nod of deference. "Yes, your

Majesty. I saw them with my own eyes. They are coming. An army of thousands, looting and burning farms and crops as they advance." He shook his head and it was only then Trystan noticed the shadows in his eyes.

He softened his voice. "Where is the rest of your unit?"

He seemed to shrink into himself and the horror was written plainly on his face. Trystan would have sworn every person in that room was holding their breath.

The man peered down at the torn and dirty uniform that hung off his thin frame, a shiver raced through him. When he spoke, his voice sent a chill through Trystan. "We were tasked with evacuating the villages along the border of Aldorwood and Isenore."

Trystan nodded. He'd sent many men to aid in the relocation of his people, hoping to get them out of harm's way. "Go on."

"The village emptied rather quickly. By the time we arrived, the people had received your messengers and were prepared to make for Whitecap. So we loaded every wagon we could find. Every animal that could carry children or elderly did. It was only a few days ride to Whitecap from this particular village, even with the train of people."

He sucked in a heavy breath. "Night came on the first day and the men we'd sent on to scout ahead returned. They'd found another one of your patrols. Dead."

Trystan closed his eyes, imagining what was coming.

The man wiped a hand across his haunted eyes and sighed. "We sent our night sentries out to the perimeter of our camp. By the time they were meant to switch with the next shift, we knew something was wrong." He met the king's eyes. "They didn't return. Half the camp was still asleep when the enemy soldiers came barreling out of the woods like the devil himself."

Someone gasped, but Trystan's mind raced. His people. Slaughtered as they fled for safety.

"Oh my earth." Rissa covered her mouth with her hand.

Trystan didn't have the luxury of shock, only action. "And you are the only survivor?"

The soldier nodded. "We had a plan in place. If we were ever attacked, because we knew what it was we were looking for—not just outlaws or miscreants, but armies—the first one to get to a horse was to abandon their duties and ride hard to the king."

Avery set her shoulders, showing no emotion, as ever. "A day's ride from Whitecap. Sire—"

"I know." He rubbed his eyes. The closest village to Whitecap was the one where Mira's family lived. He turned to the soldier once more. "How far behind you are they?"

"Hours." His eyes bore into the king. "My horse threw a shoe a day back and I lost all advantage I had. They're coming, your Majesty. And they're coming before dawn. I'm sure of it."

So they had but mere hours to prepare? Then they didn't have a moment to lose.

"You've been through a great ordeal, soldier, and we are in your debt." He turned to one of the guards at the door. "Take this young man to the kitchen and see he has a decent meal and a bit of rest. It will be a long night."

The soldier nodded and escorted the man from the room. Trystan didn't even allow the heavy oak door to close before he turned to his advisors.

"Seems Eisner is bringing the war to us. Captain Brown, update please."

"The orders have already been given, your Majesty. Every

garrison will be in place. The archers and crossbowmen will take a position on the ramparts. Our gunners are in place to operate the catapults and the ballista. Men will be placed underneath the castle and all around the foundations in case they send in miners, we'll be ready for them."

"Miners?" Rissa asked and Trystan looked at his sister in surprise. Rissa had become so adept and powerful since this had begun that he almost forgot she was not as well versed in war preparations as he was.

"Soldiers that tunnel underneath the castle walls and place tar-soaked beams to burn through the foundations so the wall collapses, allowing them entry."

Rissa lips thinned into a grim line, but she asked no more questions.

"The boy said thousands. We have over a thousand troops stationed within the castle walls, yes Avery?"

The sword master ducked her head in agreement.

"It will make for a strong defense force. But it won't be enough."

"I agree, Trystan." Ramsey spoke for the first time. "That is why I believe we should send a messenger straight away to Whitecap for reinforcements. We can't rely on the outlying vassals and landowners to help us anymore since we've emptied the villages and sent the abled off to Whitecap or Cullenspire for training. Whitecap is our closest pocket of allies."

"Even if the messenger rides day and night," Rissa interjected, "Whitecap is still a four or five day ride there and the same back. We will need to withstand this attack for eight to ten days. Are we prepared to do that, Trystan?"

Trystan wasn't the one to answer his sister's question. Davi did that for him. "Since it is Eisner attacking and not Calis, I assume that force will not be the main agenda. Most sieges are not about battle, but a waiting game. My guess is Eisner is aware we are overstocked with extra mouths and understocked in supplies. He will attack our stores first. Use catapults with fire bolts, no doubt, to burn down our supplies. He can cripple us without even one attempt on our walls."

"Then we cover the store's roofs with as many hides as we can find to prevent the fire from taking hold. Protect them the best we can. Fields, see that is done and send a messenger to Whitecap with the greatest of urgency."

"Yes, your Majesty." Fields bowed and left the room to do Trystan's bidding.

"Lonara, split those who've been trained in magic into two crews. Yours on the stores, spread out enough to protect our supplies day and night. Ramsey, you and the other wielders on the ramparts. Eisner will surely try to use magic to get in as well as to damage us. We must have some sort of barrier in place at all times."

"It will be done, your Majesty. I will oversee it."

"Good. If it's a waiting game Eisner will bring us, then we will play it better than he. We will keep ourselves protected while we wait for reinforcements and then we battle if we must." His eyes flicked back to his sister. "Rissa, check with the armory and ensure we have enough armor and weapons to equip everyone. Most of our soldiers are still untrained in their own magic and will resort to fighting any way they can. Inform the blacksmiths and fletchers to work in continuous shifts to keep the supplies of arrows and bolts up. Remember, they will need to see the strength and courage of Dreach-Sciene's princess right now to bolster them."

Rissa gave a curt nod.

"Alixa." His gaze fell on the face that had become so important to him. "I'll need you to help move the old folk and the children who've arrived from the nearby villages inside the keep for their own safety. Do so without inciting panic. Ensure they have plenty of food and water and blankets. If the outer walls of the castle do fall, at least the children will be safer in there."

"Of course, your Majesty." Her words were said in agreement, but Trystan understood her look. She would do what he asked, but she wasn't planning on staying in the keep with them. He knew when it came time, she'd be by his side.

"Sire," Brown said. "There's one last thing."

Trystan gestured for him to continue.

"If you should fall..." He paused. "Your Majesty, you are no longer the Toha where a second-in-command is an asset but not a necessity. You're the king. If the worst should happen and you are killed in this battle, the men need to know who to look to. What orders to take as they fight for their lives. Your own father was forced to take command when his father died during a fight. Earth forbid, you should follow your grandfather, but..."

"But if I do the men would have no one leading the army and Dreach-Sciene would be lost." Trystan knew he needed a second for the army, but he'd been delaying naming one. Now it was time.

Who could lead the army? Who did he trust with his kingdom? There was only one person he wanted.

Rissa stood and crossed the room to speak so others wouldn't hear. "Avery," she said. "She's the only one you could possibly consider."

His eyes drifted to the sword master. She was a woman who would jump into the fight no matter the cost. She was skilled. She was loyal.

He shook his head. Avery had never wanted to be a leader. She'd never agree because it would mean possibly leaving his side to command a second unit.

Rissa could do it, but she didn't have the training to lead in combat.

He eyed her carefully. The people would follow her, no doubt. Maybe she didn't need the training. Rissa gave orders as well as anyone else. Her mind was possibly one of the best in the kingdom – as was her aim with the bow.

She met his eye with a shake of her head. "No, Trystan. I will follow you into anything and do what I have to do, but you and I both know I'm the wrong choice." Her hard eyes scanned the room. "The men would follow Brown."

Brown would have been an excellent choice. For his father.

Trystan's second was supposed to be his partner. As those still in the room waited, Trystan's eye caught Davi inching toward the door.

"No." Trystan's voice was dangerous.

Davi froze, his shoulders tensing. "What?"

Trystan saw no other face but his brother's before him. Not evil Davi. Not the orphan kid who'd first come to the palace. He saw the boy who taught him how to evade the palace guards. The man who agreed to accompany him on a quest they didn't seem to have any hope of finishing.

"You don't get to decide where my trust lies." Trystan pinned him with dark eyes. "That's not how this works, Davion Bearne." He'd never spoken his full name before, acknowledging his true parentage. But if he wanted Davi back, he had to accept all of him, every dark part.

Davi ran a hand through his night-black hair and breathed heavily. "I can't—"

"You can." Trystan advanced until he stood only feet away.

"You have always been my second, Davi. I won't allow you to give the title back."

Davi shook his head.

"I trust you." Trystan reached out and grasped his shoulder. Davi's muscles clenched under his hand.

He released a shaky breath, his eyes glassing over. "You don't understand." He clutched at his shirt right over his chest. "I don't trust me."

Trystan brought his other hand up to grip the opposite shoulder, holding Davi in place. "That's okay. I have enough trust for both of us." Trystan dipped his head to make Davi meet his gaze. "Truwa Brathair."

Davi sucked air through his teeth, his next words leaving on a breath. "Trust." He nodded. "Brother."

Trystan grinned, a weight lifting from his shoulders despite the impending siege. He stared at Davi for a moment longer before patting him on the side of the head. "Davion Bearne is the king's second." He stepped away, his eyes finding Rissa. She nodded in approval.

"Come." Trystan made haste for the door. "We must be ready when dawn arrives."

They arrived before the sun crested the top of the mountain. The chilling sound of thousands of feet marching to the beat of a war drum rolled across the valley. The flanking soldiers carried torches, lighting up the army, filtering through the trees and filling up the valley floor. A moving sea of enemies.

Trystan stood with his people on the ramparts watching their approach, no one speaking a word. Lines of archers and crossbowmen, soldiers and common folk who'd come to fight at his back, all wearing identical masks of fear. Trystan didn't begrudge them that. He wasn't immune himself. For most of these men and women this was their true first taste of war. It was unappealing. But underneath the fear there lay more. A current of courage and strength. Trystan had a sneaking suspicion the emotions were being magically enhanced by Ramsey.

Davi and Brown flanked him while Avery and Ramsey stood at his back. His advisors. Only two of them had seen the last war. For most of them this was new territory. It was overwhelming watching as the rising sun highlighted the army surrounding the castle on all sides. His father had been his most trusted advisor in every aspect of his young life, and if there was ever a time Trystan wished to hear his advice, it was now.

A hand gripped his as Rissa slipped between him and Davi. Trystan glanced sideways at her.

"About time you arrived, sister." His voice was solemn.

"I had to finish preparing my archers."

He nodded at her explanation. He'd given control over the army's archers to Rissa without question. There wasn't anyone who could lead them better. As he met her eye, he caught sight of the challenge that always gleamed there. It was as if she dared anyone to question her place in this battle.

There was a time when he would have. Not anymore.

"Your Majesty." Alixa's voice joined Rissa's from over his shoulder.

He scanned her face, surprised at the shock of white paint stretching down the center. She stared ahead with a fierceness he'd come to expect from her.

The movement below them fizzled to a stop, but the drums kept going. The sound echoing through the valley rattled Trystan's nerves. It was nothing but a fear tactic, he knew that. Albeit a successful one.

"I wish we had thought of drums," Davi leaned past Rissa and whispered at Trystan. It was such an idiotic, Davi thing to say that Trystan couldn't help but grin as Rissa snorted in his ear.

"Sorry, Dav. I was a little occupied preparing for this invasion. I didn't think of everything," he whispered back out of the corner of his mouth. "Besides, I think drums are something a second in command should be in charge of, don't you?"

Davi nodded in all seriousness. "Duly noted. I'll be prepared next time."

Trystan knew Davi's triviality was only a mask to cover his fear, but it was a welcoming break in tension.

"Next time? Are you aware of other enemies that will try to siege our castle as well?"

Davi shrugged, a tiny smile burgeoning on his lips. "That royal stick up your butt makes you very unreasonable at times. You aren't the most easy-going of kings, Trystan Renauld."

"Not the time for both of you to show your idiocracy," Rissa grumbled at them both, even as her own smile threatened to erupt.

The drums stopped. Just like that. An unearthly silence followed, encompassing them like a shroud. The sun was just peeking over the forest. There should have been a cacophony of sounds inundating the air, but there was nothing. Trystan wasn't sure what was worse, the drums or the silence. He glanced at Brown, but the captain looked as unsure as he did.

A line of soldiers on horses spanned the front of the army. Trystan focused his attention on them. Although they rode with Dreach-Dhoun banners, Trystan recognized Eisner right away. He pulled ahead of the rest of his soldiers, sitting atop his horse and staring up at the castle walls. Looking at them. He was too far away to make eye contact, but Trystan could feel the hatred and contempt emanating from that look. This was a man who rode here with one intent. Revenge for his son.

"Strange that Calis would send his *lapdog* instead of coming himself," Alixa spat the word with just as much contempt. She had long since ceased thinking of Eisner as her father. Not for the first time the same thought entered Trystan's head. This was a momentous attack on the castle of his supposedly mortal enemy. Why would he send Eisner to do his dirty work?

Ramsey stepped forward as he answered Alisa's question "Calis doesn't want the castle. Not yet. He wants control of your lands. The death of your people. He wants you to suffer before he comes for you. Eisner is just a taste of what's coming."

He heard Rissa's sharp gasp as a movement began below.

"Archers prepare," Rissa ordered and they all snapped to attention as one, readying their bows and preparing to strike as soon as their enemy came into range. "On my command."

But the moving army did not attempt to run at the castle walls. Instead they spread out, making room as soldiers dug into the lands surrounding the castle, just out of their attack reach. Trystan's brow furrowed in puzzlement.

"At ease," he commanded the soldiers as he turned the captain's way. "What are they doing, Brown?"

The captain observed for a moment before reaching a conclusion. "They are building their own lines of defense, Sire. Digging up banks of earth which they will re-enforce with wooden palisades. A wall of circumvallation." Brown's eyes fell on him. "They are planning to stay awhile."

Hours turned into days, but still no attack. No trying to break through the gates. No attempt to mine the walls. No fire bolts to burn down their store of supplies. Eisner and his men did nothing but sit outside the walls and beat those drums. Was that the ploy? To drive them all insane? To beat them all down into surrender? They hadn't even used their magic.

Trystan rubbed at his weary eyes as he surveyed the

exhausted members of his council sitting around the table with him. Their collection of dark, bruised eyes and pale, drawn features were a testament to their lack of sleep. None of them had gotten any more rest than he had over the past few days. Maybe Eisner's plan was working after all.

"Report," Trystan snapped at Davi the moment he stepped into the room. It had been his watch last night. Although he had been the one to stay on the walls last night with the men, he seemed to be more energetic than the rest of them combined.

"Good morning to you too, sire." Davi grinned at Trystan, giving him a mock bow. "It's nice to see the night's rest has put you in such a good mood."

"Report, Davion," Trystan growled again and Davi sighed.

"As always. No movement. They are just sitting there watching us. Not one attempt to scale the walls. The men are getting restless, Trystan. I had to stop a couple of the fools from trying to pick off a few of Eisner's horses that had wandered close, just to ease their boredom."

Trystan pushed himself away from the table and stood up. Pacing around the room, he could feel the eyes of his councilors watching his every move.

"What does he want? If the surviving soldier is to be believed, they have treated no other settlement with mercy. Why have they not attacked us with the same ruthlessness? Is the true plan to starve us out?"

"That could take months," Rissa said.

"And doesn't make a bit of sense," Alixa added. "That is not Eisner's way. He is a vengeful man. He will want blood for Royce's death and my betrayal. No, he has something else planned. *Calis* has something else planned."

Trystan stopped pacing and nodded. "I agree. Lona, how..."

An urgent rapping on the door diverted Trystan's question. The soldier standing guard reacted to Trystan's nod and opened the door as a young messenger stumbled into the room. His eyes searched out the king right away as he performed an awkward bow.

"Speak." Trystan ordered.

"Your Majesty, Captain Brown sent me to tell you an army envoy approaches the castle. He requests your command, sire."

"Tell the captain I will be there shortly."

The young man bowed again and left the room without another word. Trystan's gaze flitted to those seated at the table.

"Eisner sends an envoy. Seems we are about to find out the terms of our surrender." His gaze moved to the sword master. "Avery what is the protocol to meeting this envoy?"

"An envoy is treated with respect, sire, and is not to be attacked. We need to send our own to meet the envoy halfway and discuss. I volunteer to do as such."

Trystan shook his head. "No. You are far too valuable and carry far too much information."

"Mistress Payne will be in no danger." Ramsey's smile was filled with indulgence as he studied his grandson. "Eisner wishes to speak to us. If he meant to do us harm without speaking first, he would have already done so. And in the off chance that this is but a mere trick to get us to open the gate, none better than mistress Payne to keep the attackers at bay until we manage to close the gate again. Avery is the best choice to do this."

Trystan still wasn't convinced.

"Trystan, we will keep Avery shielded with our magic. We will not let any harm come to her."

Trystan knew Lonara was as good as her word, but still he weighed his options.

"We don't have a choice, brother." Rissa joined in. "I no more wish to expose Avery to our enemy than you do, but we need to know what Eisner's terms are. Besides, I'll go myself if it means a night with no more drums pounding through my head."

Trystan sighed knowing Rissa would do just that. "Fine. Avery, you will be our envoy. We will keep a close eye on you. If you suspect anything out of sorts, raise your sword and we will launch an attack. Understood?"

The sword master gave a curt nod. "Yes, sire."

"Good. Now let's go find out what Eisner requires."

TRYSTAN COULD HEAR the unmistakable sound of the gate beginning its ascent. It would only be lifted enough for Avery to squeeze out with the direct order to drop it and close the heavy wooden doors if there was even so much as a twitch from the enemy army. Rissa and Davi stood watch at the gates while Trystan and Lonara observed Avery's mission from the wall, watching for any deceit on Eisner's part.

Trystan never took his eyes from the field, even as he sent an order Captain Brown's way. "They so much as cough the wrong way, send a volley of fire against them, understood Captain? No harm must fall Mistress Payne's way."

"Understood, your Majesty."

Lonara smiled as the captain sauntered off to speak with his men, leaving them alone. "You care much for your sword master, Trystan. She is lucky to have such a caring king."

"No you're wrong, Lona. It is I who is the lucky one. Avery has been with my family since before I was even born. She's taught me everything I know about being a soldier and so much more than that. She helped mold me from that silly boy into who I am today. Rissa and I both owe her much. Avery may not be big on emotion, but she is big of heart. No one has been more loyal to the Renaulds than her. Do your best to keep her from danger out there."

Lonara tilted her head as she smiled. "As you wish, sire."

A lone soldier stood in the middle of the open field between the castle and the encroaching army. He waited as Avery began her cautious approach. Trystan's gaze bounced between her and Eisner, but not one horse moved out of line to disrupt the talk.

The two envoys conversed for a few moments. At one point Avery seemed to reach for her sword and Trystan tensed. The sword master glanced toward the castle, but then continued the conversation, dropping her hand from her sword. Finally the two drifted away from each other and Avery returned to the castle.

Trystan did not hesitate. As soon as he saw Avery heading back he sprinted for the stairs. Taking them two at a time, he hit the courtyard the same time Avery was squeezing in under the iron gate. As soon as she was inside, the guards dropped the portcullis the rest of the way and bolted the heavy doors behind her.

Trystan stared at Avery, trying to gauge her mood, but her face was impassive as always. Beckoning to her to follow, he headed inside to his council chambers and away from listening ears. Whatever Avery had to say was sure to cause a panic. That was something he wanted to avoid at all cost.

He waited for all of his advisors to be present before he addressed Avery.

"So tell us, Avery, did you find out why Eisner has not attacked us yet? What does he want?"

The sword master glanced about the room before her eyes pinned Trystan. She swallowed hard. "He has given his demands, sire. We have until dawn to hand over Davion, Alixa, and Lorelai to be taken back to Dreach-Dhoun and punished for their crime of treason. If we do not comply, Eisner and his men will attack at first light with orders to leave no one alive."

"Out of the question, Davion." Trystan's gaze could have cut glass. He'd ordered Davi, Alixa, and Lorelai to the throne room and shut the door. His guards would keep anyone from coming in or out.

The four of them stared at each other, waiting for someone to break the standoff.

"Trystan." Alixa bit her lip and sighed.

Trystan's eyes snapped to her. "What, Alixa? What would you like to say here? Because if the next words out of your mouth are what I expect them to be, you'd do well keeping them to yourself."

Lorelai crossed her arms over her chest as she scrutinized him. "What are you going to do, your Majesty?" Her voice held an eerie threat. "Keep us here with your magic?" She lifted her chin. "Try."

Davi's eyes widened, but he wisely stayed quiet.

Lorelai narrowed her icy eyes. "You can't, can you?" She

stepped toward him. "Your magic is weak. The earth doesn't answer you." She cocked her head. "You expected the magic to return to Dreach-Sciene and make you the all-powerful king you needed to be to win this war, but that didn't happen. You really know nothing, do you?"

Trystan stepped back, needing space between him and the seer. Every word she spoke was the truth. He'd tried more times than he could count, but his magic could barely even start a fire. He was the king and he was weak.

When Davi finally spoke again, his voice held none of the confidence Trystan knew him for. "This is the only way, Trystan. Surely you can see that. There are hundreds of people—soldiers and villagers alike—within these walls. If we can save them…"

Trystan clenched his jaw and met his friends' haunted eyes with ghosts of his own. "I won't lose you again." His stern gaze swept the room. "Any of you." He pointed toward the door. "Do you think that will be the end? That we'll hand you three over and Eisner will run back to Calis and tell him this war is over." He dropped his arm. "This isn't about you."

A pounding sounded on the door and Rissa's voice reached them as she yelled at the guards to let her through. The door burst open and she barreled toward Davi, her hands stretched out in front of her. When she reached him, she shoved him backward until he hit the wall.

"Idiot," she seethed. "Of all the…" A growl ripped from her throat. "They're trying to break us and you're stupid enough to play right into their hands. Dammit, why couldn't I have fallen in love with Avery? She's at least the practical one of you lot. Ugh!"

"Ri." Trystan tried to grab her arm, but she ripped it away.

"I've got this, brother." She snapped her hand open, and Davi's arms stuck to the wall.

"Rissa." Davi tried to break free of her magic, but she was stronger. "Let me go."

She leaned close so they were nose to nose. "No." She glanced over her shoulder at Trystan. "I can handle him. You take care of those two."

Trystan stared at her for a moment longer, torn between wanting to make her back off Davi and thanking her.

Alixa scowled. "Don't even think of sticking me to a wall."

"He doesn't have enough power." Lorelai looked to him in challenge.

The sound of Davi struggling distracted him for a moment before Trystan's shoulders dropped. "There has to be a better way to end this. We have enough grain to last us long after the reinforcements from Whitecap can get here. I refuse to give Eisner what he wants. We have no guarantee he'll let us be."

Lorelai relaxed her stance. "You're right, your Majesty."

"I am?"

"He is?" Alixa parroted.

"My uncle has no loyalties. The closest thing I've seen him come to love was Davion. But he's been trying to destroy Dreach-Sciene for much longer than Davi has been alive. I don't know why Duke Eisner requested Davion and myself to turn ourselves over, but I can assure you, Calis Bearne would never agree to a truce to secure our return."

"Ri, do you hear that?" Davi asked. "We aren't going. You can let me go."

Rissa tapped one finger against her chin. "No, Davion. I know you want to do what you think is best and that means your judgment is suspect." She lifted her hand and Davi sprang free from the wall. "Sit." When he didn't obey, she forced his legs to bend. "You will remain here until the deadline has passed."

His mouth gaped open. "That's hours from now."

She shrugged. "Next time, maybe you won't be so impulsive."

Someone shook Rissa's shoulder, but she didn't have the strength to lift her eyes to them as she focused every bit of her waning magic on Davi.

"Rissa." That was Ramsey's voice. She heard it, but the words didn't register in her mind. "The deadline has passed."

She felt Davi fight against her magic every second even as he promised her he'd let go of the insanity that had him wanting to give himself up to save those inside the palace. Had he realized his capture was nothing but another lie?

But a flashback to the night Davi was lost to them in the mountains of Isenore overtook her mind, and she couldn't think of anything other than the simple fact that she couldn't lose him again. Dreach-Sciene needed him, her brother wanted him by his side, but those reasons were of little importance to her. She'd been so afraid of his dying again because if he was gone, she'd lose herself as well.

Because Rissa Renauld, princess of Dreach-Sciene, stubborn and independent as she was, wasn't anything without Davion. He was the only thing that made her whole.

So, in the middle of a siege on the palace walls, she used every bit of magic inside her to keep him pinned to the same spot. To keep him safe.

He sat beside the throne. Every time he tried to stand, she used her power to push him back down.

"Did you hear me?" Ramsey's voice was louder this time, bouncing through the spaces in her mind.

"Forget it, Ramsey." Davion sighed. She heard his words but didn't react as she listened to them absently. "She stopped listening to me hours ago."

Ramsey straightened. "Eisner knows by now we aren't handing you over. Now we're waiting to see his response."

"Do you think we made a mistake?"

"Son, I know Calis and Eisner better than you could ever hope to. So, no. I don't think it was a mistake. I have no loyalty to you. You aren't my blood. I love Lorelai like my own, but even her sacrifice would be acceptable if I thought they'd really let us be. Trades and deals aren't going to end this. I'm very much afraid only bloodshed will."

Rissa's remaining power unraveled within her. She tried to grasp it as if fumbling for a loose string, but it slipped through her fingers and she slumped back against the wall.

Davi's body surged forward as her hold released him. He fell onto his hands. Without wasting a minute, he scrambled across the floor to kneel in front of Rissa.

"Ri." He put his fingers under her chin and tilted her head up so he could look into her unfocused eyes.

"She used all her magic to keep you with her." Ramsey's voice held a chastisement in it.

Davi said something else but his words jumbled in Rissa's brain. Strong arms lifted her and it was as if she was floating.

The castle blurred around her and a singular thought entered her mind. The earth. It needed her. To take its magic. To protect it. She'd never been so drained, but even without the power in her veins, its connection was strong.

The stone fortress around her suddenly didn't feel like

protection, but instead served as a cage, keeping her from the earth. Where were they taking her?

"She needs magic," Ramsey said.

No crap, she wanted to respond, but her lips wouldn't move. She vaguely knew of people scrambling to get out of their path.

They entered the great hall, which sat at the center of the castle. The keep was the most secure part, fortified against any invasion. Villagers crowded into the small place.

"Up here," Davi said, pushing his way through.

Rissa hadn't had a need to spend much time in the great hall since Trystan's Toha ceremony. At that thought, she knew why they'd brought her here. Beyond the rows of wooden benches was a broken area in the stone. It had been created many generations before in order to perform ceremonies with the earth's presence.

Kings were crowned here. Tohas were named here. Royal marriages were blessed.

Because it was the one place inside the palace other than the walled garden where the earth entered their lives.

Davi sat her on the cool ground and took her hand to place it on the small patch of dirt. Nothing grew threw the cracks, but the earth still thrived. Her strength snapped into her as warmth flooded her veins.

She breathed in deeply and blew out when she peered up at Davi. "You're still here." A smiled spread slowly. "I knew I could stop you."

He shook his head. "I told you once I'm never leaving you again. I don't intend to break that promise."

Ramsey helped her to her feet and the three of them left the keep behind, nodding to the guards as they did.

They walked through the halls until a door led them into

the courtyard where several soldiers were milling around waiting for orders. Waiting wasn't easy on any of them.

"Princess," a few murmured tiredly as they passed. Davi got more formal "Sirs". Ramsey was ignored as usual. Those who knew who he was still didn't know what to make of the young-looking Tri-Gard member.

Alixa stood at the bottom of the narrow stairs leading up to where Rissa's archers lined the walls. She looked to Rissa in question. "Trystan said you had Davi trapped?" She raised an eyebrow.

Rissa shrugged. She wasn't proud of her fear or her dependence on Davi.

Davi held out his hand and gestured to the stairs. "Together?"

She nodded just as a shout came from above. "Fire!"

Armor-clad feet ran down the stairs, shouting as they did, before running across the courtyard.

Rissa sprinted up the steps where she found Trystan shouting orders. He caught sight of them. "Ramsey, I need you at the eastern grain stores now."

Ramsey took one look at the flames rising toward the sky across the parapets and took off.

Rissa didn't wait for a command before stepping forward. "Archers." She picked up a discarded bow and drew the string back, narrowing one eye.

A handful of men were in the distance throwing magically created flames toward the Dreach-Sciene grain stores.

"Davi," Trystan barked and jerked his head toward the west. "Take some men who use their magic well and protect the rest of our stores."

Davi left to organize those in the courtyard.

"We're going to take out magic wielders," Rissa told the

archers along the wall. "While they're still occupied with their fire." She glanced to the side to see them all lift their bows. "Draw. Aim." She marked the farthest magic wielder for herself. "Fire!"

A volley of arrows arced through the sky, but they were too far. Rissa used her magic to urge her arrow farther than the rest, but most of the strong magic wielders had been separated from the archers for their skill.

Rissa's arrow struck her target and the rest fell short.

Screams rent through the air as the buildings housing the stores to the west burst into flames.

Fear stabbed her gut, but she shook it away. Davi would be okay.

"Your Majesty." Avery stepped up beside him. "The Duke will try to starve us out. If Lonara and Ramsey can't put out the flames before all the stores have caught fire, we won't be able to sit here waiting for him to make a move anymore. We need to act."

Trystan tore his eyes from the overwhelming army below and fixed them on Avery. "You're right, Avery. I will not give up this castle." He flicked his eyes to Rissa. "Eisner doesn't know us as well as he thinks he does. We will fight for Dreach-Sciene until we reside within the earth." He turned toward the stairs. "Avery, wake the rest of the troops. Rissa, prepare your archers to provide support. It's time we deal with the traitor at our gates."

"Down!" Rissa ordered as the arrows and iron bolts from the ballista flew overhead. She pulled her magic from deep inside, adding it to the projectiles launching toward their enemy. "Put your magic behind it," she yelled at the archers, hoping this time to succeed. The last attack had been blocked with a protective barrier. She hoped this time their magic was strong enough to pierce that barrier and take out some of their enemy. Holding her breath in prayer, she watched helplessly as the arrows and bolts bounced off the shield and fell to the ground.

"Dammit," She growled, and gripped the back of her neck in frustration. Eisner's men were strong. Stronger than she expected. But then again, out there among the grass and trees the magic grew strongest. They could rejuvenate a lot quicker than their army in here. The sandy bits of soil not covered by cobblestone and rock were already running dry. It was getting harder to pull magic.

She heard the groaning and clanging of the portcullis as it lifted to allow Trystan and his troops access to the enemy. Each clang tore at her heart. Dreach-Sciene's troops were far outnumbered. It was pure craziness to go into hand to hand battle. But they had no other choice. If they stood by and did nothing, Eisner would slowly chip away at their stores. He'd practically burnt the whole castle's supplies to the ground with that last stunt. Only Lonara and Lorelai's quick thinking had allowed them to put out the fire. And the fire after that. It just kept coming. Eisner needed to be stopped and from behind these walls it was impossible. It needed to be done from outside the gate.

She buried her fear for Davi and Trystan and the others down deep, along with her resentment. Last night had been all for naught. She knew Davi. Knew him better than he knew himself at times. He would have sacrificed himself last night for the rest of them without a second thought. All of them would have. She did not regret for one moment Davi's captivity if it meant keeping him alive. But all her efforts had been in vain, for he was now going into battle with Trystan against an enemy that outnumbered them in troops and magic.

And it was killing her knowing he was riding into battle without her by his side. As much as she wanted to be out there on the field with them, to help protect those she loved, she knew she was of better use here, with the archers. Once Trystan and Davi got that shield down, the archers would do their best to pick off the Dreach-Dhoun soldiers, even if they had to do it one-by-one.

The sound of the battle cry reached her ears as the Dreach-Sciene soldiers emptied onto the field below. As if her eyes had a mind of their own, they rifled through the hundreds of soldiers flowing from the castle gates, some on horseback, searching for those she loved. She saw Trystan immediately, the gold and purple of his plate mail reflecting the sun's rays as he sat tall atop his steed. Davion flanked his right, Alixa and Avery his left. Her eyes glued to them even as her words were meant for the troops bordering the wall awaiting her orders.

"Once that shield goes down, shoot anything that comes at our troops." She yelled, as she walked up and down the wall, her back stiff and her voice sure, while inside she quaked with fear. "Do not hesitate to kill. They won't. We will do our part and keep our troops from harm down there. We will not give up, no matter how futile it seems or how fatigued we get. Reach deep and keep shooting. We do this for our king! We do this for our families!"

The roar of agreement rose up loud as it echoed down the ramparts. They would do this. They had to do this. No one she loved would die today. Not under her watch.

TRYSTAN PULLED his sword and screamed loud as he kicked his horse, his voice lost among those of his troops. He glanced over at Alixa as she rode beside him, her face a mask of beautiful rage, her skin a light bronze in the morning sun. The white streak of war paint ran from her forehead down between her eyes. Two more decorated her cheekbones. An addition from Lonara. A symbol of magic protection. Many of his people had let Lonara paint them. She believed in it, and truth be told they needed all the help they could get at the moment.

He tore his eyes away, choosing to concentrate on the enemy instead. It hurt too much to look at her. It hurt too much to look at any of them and wonder if it would be the last time he'd see their faces.

The Dreach-Dhoun soldiers appeared as a dark mountain range on the horizon. So many of them spread as far as the eye could see. His gaze flitted over them as they drew closer to their enemy, searching for the one who called the shots. Calis' right-hand man. Eisner.

Trystan spotted him at the front of the line. Him and one other he had not expected to see. Briggs Villard sat atop his own horse, overseeing the battlefield like he belonged. This was not the same weak old man Trystan remembered. This man was strong. Controlled, magic rolled off of him in waves. He could almost see it. Eisner rode around Briggs barking commands, his words lost in the roar of the battle cries, the beating of the drums.

The ground shook as Dreach-Dhoun's troops finally responded. Two armies, soldiers of all sizes. Men and women from both sides, rushing toward each other in a mad dash for survival under the calm blue sky. The two armies came together in a clash of clanging metal, bucking horses, and screams.

Trystan quickly lost sight of Davi and Alixa. They disappeared in the parade of Dreach-Dhoun soldiers. Instead, his world filled with flashes of steel as his horse reared up to avoid a mass of soldiers, bucking Trystan off in the process. He rolled to his feet as his horse trampled through the stream of soldiers.

Screams of pain, smells of blood and death. For every man and woman who fell under his blade, a tiny part of Trystan's soul withered. But still he kept slashing and parrying. Piercing and slicing, killing anyone who threatened him or his people.

Trystan put his foot against the soldier refusing to part

from his blade and pushed him off the sword. He came away with a sickening wet sound, falling at Trystan's feet. A rush of air on his neck gave Trystan the warning he needed that he was about to meet a similar fate and he nimbly rolled sideways and back to his feet, facing his attacker.

A woman stood before him with a curved blade. Her eyes looked empty, emotionless and her awkward form told him she was no soldier. Why was she even here?

"Walk away, mistress," he called to her, reluctant to take her life, even if she had every intent to take his. "I do not wish to see you die today."

"Then you will die. All of Dreach-Sciene must die."

She swung wide, but Trystan dodged her blow. "Please, just walk away."

The woman snarled as she leapt his way again, spittle flying from her mouth. Trystan sidestepped her, and she stumbled as her momentum threw her off balance. He kicked at her backside, sending her flying to the dirt. She disappeared under the throng of bodies and horses just as Trystan was tackled and knocked to the ground. A weight fell onto his chest as a blade slashed across his throat. Trystan drew back, pressing his head as hard as he could into the grass and away from the blade. Wild, empty eyes stared into his. The soldier didn't even recognize him. He didn't even care. "All of Dreach-Sciene must die." He echoed the woman word for word and Trystan had a fleeting thought.

Something isn't right.

Warm blood rained over Trystan's face as an arrow sank right between the man's eyes. Lonara and Ramsey had broken the shield allowing the archers access.

The wild eyes went vacant and the man slumped over, sliding off Trystan's chest. Trystan grabbed for his sword and made it to his knees before the same woman ran from the tangle of bodies, her sword raised high above her head, screaming as she attacked. Her blade flashed in the sun and she brought it down with both hands toward Trystan's head. He raised his own blade just in time, stopping the woman from splitting him down the middle.

She was strong. He could feel the magic behind her attack, but it didn't seem right. Something was off. Before he could figure out what it was, the woman screamed as a blade ripped through her chest and she fell to her knees, Alixa at her back.

Alixa held out a hand to Trystan and pulled him to his feet. Someone barreled into his back and he whirled, blade ready only to find Davi, a tight smile across his face.

"It's good to see you still in one piece, brother," he called out to Trystan.

"You too. Both of you. But I fear we won't be much longer. We can't keep up this pace. I have a theory. Briggs Villard is here." He pointed with his chin toward the man still on horseback, his face a calm mask. "I believe he's the one controlling these people. Him and Eisner. Find Lonara and Ramsay. We need to stop Briggs."

Trystan saw Alixa's brow go up in puzzlement, but she didn't question his order. Instead she nodded toward the surrounding throng. "You heard the man, Davi. Let's find the Tri-Gard once again."

He felt their collective pull of magic as they barreled through the crowd, seeking the magic wielders. Trystan spotted Avery and yelled her name over the din. She quickly disposed of the soldier in front of her and headed toward him. Trystan pointed with his blade to Briggs and Avery's face tightened in understanding. They cleared him a path, fighting their way to Eisner and Villard, Trystan praying his hunch would prove true. Some soldiers under Eisner's command didn't appear to be soldiers at all or even acting under their own will. Like they were being controlled by dark magic. All he could think of was the way Davi had reacted when he too had been drunk on magic. Was this kind of the same thing Villard was doing to these people?

Trystan was almost there. A small gap in the crowd allowed him open access to his enemy, and he made a run for it, only to skid to a stop as an ox of a man carrying a thick, metal chain stepped into the clearing, blocking the way. The chain snapped forward with enough force to crack Trystan's head open like an eggshell if he hadn't flattened himself to the ground in time. The chain missed him and snapped back into the man's hands. Before he could attack again, Trystan was already moving forward, acting before even thinking about what he would do. With a loud cry, he leapt and landed on the humongous chest. The force of his momentum as well as his weight knocked the gargantuan flat on his back. Trystan allowed himself to fall with him and landed straddling the man's waist. Without wasting a moment and allowing the giant a chance to recover, Trystan raised his sword with both hands and brought it down hard, infusing it with as much magic as he could muster. The blade sank through the man's chest and the roar on the man's lips faded along with the light in his eyes. Trystan jumped from the dead man and landed in the barren circle surrounding Briggs' horse. The circle was barren of any life, the grass withered and brown, the soil parched and dry.

Briggs stared down at him in contempt. "Impressive, young king. Trojo was my strongest bodyguard. You've grown in your abilities."

"Stop this now, Villard," Trystan yelled above the din of the battle at his back. "Whatever you are doing to those people, release them. I know you're controlling them through magic."

Briggs narrowed his eyes. "You are wrong, Renauld. The people of Dreach-Dhoun hate you and all you stand for. I'm not controlling them, I'm just, shall I say, enhancing that hatred."

Trystan snorted in disbelief. "You lie. The people of Dreach-Dhoun no more want war than we do. You are doing this. All of it. You and Calis are imposing your will on these people for your own vile reasons." Trystan took a stance and held his sword at arm's length. "I command you to get down from there and fight like a man instead of the coward I know you to be."

Briggs threw his head back and laughed. He actually laughed as if the piles of bodies and stench of blood did nothing to affect him in any manner. Trystan growled and coiled, aiming to knock Briggs out of that saddle and onto his ass.

Excruciating pain jolted through his arm as the blade sliced deep. Trystan cried out, dropping his sword and gripping his arm as Eisner rode past him, his blade dripping with Trystan's blood. The little man grinned, his eyes glittering with the mad taste of revenge as he leapt from his horse and approached the now weaponless king.

"Not yet, Eisner," Briggs ordered, and Eisner halted in his tracks, though his eyes glared over his shoulder at Villard in disappointment.

"Spoils of war, Villard," Eisner snapped, the tip of his sword pointing Trystan's way. "He killed my son. An eye for an eye."

"I said not yet." His icy gaze reverted back to Trystan. "You've surprised me, boy. We expected to scare you into submission. Have a little fun with you and this siege. I thought you'd crumble like a dried leaf. I really did not expect you to fight back."

Trystan raised his chin in defiance. "You will never take Dreach-Sciene. Not while I still stand."

"Well that isn't the plan." Briggs arched a brow. "Not today anyway."

As if on cue a bugle echoed over the valley as soldiers on horseback came flying out of the forest all along the tree line. Trystan feared for a moment it was more of Calis' men and his heart sank to his knees. They wouldn't be able to take on more. But then he saw the banners of Aldorwood snapping in the breeze and he grinned in relief. Whitecap Troops.

"Dear me, time to go," Briggs called out to Eisner and without another word, yanked his horse's reins and rode away. Eisner stared after him, a look of disbelief etched on his face. "Wait!"

Briggs kept riding.

Eisner quickly overcame his shock. Pulling a horn from his saddle he blew two loud whistles. "Fall back!" he yelled as he tried to mount his horse. An arrow whizzed over Trystan's head and struck Eisner in the back of his leg in the stirrup. Rissa's doing, Trystan had no doubt. His leg crumpled, and he fell out of the stirrup and hit the ground hard. Another arrow hit the horse's rump and it neighed in panic and bolted, nearly crushing Eisner's head under its hooves.

The call for retreat seemed to stun everyone. Dreach-Dhoun and Dreach-Sciene soldiers alike glanced around, not understanding what was happening. The sight of Briggs fleeing was the catalyst for some. For others it was the sight of the approaching Whitecap forces that made them run, but soon the field was filled with fleeing soldiers.

Eisner limped to his feet, trying to make his own retreat,

but Davi appeared out of nowhere and his blade under Eisner's chin made him halt in his tracks.

"Don't think so, mate," Davi narrowed his eyes at the little man.

"Trystan," Alixa called in panic as she and Lonara ran to Trystan's side.

"I'm okay," he assured her as she wrapped her arms around his neck. "Lona, Briggs is escaping." He pointed to the horse off in the distance and Lona reacted immediately. Closing her eyes, she hit the ground with her palm. You could see the power ripple through the ground and the fleeing soldiers in its path fell over one by one. But Briggs remained unaffected and he disappeared through the mountain path toward Isenore.

"My apologies, Trystan. Breaking through the barrier and trying to keep our people alive has drained me." She truly looked distraught and Trystan gripped her shoulder with his good hand, leaving a bloody handprint. "You did well, Lona. You and Ramsey both. And we are not empty handed." He pointed his chin at Eisner, still hovering at the tip of Davi's blade.

Trystan felt Alixa stiffen beside him. Without a word she walked toward her father, hatred on her face deepening with every step. Stopping at Davi's side, she stared at Eisner in silence. Gripping the tip of Davi's blade she pushed it down, away from her father's throat. Eisner sighed in relief. "Thank you, daughter."

"Davi won't kill you, father," she said as she raised her own blade and stuck the tip against his heart. "For he knows that honor belongs to me."

"Alixa." Eisner's eyes filled with fear. "You don't mean that. I'm your father."

"You are no father of mine." She spat at his feet. "You lost that title when you took my mother from me. When you took everyone I have ever cared about from me."

"Were you there?" His demand lacked any power behind it as he looked at his daughter. "Did you watch these vile people slaughter your brother?"

She clenched her jaw. "You mourn Royce but you can't give a care for my absence. Do you know why I betrayed you, father? It wasn't for any loyalty to Dreach-Sciene for I held much contempt for the prince. No." She pressed her sword harder against him. "It was because of my hatred for you. You drove me away. But I don't need you. I've never needed you. This will not end well for Calis, father. And it's already ended for you."

She stepped back, her sword still raised. No emotion shone in her eyes. With a blank coldness, she nodded to Davi and lifted her voice. "Duke Eisner of Isenore is now a captive of the realm. Take him away."

Davi used his magic to give Eisner a push forward toward the waiting guards. "Take him back to the palace. Make sure he doesn't draw any power from the earth and lock him in the farthest cell from any exposed land."

"Yes, sir," they said in unison as each gripped one of Eisner's arms.

Trystan studied Alixa's face once her father was out of sight.

She sent him a scowl. "Don't you dare ask if I'm okay."

Trystan held up his hands in defense. He knew when to back off. Adrenaline still coursed through his body, stronger than any magic he'd ever felt. Most of his soldiers lacked much power as well. Just because the land held magic, didn't mean it gave it freely to all who desired it.

Yet they hadn't been bested in the fight. For the first time, he felt like not having the kind of power Rissa possessed didn't make him any less able to lead this army. He still knew how to fight.

Lord Coille rode up beside him and dismounted from his horse.

"Your Majesty," he said in relief as he gripped Trystan's shoulder. "I feared we would be too late. Like Isenore."

The relief Trystan felt at seeing Coille curdled in his gut at the Lord's words. "What do you mean, Coille? What about Isenore?"

Coille wiped a weary hand across his face. "The attack on the castle was a distraction, Trystan. They never meant to take the castle. They meant to keep you occupied. To keep you from aiding Cullenspire. The real attack happened in Isenore. Cullenspire and all of Isenore has fallen to Calis."

"The earth's memory is long." Lorelai's voice drifted out over the barren land in front of them.

How could this happen?

Rissa placed her hands on the ground. "Nothing." She lifted her face and tears fell from her lashes. "I feel nothing. No magic. No song. It's as if the earth has abandoned this place."

Lonara and Ramsey sat on either side of Rissa with matching agony on their faces.

Trystan paced back and forth before stopping in front of his grandfather. "You felt this."

Three nights before, they'd been camped on the Aldorwood border, palace troops and Whitecap soldiers alike, when Ramsey woke writhing in pain. He didn't need to answer because they all knew.

The Tri-Gard felt every drop of magic that was drained from the land stretching between them and Cullenspire.

Davi trudged toward them, dead leaves and sticks crunching underneath his boots. He shook his head when he stopped. "It stretches all the way to the fortress where the legions are camped." His brows pulled together. "This was my father."

"How could he do this?" Rissa's voice shook. "The earth gives us its power to guard and protect. This destruction goes on for miles." She met Davi's eyes. "Miles of earth he just… drained. It's like what we saw in Dreach-Dhoun… but he left nothing behind this time."

"You forget," Ramsey started, taking her hand in his. "This is the same man who made us take all magic from Dreach-Sciene."

"This is different." She wiped at her face. "He didn't perform some ceremony this time and put all the magic into three crystals. He bled the land dry."

"This isn't the first time," Davi said to Trystan. "The lands around the palace of Dreach-Dhoun are identical to these. Blackened, dead. We saw it when we went back."

"Lorelai." Trystan faced the seer. "What did you mean the earth's memory is long?"

Ramsey was the one who answered. "It's something your mother would say. Marissa told us the earth remembered every slain soldier, every battle, every scar."

"I remember those words from her." Lonara smiled sadly.

Rissa sucked in a breath. "She was right. It's the tenelach. I can feel it… struggling."

"And we've been here before." Trystan didn't realize when Lord Coille walked up.

All eyes snapped to him.

The duke's tense shoulders dropped. It'd been a trying time for him. Within hours of the messenger from the palace arriving in Whitecap begging for reinforcements to help lift the siege, they'd gotten word Cullenspire had fallen. None of them knew the fate of their friends inside.

Coille sighed. "Cullenspire. This land. The battle that is sure to happen here. It's exactly as it was twenty years ago. I rode beside Marcus and Hendry Yaro as we faced Calis' army. We failed that day."

Trystan put a hand on his shoulder. "This time it will be different." He turned to the others. "Pull the army back past the magic line." He didn't have a better word for it, but he wouldn't have his people camping where they couldn't draw power. They needed a plan.

THE EXPERIENCED SOLDIERS set up camp quickly, but the villagers who'd joined the cause took quite a bit longer. It was an army of disjointed pieces. He had a handful of those with strong magic. The palace guard who'd spent years training under Avery and Brown. The Whitecap forces, which were partially made up of sailors from the Isle of Sona.

How was he supposed to lead an army like that?

He rubbed his eyes, exhaustion weighing him down. He hadn't had a proper night's sleep in weeks. Had his father felt the constant worry and fear Trystan couldn't shake? The man had seemed so strong, so sure. But maybe that was what made a good king. Being the confident one even when you didn't feel it yourself.

He had to give his people something to believe in.

Trystan sat alone in his tent, his sword resting across his thighs. Lorelai's words rang in his mind. She'd been right.

When the magic was returned to Dreach-Sciene, he'd waited for his part, attempting to draw it from the ground.

He was the king. His father had been the most powerful man in the kingdom. Why shouldn't he inherit that strength?

But it hadn't come. Sure, he could do the basic things anyone in Dreach-Sciene could. If he tried really hard, it could give him extra strength. But he'd wanted more.

Rissa and Davi could do more for the kingdom with their power than he ever could as king. Even Alixa had a little.

"Your Majesty," a familiar voice said from outside the tent.

Trystan set his sword to the side. "Come in."

Rion poked his head inside before his broad shoulders followed. "I just returned with the first scouting party."

Trystan gestured for him to go on.

"The stronghold is manned, sire. Bowmen line the ramparts, but with the legions down below, we couldn't get close enough to see what other protections they've put in place."

Trystan squeezed the back of his neck. "How many men would you guess are camped at that wall?"

"A few thousand, sire."

"So, not all of them. And only the legions? Calis hasn't brought the rest of Dreach-Dhoun into this?"

"Maybe the scouts sent to the south will have better luck." Rion hesitated.

"What is it?"

"Sire…" His eyes flicked to the tent opening and then back to the king. "Our people inside Cullenspire. What do you think has happened to them?"

They all knew what Calis did to his enemies, but Trystan couldn't speak the words out loud. He got to his feet and put a hand on the young soldier's arm. "It does us no good to imagine the worst, Rion. I know Wren was a friend of yours—"

"Is."

"What?"

"Is, sire. Wren is a friend. My best friend. He's my brother as sure as Davion is yours. I would lay my life on the line for him."

Trystan met his eye with respect. "Let's hope it doesn't come to that."

The sound of horses galloping into camp got Trystan moving and he rushed from the tent. The second scouting party had returned. Maybe they'd shed light on the location of the rest of Dreach-Dhoun's forces.

The scouts were not alone. Anna jumped from her horse without waiting for help and ran straight for Alixa. Alixa caught the girl in a hug.

Davi dismounted and walked forward. He'd insisted on leading one of the scouting parties himself and Trystan envied him for the task. It beat sitting around and waiting for them to report to him.

"Your Majesty, we need to talk."

Trystan nodded. "How is Anna here?"

"She escaped. The way she tells it, her brother forced her to leave as soon as the Dreach-Dhoun army arrived."

"How'd she get out?"

"The tunnels." Lord Coille joined them. "Right?"

Davi nodded. "It seems Cullenspire holds more secrets than we were aware of. A tunnel stretches from the cellar of the stronghold to the forest."

Trystan's mind formulated a plan. "Can we use them?"

"I'm afraid not. Once Calis seized Cullenspire, he used them for his own needs. The army is split. There are a few units of black-clad soldiers camped in the forest near the mouth of the cave Anna says is the only entrance to the tunnel."

"And the other soldiers? The ones not shrouded in black armor? Where has Calis put his people?"

"According to Anna, he has the troops he's formed from the Dreach-Dhoun villagers camped in the abandoned village."

"Anna's a child." Trystan shifted his eyes to the shaking girl crying into Alixa's shirt. "Do we trust her information?"

"It wasn't only her." Davi focused on the ground. "We found her hiding with her mother's body."

Trystan squeezed his eyes shut. Lady Yaro had done everything in her power to support him. Her husband and eldest son died in their defiance of Eisner. Now it seemed she had as well. "How?"

"An arrow to the chest."

Trystan pushed out a breath. "That still doesn't explain how Anna came to be in possession of troop movements."

A small voice froze them. "It was my brother." Anna sniffed. "He knew Cullenspire would fall. Mira wouldn't leave him and the men so he forced mother to take me through the tunnel in hopes we'd find you. He knew you'd come, sire. We must save him."

Trystan found himself unable to look away from her sweet face that was now set with a hardness she shouldn't know. How could he tell her Wren was probably dead already? Or that they should hope he was because if not… He shook his head. Whether or not the people they'd left at Cullenspire lived still, he owed it to them and to all of Dreach-Sciene to recover the stronghold.

He couldn't let it stay in Calis' hands.

"All of you meet at my tent at sundown."

They were his council and it was time to go to war.

RISSA WATCHED the faces around the tent. Some were missing who should've been with them for this. Her father. Edric. Wren. Lady Destan who'd stayed behind in Sona to help those who evacuated from the villages.

But they had two of the Tri-Gard. Lord Coille who'd been at her father's side in the previous war. And more people who'd lay down their lives for the kingdom than she'd ever thought possible.

And it was time to ask them to.

She'd gone over and over it in her head. There were many paths Trystan could lead them down and her gut instinct told her each one would be their end. And she didn't need Lorelai's visions to confirm it.

She met the seer's eyes and knew exactly what she was thinking. Now was the time to tell Trystan what needed to be done.

He was their king, sure, but he'd never come up with such a plan himself because he always tried to save the most number of people first.

But this time, it wasn't about saving the lives of those fighting, but saving the kingdom itself and every single person living in it.

He had to see that.

In the aftermath of the burning of the village of Briarwood, when Lorelai first told her of this plan, she'd thought it was insane. But maybe the only way to beat a king who thrived on insanity was to use a bit of it yourself.

Arguments rose around her as they all tried to form a battle plan. Trystan kept a strong grip on the conversation but it was clear he didn't know how to win this once and for all. No more battles. No more deaths. Not after this one. It had to end here.

"Everybody quiet," Rissa hissed. No one seemed to hear her. She raised her voice. "Please." Ire churned in her, finally breaking through. "Shut up!"

The room stilled.

Lorelai nodded, urging her to go on.

"Sister," Trystan said. "If you have an idea, I'm all ears."

She swallowed. "They drained all magic from the land anywhere near the fortress."

"We're aware."

"Which means we won't be able to obtain more power once we've used ours..." She met her brother's inquiring gaze. "And neither will they." She rubbed her slick palms up and down her pants. "With magic, our forces stand no chance against the legions. Our people are untrained. Most are rather weak in their magical ability. They're counting on being able to store more than us in their bodies—which they'll be able to do no doubt."

She looked to Lorelai whose face showed no encouragement even though this was her plan.

"We need to force them to use their magic. All of it."

Trystan studied her. "How do we do that?" His face said he knew her answer but needed her to say it.

"We march against them. And don't use our magic."

The room erupted into panicked chatter as the others spoke of the dangers of such an idea.

"The cost is too high," Lord Coille stated. "Unacceptable."

"Do you realize how many people would die, Princess?" Brown asked.

"Ri." Davi reached for her but she stepped back. "Come on. Surely you see the problem with this."

Trystan didn't say a word. His jaw clenched and he scratched the side of his face.

"It's a sacrifice," Rissa admitted. "But how are we supposed to match our magic against theirs? We must exhaust theirs before using ours. We don't have a choice!"

"We'd need to cut them off from the tunnel." Trystan's words stunned the room into silence.

"Your Majesty," Lord Coille pleaded. "You aren't seriously considering this?"

"My sister is right, Adrian. We are out of options. We don't have time or the power to play it safe. What kind of sacrifice would you have made twenty years ago to win that fight? To prevent two decades of devastation in Dreach-Sciene?"

Lord Coille's eyebrows drew together. "I would have given everything."

Trystan flicked his eyes to each of his advisors as if willing anyone else to question him. Finally, he turned to Brown. "I need to know everything about these tunnels. If we are doing this, we must prevent them from drawing more magic from the woods."

Rissa's shoulders finally relaxed. In that moment, she'd been so sure of this plan. Lorelai nodded to her in approval and Ri took that as a win. She'd grown as close to the seer as one could get to Lorelai and wanted to make her proud.

The woman who'd known Rissa's mother and loved her father.

The rest of the meeting passed in a haze of planning and by the time they stepped out into the silver illuminated night, they were as ready as they could be.

Davi hung back to talk to Trystan, but Rissa needed to get

away from all of them. She needed to think. Her plan was a good one, wasn't it?

Then why did she have a sick feeling burning inside her?

All of them had been right. The cost would be high. She didn't know if Dreach-Sciene would ever be the same once the kingdom's people threw themselves against the Dreach-Dhoun's legions, ready to be slaughtered.

But what other choice did they have?

At dawn, they had to attack.

We can't risk it, Davion.

Those were Trystan's words only moments ago when he'd stayed behind to give the king an idea of his own.

We can't risk you.

He shook his head. How were they supposed to throw themselves against the walls of Cullenspire when they were horribly outnumbered?

But Trystan, our scouts have seen it. Part of the Dreach-Dhoun force has camped in the abandoned village, away from the legions. They're villagers and farmers, not soldiers.

Trystan hadn't budged.

Davi walked through the dark camp where very little chatter filled the air. None of them could speak of the horrors they were sure to see. Could anyone truly prepare for battle?

Their numbers were considerably smaller than they needed for the task ahead of them. He avoided the eyes of people he passed. Some gathered together to pray to the earth for their safe return. Others sank into their fear.

He only had one person he needed to see. No matter what Trystan said, there was something he felt he needed to do and a part of him hoped Rissa would tell him it was stupid even if they were desperate.

He found the girl in question sitting on the ground outside her tent, a knife in her hands.

Her fingers shook as she curled them around the hilt.

He rushed toward her, fear gripping him.

When he stopped in front of her, hazel eyes snapped to his.

He dropped to his knees and pried her fingers off the knife. "Ri."

She shook her head. "I told him." Her words shook. "I told him we had to do this. It was my plan."

He put his fingers under her chin and tilted her face up. "It's a good plan, Rissa."

Her shoulders shook. "You didn't think so only a moment ago." She shifted her eyes to the surrounding tents and their occupants. "Their deaths will be on me."

"They answered their king's call, knowing what it could mean. Tomorrow, they will fight willingly. You do not own their decisions." He ran a hand through his hair. "Ri, there's something I have to do and it's something only I can accomplish." He paused. "Trystan thinks it's suicide."

"Is it?"

"Maybe."

She studied him, her eyes able to read every expression. "But if it's not?"

"We can win this. We can save Dreach-Sciene."

"Dav..." She hesitated, meeting his gaze. "I can't... You can't risk yourself. Maybe Trystan is right."

He squeezed both her hands in his. "Everything in my gut tells me I need to do this. Ri, I'm so sure."

She pulled one hand free and reached it forward to cup his jaw. "Then it sounds like I need to do it too."

He unleashed a smile. "I haven't even told you want I want to do yet."

"I trust you, Dav. Always have. Wherever you go, I go."

"Okay." He'd never try to tell Rissa what to do, not anymore. She knew herself and had just as much right to take risks as he did. "We need one more person."

She raised an eyebrow but Davi pushed himself to his feet and helped her up. All sadness disappeared from Rissa's face as the determination he knew so well set in.

He swung an arm around her shoulders and pulled her into his side.

They found Lorelai near one of the dying fires at the edge of camp, her eyes trained on the sentries.

"Cousin." Davi scanned their surroundings to make sure they weren't overheard. "Want to help me disobey the king?"

Shock clouded her face, but her usual mask of aloofness soon returned. "Why do I feel like you're going to get me imprisoned one of these days?"

He shrugged. "You know the Dreach-Dhoun villagers as well as I, Lorelai. What is the one thing that bonds them together?"

She clenched her jaw. Was she remembering the mass execution they'd rescued her from? "Hatred of their king."

Davi nodded. "My father got it wrong, didn't he? He sent his legions marching into any village with even a whiff of rebel activity, but what he didn't understand, was they were bred to be rebels. It wasn't a movement. It was a way of life."

Lorelai met his eye. "Do you think Calis would unleash disloyal forces without assurances?"

"Assurances?" Rissa asked.

She knew nothing about Dreach-Dhoun, Davi realized. In her mind, a king existed to serve the people. But across the border, the people existed to serve the king. "He must be keeping those who cannot fight somewhere across the border."

Rissa's eyes darkened and Davi reached for her hand. He threaded their fingers together and squeezed.

Lorelai scratched the back of her head. "I know what you're hoping they do. It won't work."

"We're out of options, Lorelai. Trystan forbade me from leaving this camp, but I can't sit here and wait for morning to come. Not when that morning may be the last our people see."

"Our people," Rissa whispered. "You said 'our people'." A smile came to her lips.

"Aren't they?"

She nodded and released a breath. "Yeah, Dav. I'm just glad to hear you say it again."

Davi flicked his eyes from Lorelai to Rissa, unsure of how they would take his next words. "But in Dreach-Dhoun, they're my people too." He swallowed a lump in his throat.

"I know." Rissa met Lorelai's gaze. "When we don't have many options before us, we must attempt the impossible. If we die, it won't matter what we tried, only what we didn't."

Davi would've sworn he saw pride shining in Lorelai's eyes when she took in the princess. They'd been working together non-stop, but still didn't seem to like each other. Fondness wasn't a necessity for trust, it seemed.

Lorelai put the guards to sleep just long enough for them to untie their horses and lead them past the edge of camp. The fires that had lit the night now faded into the background as darkness spread before them.

The pounding of the horse's hooves was deafening in the silence of the empty countryside. They skirted the edge of the magic line, choosing to avoid the dead land where Calis' Legions patrolled.

Most of the soldiers had pulled back into the stronghold.

The village looked deserted from afar. The people had packed up everything they could carry and fled into Aldorwood. They'd known Isenore would become a battleground.

The closer they rode, the more they could see. A ring of fires circled where the bedraggled soldiers took their rest.

The troops made up of Dreach-Dhoun villagers would suffer in the battle to come, by the looks of their crude, blunt weapons. Their numbers would be their only advantage.

"Most of their magic is weak," Lorelai whispered. "Much like those who live off the land in Dreach-Sciene. But there may be a few with greater capacity. We must proceed with caution."

Davi had no time for caution. He kicked his horse and took off down the hill. Grass gave way to cracked cobblestone streets.

By the time he reached the fires, the entire camp knew of his arrival.

A warning horn sounded and men carrying rusted swords and poorly carved bows stumbled to jump into the battle they were expecting.

Rissa and Lorelai struggled to catch up with Davi.

He jumped from his horse without waiting for it to stop completely and threw his sword to the ground.

"I am not a threat!"

A burly man barreled forward. Black markings stretched

down each of his thick arms. He held a heavy ax. "What is the meaning of this?" His eyes widened when they landed on Davi. "Your… Highness?" He turned to the man at his side. "Give me a torch." When the torch finally reached him, he stepped forward to get a better look, bringing the light of the flame close to Davi's face.

Davi's heart thundered against his ribs. If he was wrong about this, they'd kill him right away.

But the man didn't raise his ax.

A growl sounded in his throat. "I was there the day you led the legions against my village. When you slaughtered those whose only crime was listening to someone speak."

Davi shrank back. It was one of the memories he wished could be taken from him. He couldn't bring himself to look at Rissa or see the disappointment that was sure to be on her face. She didn't know who he'd truly been without his memories.

"I won't apologize." Davi cleared his throat. "Because that would assume I can ever take back my actions. I can't."

The man grunted. "The king said you were dead. Killed by Dreach-Sciene scum."

Calis would never want his people to know Davi had chosen the other side, or it could break his hold on them.

Davi scanned the troops who relaxed their stances as his name bounced through the air.

"Are you here to aid us in this fight?" someone asked.

Davi ignored the question. "I must speak with your generals."

Lorelai stepped forward, and the mood shifted noticeable.

"The seer," someone whispered. "She's come for us."

Davi watched them approach his cousin and saw it from their view. Lorelai was one of them. Imprisoned by Calis. She'd even fought for her mother's life the day he brought the legions down upon them.

He turned his attention back to the man who was still studying him.

"I am General Mack. I don't trust you, Prince. But who can afford trust anymore? Come."

Davi held his hand out to the still silent Rissa, and she took it as they followed General Mack. He led them through the once deserted village, past empty shops where Dreach-Dhoun soldiers had taken over, until finally coming to a stop outside a one-room house. The windows had been broken and a long crack ran the length of the wooden door.

Once inside, Mack turned on them. "Davion Bearne is supposed to be dead. Lorelai Bearne was said to be taken by Dreach-Sciene forces." He flicked his eyes to Rissa. "And you are one of the Dreach-Sciene warriors. Tales of your flaming hair have reached even us. Tell me why you are here. And then tell me why I shouldn't turn you over to the king for being the traitors you are."

"Mack..." Lorelai spoke absently as if deep in thought. "I remember the name."

He narrowed his eyes.

"Were you part of the rebel movement?" She nodded as if answering her own question. "I was imprisoned with your sister."

"I don't know what you speak of." He glanced toward the door nervously.

Davi took the opening. "We're here on behalf of King Trystan Renauld."

General Mack froze. "So you are traitors then? All of you." He stepped toward the door to call for help, but Rissa flipped her hand and twisted her magic around his legs, keeping him in place.

"You will listen," Rissa growled.

"What could you possibly want with us?" The general spat. "Those men and women out there..." He pointed to the door. "They're not fighters. They don't want to be here. You're not going to find use in defeating us."

"What if we don't want to defeat you?" Davi crossed his arms over his chest. "General, someone has to win this fight. We're risking our lives for these kings with the hopes they'll make a better world in the broken aftermath." He leveled his gaze. "Do you believe in your king?"

"Of course." His answer was too quick.

Davi stepped toward him and dipped his head. "I believe in mine. Trystan Renauld will make this kingdom great. My father will destroy it. Why are you here?"

Mack's pupils dilated and he sucked in a breath. "I fight for my kingdom."

Davi advanced on him. "Why are you here?"

Mack clenched his jaw and didn't answer.

Davi didn't stop until he was chest to chest with the man. "Why are you here?"

The general shook his head. "My daughter. She's back in Dreach-Dhoun."

Rissa released the man from her magic and Davi stepped back. "Many people's daughters will die."

"What are you asking of us?"

Davi waited a beat before responding. "Lead your people against Calis. Fight with us."

Silence filled the room for a few minutes.

Mack shook his head. "No." He walked outside before Rissa could stop him again.

Lorelai followed him quickly, but when she spoke, it was for the men and women crowded into their large camp.

"My mother foresaw the fall of Dreach-Dhoun." She lifted her voice. "Do you remember? Right before the king killed her, his own sister. She wanted to warn you. To tell you Calis Bearne was not the man who would lead you into the light. And you listened as she spoke. So hear me now, you are on the wrong side in this. You're fighting for the man who has brutalized you for years. I was you once, blinded by loyalty. Even as he made me his whore, his assassin."

She paused. "You're scared. He has control over the people you love. But if he wins this war, that control never ends. Trystan Renauld will protect you. He will fight for you."

General Mack raised his eyes to a group of men standing on the edge of camp in shining black armor. Legionnaires. He shook his head. "We will never fight for Dreach-Sciene." The armored soldiers closed in. "Surrender all weapons. We are taking you to the king."

Davi scanned the ground for his discarded sword but he'd left it at the edge of camp. Rissa raised her arms. Right. They didn't need weapons. They were weapons.

The princess looked from Lorelai to Davi and nodded before fire erupted from her hands.

Soldiers ran for them and Lorelai threw a bolt of magic, flinging them back.

Rissa tried not to hit the common soldiers coming for them as she set their camp ablaze. Davi followed behind her, crafting a shield with his power. A few bits of magic bounced off the shield as they ran for their horses.

No one had moved the beasts and Lorelai sent power toward anyone who tried.

They climbed into their saddles.

Davi waited until the two women were ahead of him before digging his heels into the flanks of the horse and flying away from the village and the attackers they left behind.

When no pursuit came, he dropped the shield and slowed to a canter.

His chest heaved as he sucked in air. Rissa threw her arms up with a laugh. "That felt good."

He raised a brow.

"Tomorrow, I only get to use my magic for shield purposes. But now it's rushing through me. I can't believe we just got out of that without hurting anyone. They didn't have a choice in coming after us. Not with the legionnaires watching."

"No, but we're still not better off than we were."

Lorelai looked to him in sympathy. "It was worth an attempt, cousin."

They arrived back at camp to find the king waiting for them. Trystan's scowl turned to a look of relief as soon as they appeared.

"You've been gone for hours," he said, crossing his arms.

Rissa slid down and faced him. "We had to try."

Trystan sighed and rubbed a hand over his face. "I've been standing here hoping you'd return to tell me you'd succeeded. That we had some new allies."

Davi's shoulders dropped. "I'm sorry, Trystan. We failed you."

Trystan clapped him on the back and hung his head in exhaustion. "Davion, you could never fail me. Go get some rest. Tomorrow will be the longest day of our lives."

Lorelai left for her own tent right after Trystan.

"He's right," Rissa said. "We should rest."

Davi pulled her along behind him. "As long as I can hold you, Ri. Tomorrow…"

"Is in the future," she cut in. "I don't want to talk about it." She stepped into his tent behind him and slid the cloak from his shoulders.

He turned to face her. "But what if—"

She silenced him with a kiss.

"Rissa," he whispered against her lips.

She pushed him onto his cot and straddled his lap. "I don't know if we're going to win tomorrow. If we do, I don't know what our future will be. I can't see where I'll live or what I'll be doing. I think I'd like it to be away from the palace. But Davi, the only thing I do see is you. You're my future. Whether it ends tomorrow or when I'm old and wrinkly, I'm going to spend the rest of my life with you."

"If it ends tomorrow, just know—"

"I know." She pressed her lips to his. "Before our quest, I never thought I'd get to be in love with you. Sure, I loved you, but being in love is two sided. It hasn't been easy, Dav. It's almost destroyed me. But it's also prepared me for whatever we have to face. I get to be in love with you forever—even after I've joined with the earth. Tomorrow could be the end of a lot of things, but not that. Never that."

He blinked away the tears hanging in his lashes and took her face between his hands. "You're incredible."

A slow smile spread across her lips but it didn't have time to reach all the way because Davi took her mouth with his, searing his love into her.

She was right. They were forever, whether their bodies rested above ground or below. With that thought, he could do whatever was necessary to defeat his father.

No matter how many plans they had in place, no one felt ready to march into battle to fight for their lives.

Trystan took in the swarm of bodies surrounding him. His people. Some were soldiers. Others had worked their farms or run shops in the villages. Some women who now prepared to march had spent much of their lives caring for children.

Yet, they'd come. From the villages of Aldorwood to the shores of Sona. Even many who claimed Isenore as their home.

Word had wound its way through the camp in the night of the impending battle. He'd needed them to begin their preparations. To don their makeshift armor and crude weapons. The ones who had much magical ability had to draw power from the earth before crossing over to the land that was now dead and devoid of magic.

He adjusted the straps on his breastplate. The iron felt foreign on his body.

Lord Coille stepped up beside him and nodded in approval.

"Your father insisted on wearing leather armor into battle. I never understood his desire for the vulnerabilities that gave him."

Rissa appeared, her red hair pulled back and twisted around the crown of her head, making the angles of her face more prominent. "It was a desire for freedom, not vulnerability." She swung her arms, moving her own leather armor as if to prove her point. Trystan and Davion had both tried to force her to wear more protection, but she'd refused.

Fog swirled through the woods where the army waited as the dark veil lifted from the world. Tension sliced through the air, refusing to snap.

"Ri," Trystan started. He didn't know what he wanted to say next. Stay safe? I wish you weren't coming with us?

How could he when they needed her? Her archers would be at the front. They'd eventually pull back, but Rissa was one of the most powerful magic wielders Dreach-Sciene had. She'd be needed to hold the shield.

Or at least try to.

So instead of voicing his concerns for his sister, he turned his thoughts to the battle ahead. "Do you remember what it is you are to do?"

She sighed. "I don't want you to get hurt either, brother." She peered into his eyes as if reading his thoughts. "You don't need to distract me with talk of strategy and plans. I know my role. I will do it as well as I can." She touched his arm. "I'd tell you not to play the hero, but I know you will. Just… when I first got Davi back, I thought I couldn't go through that again —losing someone I love. But we're Renaulds, Trystan. We weren't raised to think of ourselves. The sacrifices required of us, the things that destroy us, might just save everyone else."

Rissa released his arm. "I love you, Trystan. Whatever

happens here this day, you are my king, my family. So be the hero. Even if you have to give all of yourself. Your kingdom deserves no less."

Tears pooled in the depths of her eyes but she didn't allow them to break free. Trystan pulled her into a crushing hug. His sister was right. Their troops were being asked to sacrifice a lot and he would not spare himself.

Davi appeared behind them and Trystan released Rissa so she could fall into his friend's arms. One day, if they survived this, he'd make sure the two of them had the chance to be together without constantly being pulled apart.

Trystan squeezed Davi's shoulder as he walked by. He reached his horse and swung up into the saddle. Others followed suit. Those who'd be making the trek on foot formed their lines.

His generals' commands ripped through the air, turning chaos into order.

It took time to get set, but with the sun rising at his back, Trystan kicked his horse out in front of the others and jerked him around.

He took a deep breath, studying the faces of his people. Many had come who'd fought in his father's war, their faces now lined with age. Others were picking up swords for the first time.

The only ones not holding weapons at the ready were the few wielders who'd be using their magic from the start to form a shield. It wouldn't hold for long, but the Dreach-Dhoun legions would throw their magic at it, not realizing their path to more power had been blocked.

At least that was the plan.

He'd gone over it in his head a million times and now it was time.

"What I ask of you today is more than anyone should ever have to give." He lifted his voice to reach even the farthest line of men. "Should we succeed; our victory will come at a cost that will change Dreach-Sciene forever. Yet… I still must come to you. I still must ask you to leave your fields and your shops and travel across the kingdom to stand alongside those who've trained for this."

He paused. "And you came. You appeared out of the darkness to show me, show Dreach-Sciene, a way to bring back the light. This is your kingdom. Not Calis Bearne's. Not Briggs Villard's. Ours." He pointed to his chest. "Twenty years ago, they stole our magic. Now they come to take everything else. But Calis Bearne does not know what I do. The people of Dreach-Sciene are not so easily beaten."

A cheer rose up through the soldiers.

"The legions have bled the earth dry. They chose this battlefield. But we've lived without magic for twenty years. It does not give us our strength." He lifted one arm to point and moved it so he encompassed all. "This is our strength."

Metal clanged through the clearing as swords crashed against shields and armor in agreement.

Trystan nudged his horse back beside Davion. His friend had a smile on his face. He held out his hand. "Truwa."

Trystan grasped it. "Brathair."

Avery flanked his other side. Her gaze was as calm as always, but it held something else as well. Pride. "Your father and mother would be proud, Trystan. As am I."

Simple words, but they meant a lot coming from this master of stony silence.

"I am lucky to have you by my side, Avery."

She ducked her head. "As I served the Renaulds before you, sire. It is where I am meant to be."

His eyes left Avery and found the familiar golden ones. He and Alixa shared a smile across the span that separated them as Trystan drank in Alixa's features.

As if she gave him the courage, finally he was ready to let go. He nodded to Brown whose "Move out" command sent a jolt of adrenaline surging through Trystan.

This battle would either be the end of his reign or the beginning of something else.

THE SIGHT of the waiting Dreach-Dhoun army as they rode toward the stronghold was beyond terrifying. They stretched for leagues into the horizon. A sea of black armor in the gray wasteland that was once Cullenspire. Calis' legion of loyal followers and powerful magic wielders. The army they would have to defeat or die trying.

Trystan refused to let the fear burning in his gut overwhelm him. He rode swiftly, his eyes taking in those around him. Even though they all knew the same, that most of them marched to their deaths, they marched strong and tall. No one showed fear. Trystan was proud to call them his people.

Cullenspire lay off in the distance, the lazy spirals of smoke still emanating from it a testament to the battle that had occurred here. Trystan had a fleeting moment of sadness for those he knew perished there. They were his people too. He hoped Wren and Mira did not follow in the path of Lady Yaro, but he didn't have much faith in that hope.

They crested the rise and stopped. The sound of hundreds of horses and marching troops ceased as an eerie silence encompassed them. Calis and his army waited below just as silently under the deceivingly calm blue sky. Trystan glanced up and down the line of soldiers that flanked him.

"Ready!" he bellowed, and at his command shields and lances were raised. Frontline soldiers interspersed with wielders to protect the line of archers behind them. "Attack!"

Horns sounded, joining the battle cries of both armies. As one they descended the hill and hurtled into battle.

As soon as they came into range of Calis' men, the sun warming their heads was blocked out as hundreds of arrows filled the sky. Trystan felt the magic shield rise around them, embracing them in its touch, as their physical shields went up as well. Their wielders would hold back on magic. Dreach-Dhoun's archers would not. There would be power behind those arrows, most likely enough to penetrate the weak shield.

He was right. Even as most of the arrows bounced away, some broke through with a crackling of power. A couple of his people shrieked in pain as the arrows found their targets.

"Now!" Lonara ordered and the magic was drawn back, the shield disappearing. Trystan heard Rissa commanding their own attack. Dreach-Sciene's arrows were not backed by magic, but the enemy did not know that. Trystan watched pleased as the powerful barrier their enemy created repelled the volley of arrows unleashed on them. A shield that strong took power. Magic they would not be able to get back from the empty earth.

"Again," Rissa ordered as the enemy's shield went down to allow their next attack. A second shower of arrows barreled over Trystan's head. The foremost of Calis' men dropped, gurgling with Dreach-Sciene arrows in their throats. The rest kept advancing, running over their own fallen soldiers as the world around them plunged into chaos.

Screaming started. Sounds of crashing steel, of rage, of pain, filled the air. Both sides taking damage and sustaining casualties. Trystan slashed at anything in black armor, but they fought back strong, their strikes fueled by magic. Again and again his blade contacted with resistance as their enemy used up their magic stores. An occasional strike against flesh stained his sword red, but Trystan feared those strikes were too few and far between.

A gust of magic struck Trystan from the side, spooking his steed. The horse neighed in fright and reared in the air, dumping Trystan unceremoniously on the ground. He rolled into the fall, his sword still in his hand, and leapt to his feet as a blade slashed by his cheek so near it burned. The soldier stumbled, and Trystan slashed at his legs, cutting them out from under him. Once the man hit the ground, Trystan sliced him through the neck, ending his agony.

Bodies were so close together, fighting surrounding him on all sides. It was hard to tell who was who. Trystan turned just in time to see a Dreach-Sciene soldier meet his bloody end. The legionnaire who took him down whirled on Trystan, the hate twisting his face with ugliness. He fell his sword at Trystan and the king blocked the blow with his blade. They snarled at each other, so close Trystan could see the red veins in the whites of his eyes.

They strained and grunted in their stalemate, neither willing to back away. Trystan knew the moment the soldier called on his magic. The pressure on the sword increased and Trystan's knees buckled from the power the soldier exerted. If he fell to his knees, it would mean certain death. He suddenly pulled away and the soldier fell forward from the momentum of his attack. He hit the ground hard, but quickly flipped over onto his back, his sword still in his hand.

Trystan was just as quick. He attacked, and the downed soldier raised his own weapon to parry as Trystan swung.

The sword froze in the air.

Trystan stumbled as he tried to force the weapon forward, but it was held firmly in place by invisible hands. It was like trying to swing through metal instead of air. Magic.

Trystan glanced around trying to find the source of the power. It wasn't the soldier on the ground. He looked just as confused. A woman stood to the side, dressed in the black armor, her red hair so much like Rissa's hanging wildly in her face and taunting Trystan with her grin. When she realized Trystan was left unprotected, she lunged, her blade slashing at his neck.

Trystan released the useless weapon hanging in mid-air and threw himself to the ground. He felt the breeze as the woman's sword swung over his head, narrowly missing him. His own blade clanged to the ground a short distance away.

He rolled, trying to dodge the next blow as it slammed into the ground close to his head. His hand shot out trying to grab the sword, only to have it yanked away by more magic.

That's right, keep using it up.

He leapt to his feet and whirled while the woman was preparing for another swing. Throwing himself forward he ducked under her arm and dashed to the side, hoping to reach his sword before she could cast more magic. With one swift movement he fell to his knees and slid along the ground the last couple of feet, grabbing up his sword in the process. He turned in time to catch the wave of magic she flung his way, hoping to leave him defenseless once again.

The gust of air hit his blade, jerking it back, but Trystan held on. Her magic was waning. He could feel it. Her look of puzzlement soon turned to anger as Trystan rolled his shoulder forward, still very much holding his sword, and pointed it her way just as she lunged for him. He didn't have time to avoid her hurtling body. The look of surprise was still clear on her face as the blade sliced through her chest, killing her instantly.

Trystan fought against the wave of disgust and nausea rolling over him as he extracted his bloody blade. The woman slumped to the ground, her wide eyes staring at the sky. In death she appeared younger, so much more like Rissa. And he'd killed her. His hands trembled as he tore his gaze away from the woman's bloody corpse and looked around.

Death and carnage were everywhere. His people as well as the bodies of Dreach-Dhoun soldiers littered the blood-soaked ground. His horrified eyes stopped on a young man dressed in Dreach-Sciene colors, blood oozing from the wound at his neck. He recognized the still face. He'd spoken to him just last night. A farmer's lad. Newly married and a child on the way. A child he'd never see. A child that would go through life never knowing its father.

Trystan wiped at the wetness gathering in his eyes. This was Calis' fault. This whole darned, unnecessary war. These people were dying because of the mad king's need for revenge and power. It had to end. Calis had to be stopped.

A shadow fell over him and Trystan reacted on instinct, his blade blocking the sword slashing his way. He was almost too late. The blade nicked his cheek and Trystan felt the pain as his flesh was cut all the way up to his temple. He pushed back at the soldier dredging up an ounce of his own magic. The soldier stumbled back and Trystan darted in quick as a snake and tried to kick the soldier's feet away, but the gust of magic from the man's upturned palm caught him unaware and blew his feet out from under him instead. Trystan landed on his back, the man hovering over him and his blade glinting in the bright sun as he lifted it high above his head, preparing to strike.

The blast of magic took the soldier by surprise. Trystan watched as the man's face went blank, then paled as he dropped the sword and keeled over, writhing in pain. Lonara rushed past the incapacitated soldier and joined Trystan, her face a mask of concern.

"You are hurt, sire," she said as she observed his bloody cheek.

"I'll live, Lona." He glanced around. "Unlike most of our troops. Too many of our people are dying. We need to find Calis. It's the only way to stop this. I know he's on this battlefield somewhere. Can you track his magic?"

She nodded. "It will take powerful magic and all my concentration, but yes. Keep them off me."

Trystan grunted in response as Lonara sank to her knees and dug her fingers into the red soil. As if Calis' army knew what she was trying to do, four soldiers barreled their way, their faces full of malicious intent. Trystan took a stance and wiped the blood dripping into his eye with his sleeve. Four against one. Not his lucky day.

As the first blade came crashing against his, he blocked it and kicked at the soldier's gut, sending him off balance. He whirled and thrust his blade again, taking the second guard through the throat and leaving him gagging on his own blood as he turned to the third. He was quick, but this soldier was quicker. He slashed at Trystan's chest and Trystan grunted as the blow sent him stumbling back. Recovering quickly, he barreled into the soldier trying to get close to Lonara. They both crashed to the ground, the soldier managing to roll at the last moment and land atop Trystan, his blade at his neck.

Before Trystan could react, the soldier was yanked off and

his spilt blood splashed across Trystan's plate mail. A hand appeared as Davi hovered over him, a tiny smile flitting about his lips.

"Looks like you could use a hand, brother."

Davi yanked Trystan to his feet as Trystan's eyes searched for Lonara and found Avery and Alixa standing back to back, protecting the Tri-Gard member from any harm. Her eyes caught his, and she leapt to her feet.

"This way," she yelled over the din. She'd found Calis.

"With me," Trystan yelled over his shoulder, and whatever Dreach-Sciene soldier within distance fell in line behind their king.

They battled their way through a sea of legionnaires and flailing swords, Lonara and Davi's power helped cut a path. They found Calis in the middle of his men, a circle of open space between him and the battle. He was standing, eyes closed and arms spread, cocooned in a bubble of protection. Trystan could see the magic emanating from him like heat ripples on a hot day. Hate for the man himself and his cowardly actions bubbled in Trystan's chest, making his voice raw with anger.

"What is he doing?" Trystan asked and Lonara was the one to answer.

"I think he's allotting magic to his people, providing them strength."

"Break his barrier, Lona. This needs to end today."

Whether through brute strength or the fact that they caught Calis unaware, Lonara did just that. The magic barrier broke like shattered glass and Cali's eyes popped open at the intrusion.

"Davion," he cried in surprise just as Trystan hurled himself at him with a roar.

The mad king reacted quickly. The blast of magic he channeled Trystan's way seared everything in its path with flames of fire, threatening to burn Trystan alive.

"No!" Davi yelled, directing his own magic at the threatening flames. The two blasts collided in front of Trystan's face with the power of a black powder explosion. Trystan flew off his feet and sailed back through the air, his very breath sucked from his lungs. He landed hard, his head reeling from the explosion and his ears ringing, deafening him to any other sound.

He watched from his knees as Calis sent Davi a look of disappointment before surrounding himself in a cloak of magic and disappearing into the surge of army heading their way.

Trystan struggled to his feet, his head swimming and tilting dangerously to the side. A Dreach-Dhoun soldier hurtled his way, sword outstretched. Trystan searched in desperation for his weapon but he'd lost hold of it in the explosion. The soldier was almost on top of him now and Trystan tried a last vain attempt to draw magic. He needed to protect himself somehow. He didn't need the magic. The soldier fell under Avery's blade as she fought her way toward her king's side.

"Your Majesty." Her voice sounded far off, like she was calling to him from a deep well. He shook his head, trying to stay conscious. Blood was gushing heavily from his wound and he knew passing out meant certain death. He needed to stay awake. If only his body would listen. Avery reached him just as he tottered. But instead of holding him up, she shoved him hard, causing him to stumble to his knees again. He peered up at her as the arrow meant for him buzzed over his head.

Avery staggered back, lifting a hand to her throat. Trystan's puzzlement quickly turned to horror at the embedded arrow and the line of blood running down the sword master's neck into her armor. Her eyes locked with Trystan's, calm as always but tinged with sadness. Hair plastered to her head and chest heaving, she reached out a hand, her lips moving as if to say something. Instead a shuddering breath racked her body, and her sword dropped from her hand as she fell to her knees.

Trystan crawled her way, trying to reach his old friend. She landed face first into the soil sending a puff of dust into the air as a pool of crimson surrounded her head like a dark halo.

"Avery!" he yelled, his voice sharp as broken glass with his grief, but she was beyond hearing him. She was beyond anything. He realized the heartbreaking truth as he fought to avoid the darkness threatening to overtake him. Death had opened the last portal for Avery, from which there was no return.

He stared at her lifeless form in shock. That wasn't Avery. Couldn't be. His fearless sword master. The woman who'd served Marissa Kane until her death. His teacher who'd joined him on the quest no questions asked.

She couldn't be… gone.

Rissa's words entered his mind.

The sacrifices required of us, the things that destroy us, may just save everyone else.

"Trystan!" Alixa yelled. "Get up."

"In case you didn't notice…" Davi ducked away from an arrow that flew past his head. "There's a battle going on."

Trystan jumped to his feet and used a move Avery taught him to block a black-clad soldier's attempt to take his head off. *Thank you, teacher.*

Another volley of arrows took flight, but their paths lacked the strength of the ones before.

"They're weakening." Trystan lifted his eyes to the fortress as a new wave of soldiers rushed from the heavy iron gates. "We have to get into that stronghold."

Because he was suddenly sure without a doubt that was where they'd find Calis Bearne and Briggs Villard.

The only way to end this was to face them.

A HORN SOUNDED. The village troops had arrived. The Dreach-Dhoun people who were not part of the legions.

The ones who'd chosen Calis' side despite years of oppression.

They were late, but they'd come.

Davi jerked his head up to watch them crest the hill. They stopped and didn't move.

Trystan appeared at his side, wiping blood from his face, and heaved out a breath. "We have to get inside Cullenspire."

"The tunnels?"

"No. They're too long and we'd have to fight through too many men inside the stronghold."

Davi met Trystan's eyes, noticing the danger sparking in their depths. "You want to blow the gate." He shook his head. "It'll use too much of our limited magic, ruining the entire plan you've set in motion."

"We have to get inside, Dav."

Davi ran a blood-stained hand through his sticky hair. "I'll follow you in anything. You know that."

One side of Trystan's mouth curved sadly up as Davi formed up with him.

"Alixa, Lonara," Trystan called. "New plan. With me!"

The four of them cut a path through the sea of soldiers until they reached the gate. It looked as though it had been hastily repaired recently and Davi knew instantly, this was how his father got in to overtake Wren.

He barely knew Wren, but he sent a silent thought into the atmosphere. Wren might be dead, but Dreach-Dhoun would not have his home.

Soldiers yelled from atop the wall as they leaned buckets over to pour boiling pitch from the heavens.

Davi jumped back to avoid the bubbling tar.

"Where's my sister?" Trystan yelled as he sliced through a man who was obviously drained of his magic.

Davi shook his head. He'd tried to keep Rissa in his sight, but she'd stuck with Ramsey and Lorelai as they tried to keep some sort of shield in place.

Worry gnawed at him. The shield had fallen quickly, and he didn't want to think about what that could mean.

Rion sprinted toward them, deep red blood spattered across his face. "Your Majesty. We're taking heavy losses. We can't keep this up. Our soldiers are no match."

Trystan drew himself up. "They have to, Rion. There is no other choice. We cannot retreat."

Lonara's gaze scanned the heavy gates. "I need someone else to do this, Your Majesty. I must save my magic for Briggs."

As she spoke, Davi caught sight of a flash of red hair. Relief spread through him. Rissa whirled, bow in hand, taking out enemy soldiers before they could get close enough to hurt her.

Her mouth was set in a grim line as she loosed another arrow.

"Rissa!"

She jerked her head up.

A row of soldiers stood between them. Rissa straightened and threw her hand out in front of her. The soldiers were lifted off their feet and thrown to the side to create a clear path.

Rissa sprinted toward them and flicked her eyes to the gate. With no explanation, she nodded. "Stand guard."

Trystan and Alixa turned their backs to each other and held their swords aloft.

But Davi didn't leave Ri's side. He may not hold as much power as her, but he could help.

Rissa clenched her jaw in concentration and her body jerked forward as she threw a wall of pure power toward the stone.

A boom cracked through the air.

Davi joined her, drawing on every bit of magic he had inside. He hurled it toward the wall in sync with Rissa.

The stones shuddered and shifted.

More boiling pitch streamed down from above, coating Cullenspire manor in darkness.

Davi and Rissa didn't stop.

Each bit of power he released depleted him more until he could barely lift his arms. If someone attacked him, he'd stand no chance.

Still, Rissa persisted.

A fissure started near the top of the gate.

"Again!" Rissa yelled.

But Davi had nothing left.

Rissa lifted her hands and the gate burst inward, sending rock raining down on all those near.

Rissa's shoulders slumped.

A horn sounded again, and Davi had just enough energy to peer over his shoulder. The village troops barreled toward Dreach-Sciene's farthest lines.

They'd overwhelm them in moments. It was almost over.

Trystan's panicked eyes found his. "We have to find Calis."

How were they supposed to defeat Calis when they found him? Lonara and Ramsey had to deal with Briggs. Rissa used all her magic just to take down the gates.

And now a second army threatened to collide with their dying one.

They'd lost.

How could Trystan not see that?

The two armies crashed together and Trystan prepared to run into the stronghold where Calis was. Legionnaires poured through the now destroyed gate, but stopped as they saw the sight first.

The village army wasn't fighting Dreach-Sciene. They raised their swords only against those in black armor.

Trystan, a new strength in his eyes, raised his sword. "Charge!" He ran toward the blown gate and jumped into a fight with the legionnaires. Dreach-Sciene followed their king, hope once again existing in their minds.

Davi lifted his sword, all exhaustion fading away as adrenaline kicked in. He ran after Rissa.

"Dreach-Sciene!" Trystan yelled. "Use your magic!"

The Dreach-Dhoun soldiers were drained of all power, the emptiness forcing a weight into their limbs.

Davi slammed his shoulder into a woman as she yelled orders and he tumbled to the ground on top of her. He rolled off and jumped to his feet. The woman leaped up, knife in hand.

Her eyes went wide as a rusted blade appeared protruding from her chest.

Blood ran from her mouth as she slid forward off the sword, revealing the man behind her.

Wren's crazed eyes stared back at him.

"Thought you were dead!" Davi yelled over the grunts and clashes of steel behind him.

"Long story," he responded. "Come on, Calis is upstairs."

Trystan caught sight of them. "Wren, earth, it's good to see you. Mira?"

"Alive." He grit his teeth. "Calis has her."

Another wave of Dreach-Sciene soldiers pushed into the stronghold, their remaining magic evening the fight with the weakened enemy soldiers who outnumbered them. When no more Dreach-Dhoun soldiers stood in the courtyard of Cullenspire, Trystan sucked in a breath.

Ramsey's head popped up among the Dreach-Sciene men guarding the gate.

Davi scanned those present. Many of their people continued to fight outside the stronghold. But his eyes found Lonara, Lorelai, Alixa, and Rissa.

Trystan seemed to be looking in the same direction. "Lonara, Briggs, with me." He sprinted for the stairs just as more soldiers in black poured from the upper floors.

Calis' unmistakable voice boomed throughout the hall. "Bring them to me!"

Davi fought with everything he had left, and he knew it still might not be enough. The Dreach-Dhoun soldiers pushed them back into the courtyard.

Calis and Briggs appeared as a line of enemy soldiers circled the Dreach-Sciene fighters who'd entered the fortress.

Calis' lip curled and Davi knew instantly. His father still had magic stored in his body.

He saw the flick of his father's hand an instant before chaos broke free and a spear of power was aimed directly for Rissa.

Davi leaped through the air, colliding with her hardened

body. The magic pierced his side, sending a searing pain into every part of him.

He screamed.

"Davi," Rissa yelled.

He couldn't hear anything that happened next, but he saw every motion.

Briggs held a ball of fire in one hand before throwing it toward Trystan. He hurled them in every direction, sending flames stretching across the courtyard.

A scream ripped through the air. Alixa. Briggs' magic pierced through her. The flame was easily put out, but the power behind it tore through her skin. A gouge opened in her side, letting the blood pour through as she collapsed to the ground.

Trystan tried to run for her, but Briggs' held him in place.

Lonara and Ramsey advanced on their fellow Tri-Gard member, but he waved every bit of their power away.

Briggs picked up a spear and everyone jumped into motion. Still Davi couldn't move as the pain held him captive. He couldn't roll out of the way as Briggs aimed the spear.

He couldn't even flinch as it sailed through the air with every bit of strength Briggs' magic held. Rissa, Lonara, and Ramsey threw their own power toward the spear to stop its momentum, but their power couldn't match Briggs'.

Davi met Rissa's eyes as she tried to stop it. To prevent the inevitable.

Sacrifice.

It was all they'd ever known.

And it seemed it was all they'd ever get.

I get to be in love with you forever—even after I've joined with the earth. Tomorrow could be the end of a lot of things, but not that. Never that.

He closed his eyes, wanting Rissa's words to be the only thing in his mind.

A body collapsed beside him and he snapped his eyes open, the world crashing back into focus around him.

"Davi." Rissa squeezed out from under him and rolled him over.

How had Briggs missed?

Then he felt the blood inching toward him and he shifted his eyes. Calis Bearne laid unmoving in front of him. His father.

The pain faded from Davi's limbs, traveling to his heart instead.

"Father?" He rolled to his side and scrambled to his knees. "Father."

The spear had torn straight through Calis Bearne's torso, the shaft leaving a hole behind. His wide eyes stared at the sky as if still in shock.

Ramsey and Lonara were locked in a magical duel with Briggs, but all Davi could see was his father who'd just given his life to save him.

He had proven in the last moment of his life there was something more important to him than power.

Rissa put a hand on Davi's back and he turned to clutch her to him, half in relief to still be with her and half in grief over a father he wasn't sure he was allowed to grieve.

She clutched him, her own sobs matching his.

"You're still here," she whispered.

A blast of power shook the stronghold, bringing dust down upon them.

Davi watched Lonara and Ramsey fight as Lorelai ran into the room and froze when she saw Calis.

"Oh my earth," she whispered. "Davi… who managed to…" She couldn't finish her question.

Davi glanced at his father once more. "He saved me."

She swallowed thickly.

"Lorelai," Ramsey called. "If you still have power, we could use some help."

Lorelai twisted her hand and sent a tunnel of air to slam Briggs up against the wall, pinning him there.

Ramsey looked to Lonara. "Now!"

They advanced as one, sending their magic straight into his chest.

"The Tri-Gard is broken," they chanted. "Take our pieces and make us new."

"No!" Briggs roared, expelling his power in every direction to save himself.

Lorelai made no sound as Brigg's last effort at freedom struck her in the chest, cutting off all air. She fell back, clutching at her neck, her skin turning ashen, before collapsing to the side.

Briggs' faced seemed to grow even older as he withered right in front of them.

Davi's jaw hung open as Lonara and Ramsey snapped their magic back and the husk that had once been Briggs Villard fell to the ground before exploding into dust.

All Trystan saw was blood.

He felt as if his own life-force drained out of him at the moment of Briggs' death.

Blood and death... but they'd won.

Shouting still rang out from the courtyard. Two armies were still locked in battle.

Trystan stood in shock. Around him, his friends suffered. The two remaining Tri-Gard members huddled over Lorelai who hadn't moved in too long.

Davi stared wide-eyed at the ceiling above with Rissa clutching his hands.

And Alixa. The thought of her spurred him into action. Her breath wheezed in her chest as her face twisted in pain.

Her leather armor had split open at the side to reveal a long gash. She squeezed her eyes shut.

"Alixa." Trystan pressed a hand over her wound to staunch the flow of blood. "Alixa, open your eyes."

When she obeyed, her gaze held a hazy quality as if she wasn't really seeing him.

"Stay with me, Alixa."

"Trystan," she whispered, a tear tracking down her face.

"No. You're going to be okay. Alixa..." He pressed his forehead to hers. "I can't do this without you. I won't."

She tried to lift her arm and failed.

"Trystan," Rissa whispered as she put a hand on his shoulder. "Is she...?"

"She will be fine," he snapped as he slid his arms underneath her.

As he hoisted her into the air, the ground shook.

"What's happening?" Davi yelled, finally sitting up.

Rocks rained down around them as the ground shifted under their feet.

"We have to get out of here," Ramsey yelled, lifting Lorelai. "Now."

Rissa helped Davi to his feet and Trystan followed them out. They passed bodies strewn along the halls.

Chaos reigned in the courtyard below as legionnaires and Dreach-Sciene soldiers alike scrambled to get distance from the crumbling walls.

Felled soldiers littered the land surrounding the fortress.

"Hold on, Alixa." Trystan grit his teeth and picked up speed.

Both armies fled as if the ground would swallow them whole. Horses ran wildly across the battlefield.

"We have to get them back to camp," Trystan yelled above the chaos. "To the healers."

Ramsey nodded and shifted Lorelai higher into his arms.

"Your Majesty." Wren's voice reached them.

Trystan glanced back to find Wren and a bedraggled Mira leading horses from the Cullenspire stables.

Trystan didn't pause before lifting Alixa onto the saddle of one of them and climbing on behind her. He kicked hard, not looking back to see if any of the others followed.

The horse cantered across the magic line, supposedly going from dead land to land thriving with power. But the tingling he'd grown used to didn't come.

His horse jumped to avoid a felled tree as the ground finally stopped shaking.

When he got to camp, a healer took Alixa from him and he was left to pace outside the tent. His people swarmed around him, searching for loved ones. Some mourned for the lost and he knew there'd be much time for that.

A few other horses galloped into camp. Rissa slid down and ran toward him before throwing her arms around his shoulders. "Is she okay?"

He only shrugged.

A sob wracked her body. "It's gone. All of it. Do you feel it?"

He held her at arm's length, imploring her to explain.

Her lip quivered. "Was this what it felt like before when the magic was drained?" She clutched at her chest. "I could feel it was happening, in here. The earth's agony." She shook her head. "What happened?"

Ramsey appeared and lowered Lorelai to the ground.

Rissa released another sob. "She's dead, isn't she? And Avery… I told you our sacrifices were worth it. That they were needed for our people, but…" She shook her head. "Avery was mother's guard, her friend. She helped raise us. Taught us. Protected us. And now she's gone."

Ramsey lifted his tortured eyes to Rissa's. "They're never gone. Everything Avery taught you is still inside of you. Alixa has not left us yet. And Lorelai…" He looked down into her face. "She's finally at peace."

"What happened?" Rissa asked, jumping toward her grandfather. "What did you do this time? Why is the magic gone?"

An arm wrapped around Rissa's waist as Davi yanked her back.

Lonara was the one who answered. "There must always be three. The Tri-Gard are the earth's balance. Without each one of us, magic cannot exist. We have light and we have earth, but Briggs Villard was the darkness all magic must have."

"You knew this would happen." Trystan was suddenly so sure. "From the moment we found you."

Ramsey brushed Lorelai's hair out of her still face and sighed. "Briggs had to be stopped."

"Why didn't you tell us?" Rissa ran a shaking hand over her blood-caked braid.

Lonara watched her sadly. "We are not protectors of man. It is not our job to give you power. We are stewards of the earth. Briggs would have used the power to destroy everything."

The healer emerged from the tent and beckoned Trystan forward.

"This girl was very lucky you got her here so quickly. I was able to close the wound before she lost too much blood."

"She's going to live?"

The healer nodded. "Now, will you let me look at that cut on your face?"

Trystan barely even remembered the injury after everything that happened. "Later. Please." He touched the place where crusted blood covered the cut.

A breath whooshed into Trystan's lungs as if he hadn't breathed in days when he pushed into the tent to find Alixa laying on a cot.

Kneeling beside her, he kissed the side of her face.

Her eyes slid open slowly. "Trystan."

"I thought I'd lost you."

"Didn't you know I'm more stubborn than that? You'll have to try much harder than an epic battle against a powerful sorcerer and evil king to get rid of me."

He released a relieved laugh and rest his forehead against her chest. "Earth, I love you."

A smile spread across her face. "So, we won. We're safe?"

He shook his head. "The magic is gone again."

"But we're safe?"

He nodded against her. She was right. His people were safe, for now. He'd have to deal with the remaining legions and send his army into Dreach-Dhoun to make sure the villagers were unharmed.

And then when the land started suffering for the lack of magic again, he'd find a way to save it.

As if she too was thinking of the suffering, her eyes squeezed shut. "My father. He's the only one of them left. I don't want to kill him, Trystan." She opened her eyes to search his face. "I once thought I did... but I think we've had enough killing."

He ran a hand over her dark hair. She would never stop amazing him. "You're right. He will remain our prisoner... but we have enough dead to bury."

Tears shone in her eyes and she nodded as she turned her face into his palm.

He leaned his forehead down against hers. "When I thought you were gone…" He sucked in a shuddering breath. "I didn't like how my future looked. I can't do this without you."

"Of course you can," she breathed.

He closed his eyes. "Fine, then I don't want to do it without you."

"What are you saying?"

"Alixa Eisner…" He opened his eyes to find her staring at him. Was that fear or awe he saw in her gaze? "Dreach-Sciene needs you. I need you. You almost gave everything for this kingdom and what I want from you isn't going to be easy."

"Trystan." Her eyes widened. "I'm going to need you to spell it out."

"Marry me," he whispered. "I know you only just started not to hate me. We still have so much to learn about each other. You think I'm a sexist asshole. I know you're a handful. But Alixa… you almost *died*. We almost didn't get our chance. My mother and father only had a few years together but that time defined their lives. Let's take our chance. I don't want to wait until it's too late."

A smile graced her lips and she placed one finger against Trystan's mouth, stilling his words. "You're rambling, my king." She trailed her finger down his chin to his neck where she could feel his heart beat strong.

He released a groan as she continued to consider him. "You're killing me here."

She laughed softly. "In the past few months, my family has betrayed me. I've washed my hands in blood. Every part of my life has crashed down around me. And then you came like a knight in friggin' armor. My king. You saved me. You saved the kingdom. I don't want to exist in this life without you."

"Yes?" He asked tentatively.

She nodded. "Yes."

Trystan grabbed her face between his hands and kissed her. Magic may be gone, but they'd survive just as they had before.

Shouting reached them from outside.

Trystan stood with, unable to wipe the grin from his face. "The army is returning. They'll be frightened and exhausted. I'll be right back. I promise."

She nodded, matching his smile. "Go be king."

He found everyone within sight hovering over Lorelai.

A faint buzzing traveled over his skin. *Magic.*

When he pushed his way through the crowd, he found a mass of weeping and astounded people. At the center of them was Lorelai sitting up and staring ahead with wide eyes.

Rissa lunged for her, gripping her shoulders in a hug.

"It's back," Davi said to no one in particular.

Lonara and Ramsey spoke in hurried tones.

Rissa released Lorelai and glanced down, her mouth opening and shutting rapidly. Marked onto the skin of Lorelai's forearm was a symbol. Trystan has seen it before in the mountains of Isenore when it had defined Briggs Villard.

The sigil of the third Tri-Gard member.

"The earth chose a new steward," Lonara said.

Trystan scanned the camp where soldiers were making their way back from the battlefield. He breathed in. Dreach-Sciene was going to move on just as he'd already behung to. They were going to create a new world.

A flash of blonde hair bolted past Trystan as Anna tore through camp with a cry on her lips. Wren had barely dismounted from his horse before she threw herself at him.

She sobbed loudly.

Wren squeezed her tightly. "Where's mother?"

Anna cried hard before finally shaking her head.

Wren's eyes shuttered with sadness and Trystan couldn't make himself look away, feeling guilty for the brief moment of joy he'd experienced with Alixa. Each of them had been touched by loss.

Mira took Anna from Wren's arms and Wren walked toward Trystan. "Your Majesty." He blew out a breath and ran a shaky hand through his hair. "Thank you for coming to protect Isenore."

Trystan met his gaze, turning from newly engaged man to determined king. "I am not only king of Aldorwood and Sona. Isenore is a part of Dreach-Sciene. I only wish we had come sooner. The palace was under siege."

"I know. I heard many of Calis' plans while in Cullenspire with him."

"How did you survive the initial attack when others didn't?"

Wren smiled but the gesture didn't reach his eyes. "After the last battle at Cullenspire, my father went to work preparing the stronghold should it ever face war again. Tunnels. Hidden rooms. Places where the stone opened to the earth. My father always had faith the Renaulds would recover the magic."

Trystan's eyes widened. "So you've just been hiding?"

"Calis found Mira only a few days back. After we got my mother and Anna through the tunnels, we started having a little fun creating havoc for the legions stationed inside the fortress."

Trystan reached out and gripped his shoulder. "We are in your debt. I am sorry for all you and Mira have lost."

"You can never lose what you keep in here." Wren pressed a hand against his chest.

Another man ran toward them, skidding to a halt to avoid a collision with Wren. Rion stared as if not quite believing his friend stood in front of him. Slowly, a grin spread across his face.

Trystan gave wren's shoulder a final squeeze and left the two to their reunion as he joined Davi. A man he'd never seen before hovered at the tree line before making a straight line for them.

"General Mack." Davi grinned. "You have our eternal gratitude." The two men shook hands.

Trystan joined them.

"General." Davi clapped Trystan on the shoulder. "Let me introduce you to the king."

The man's eyes widened and he fumbled through a bow.

The Dreach-Dhoun troops who'd turned against their king changed the tide of the war. Trystan eyed him. "Do not bow to me, General. Not here. Not when you have saved so many of my people." Trystan bent at the waist. "We owe you everything."

The general cleared his throat. "Sire, Dreach-Dhoun suffers. Calis Bearne tore our kingdom apart and now we find ourselves with no direction. We have many across the border who are still being held. The prince told me you are a king who will build a better world. We need a leader."

Trystan hated the next words he spoke because he didn't want to think of his best friend leaving him. But there was only one person who could rebuild that kingdom. "You have a leader. Davion Bearne is the rightful heir to your throne."

General Mack grinned. "My thoughts exactly, sire. Most across the border will follow him."

Davi shook his head. "I'm sorry, your Majesty. General, I am no king. I have lived my life as a common man, not a prince. There is one better to lead." He paused. "Dreach-Dhoun and Dreach-Sciene were split centuries ago by sorcerers who lusted for power. As long as it exists as two kingdoms, the people will never see themselves as one. Maybe it's time to cease the endless wars for good."

General Mack smiled proudly. "A new world?"

"Peace."

Trystan peered over his shoulder at the new Tri-Gard

member. Would they help him? They had a lot of work ahead of them, a lot of struggles.

And every bit of it was worth it if his people had the peace they deserved. Could he rule two kingdoms?

No. That was the simple answer.

But they weren't asking him to do that. He wouldn't be king of Dreach-Sciene and Dreach-Dhoun.

"Dreach," he said, reverence tinging his tone. "We are one people."

General Mack bowed once more. "I must return to my camp. They need me. Goodbye for now… my king."

Trystan watched him go and rubbed his eyes in exhaustion. "I need to speak to all those who've returned."

Davi shook his head. "There will be time for speeches and king duties later. Right now, you look as if you might fall where you stand."

Trystan sighed and let Davi lead him back to Alixa's tent. Rissa sat at her side.

Trystan dropped onto the end of the cot and put his head in his hands. His exhaled in exhaustion as the day's events crashed over him.

They'd done it, but they'd lost too much along the way.

Their youth and innocence.

Friends and loved ones. Edric. Avery. Marcus Renauld.

Their hands had been stained with blood.

"Our quest is finally over," he whispered.

Rissa leaned forward to grip his arm. "Calis hadn't planned for this. He manipulated us into war and we're finally free. No more ploys or secret plots. His game has ended."

Davi's eyes darkened at the mention of his father.

Trystan met their swirling depths. "I'm sorry for your father's death."

Because he was. Calis' death was what they'd hoped for. He was trying to destroy them. But in the end, he wasn't the dark king. In his final moments, he'd only been a father protecting his son.

Davi wiped away a tear. "Thank you for saying that. For… understanding."

Rissa stood and walked around the bed so she could wrap her arms around Davi. "You were his one weakness, Dav."

Davi rested his chin on her head. "No. Ri, I've been telling you this entire time, emotion isn't a weakness. When you cry, you're showing the world your strength. When you love someone, you're showing yourself your strength. I think the moment my father decided not to let me die was when he finally became strong."

Trystan closed his eyes, letting his friend's words sink into his mind. Calis Bearne commanded armies, tormented towns. He had a Tri-Gard member to do his bidding. But he'd lived his life in fear of losing himself. He sent his son away and had his sister executed.

For the first time, Trystan saw the dark king as he really was.

And that's when he realized what he should have known all along.

Dreach-Sciene was always going to win this war. His people loved their kingdom and they loved each other. They were stronger than any legion of well-trained, emotionless soldiers.

Because they didn't fight out of fear.

"Thanks, Dav."

"What for?" Davi asked.

"For helping me learn how to be king."

"Truwa." Davi held out his hand. "Brathair."

Trystan had never truly understood what those words would mean to him one day. Now, they were everything.

He gripped Davi's hand and met Rissa's glassy gaze. "Trust." His eyes shifted to Alixa as if the phrase now encompassed all four of them. "Brother."

EPILOGUE

"Trystan, I have something to say to you…"

Rissa shook her head. No, that sounded wrong.

"Brother, you know I love you, but…"

Her voice rang foreign in her ears as she paced from one end of the room to the other.

He wasn't going to be okay with this. With her request. Would he agree to it?

Her heavy steps echoed off the stone floor, and she flattened her palms against the lace bodice of the gown they'd stuffed her in.

She couldn't breathe.

In. Out.

It was too tight. Her fingers clutched at her chest. How was she supposed to get through this day if she couldn't breathe?

She stopped near her bed and sat down. When she tried to lean forward to put her head in her hands, the corset squeezed so hard she worried her eyes would pop right out of her head.

Her bright hair, the color of a good wine, had been arranged in spirals that now fell over one shoulder.

The door to her room opened, but she couldn't look up.

"Rissa." Willow rushed toward her and kneeled.

"Is she okay?" Alixa asked, entering the room.

Willow took Rissa's hands between her own. "Princess, calm down. You're okay."

Rissa snapped her eyes to the porcelain face in front of her and sucked in a breath. "I'm okay."

"Of course you are." Alixa crossed her arms over her chest. "We're all okay."

That was a lie and each girl in the room knew it. The war was over, but the earth never forgot. The scars would live on long after those involved ceased to be. And the images… Rissa glanced down at her hands.

She hadn't been able to make herself use her magic in the months since the final fight. Life was beginning anew for the people of Dreach, no longer split into two kingdoms. Yet, each night, the fight returned.

She saw it in Davion as well.

It was going to take a while.

But this was a start. This day. This new world. She was getting the one thing she'd ever wanted in life.

Alixa stared down at her. "Ri, you don't have to speak. Blink once if you want to go through with this and twice if you need me to 'take care' of Davion for you."

A laugh broke free of Rissa.

Willow threw a scowl over her shoulder. "You'd kill Davi just so Rissa doesn't have to marry him."

Rissa bit her lip to hide her grin.

Alixa shrugged. "I've never liked him much."

Willow scrunched her brow as if she thought Alixa would really do it.

Rissa squeezed Willow's hand. "Relax. I'm only considering it." Then she blinked twice. Hard.

Alixa couldn't control her laughter as it rolled through her and Rissa was grateful for the distraction.

Maybe Alixa had been right. Maybe they all were okay.

"Knock knock," Lonara called from the doorway.

Lorelai followed her in.

The Tri-Gard had been busy dealing with the final threads of Bearne power in what had been Dreach-Dhoun. They'd made the journey to the palace the week before.

Rissa's chest loosened, but then she remembered the request she was going to make of Trystan. It meant being even farther from these women.

She stood and Lonara stepped forward to wrap her in a hug. "Your mother would be so proud."

Rissa laughed roughly. "We've just saved two kingdoms and she'd be proud of me for getting married?"

Lona leaned back. "No, she'd be proud of you for being you. Rissa, your worth isn't wrapped up in your skill with a bow or the tenelach. Marissa would be proud of this." She pressed her hand over Rissa's heart.

A tear tracked down Rissa's face. How could she believe Lonara's words? She'd done so much wrong. Killed so many people. Almost lost herself.

Lorelai met her eyes in understanding. "You are good."

Rissa's tears fell faster as she thought of her first training session with Lorelai when she'd uttered those words. *I want to be good.*

She nodded and sniffed before releasing Lonara.

"It's time."

The women surrounded her in support as they walked toward the great hall. Ramsey met them at the door.

One by one, the women filed through. A single violin lifted its song to the rafters.

Rissa wiped her thumbs under her eyes and slid her arm through her grandfather's. She'd never seen him looking more regal in black trousers and a black jacket with his Tri-Gard symbol emblazoned on the lapel.

He breathed deeply, his eyes glassing over as he watched her. "I never thought I'd have a place in your life. I only wish your mother could as well."

She squeezed his arm and prepared to follow the others into the cavernous room. She couldn't voice her own wishes without breaking down. As a young girl, she'd known she'd have to marry a man of her father's choosing.

She almost did.

He'd walk her down the aisle and give her away to someone who would then be tied to the kingdom. That was the only hope.

But she liked to think if he were still alive, he'd have eventually seen Davion as the only choice. A prince who no longer had a kingdom. An orphan who had been no orphan.

A Renauld who didn't bear the Renauld name.

Because he was one of them.

Her eyes found him at the end of the aisle, waiting for her as if he'd been right there her entire life. Trystan stood at his side like he was always meant to.

With her grandfather giving her strength, she stepped forward.

MUSIC DRIFTED out of every part of the palace as the kingdom danced and feasted.

Rissa peered over her shoulder once more before ducking around the corner and escaping the commotion.

She pushed through the door to the walled garden that had been her sanctuary even when it failed to thrive.

The moment she stepped into it, magic buzzed along her skin. Her feet took her to the familiar tree and she sank to the ground, unconcerned about dirtying her white dress.

She let the power flow into her, but released none of it. She hadn't been able to let it free without flashes of the battle returning to her.

But there, in that place, she wanted nothing else.

Crossing her legs in front of her, she concentrated on the grass surrounding her. A moment later, yellow flowers shone bright in the darkness of the night.

A smile crept across her face, and she breathed in the scents. The flowers weren't real, but they still gave a sense of peace.

She leaned forward to run her hands along the smooth bark of the tree. How was she supposed to say goodbye?

Footsteps alerted her to someone else's presence, and she knew who it was without turning.

"Ri." The voice grew closer. "Rissa, what are you doing?"

She smiled and laid back to watch the stars shining overhead. "Just thinking of the man my family made me marry."

The day she'd realized she loved Davi under that tree felt like a lifetime ago. She'd only just found out about her impending marriage to Royce Eisner.

Davi lowered himself to the ground beside her. "Yeah? Is he a horrible brute?"

"The worst." She turned onto her side. "He abandoned

everyone at our wedding ball to meet some girl in the garden. Terribly rude of him."

Davi turned his head and grinned. "I'm really glad you aren't my sister."

A laugh burst out of her. "Don't make me laugh. It's already hard enough to breathe in this dress."

"I can help you with that."

He reached over to play with the laces on her dress, and she swatted his hand away. "I am a princess, good sir."

"Well, I am a prince."

"Oh good. I wouldn't be seen with you any other way."

He rolled toward her and pinned her to the ground. "We have guests inside the palace."

She shrugged. "That's why we gave them so much wine."

"Are you saying you got the entire palace drunk so you could take advantage of me?" He smirked.

She laughed.

A third voice entered their peace. "Not looking. Not looking. Ow!"

Rissa jerked her head toward the sound. Trystan held a hand over his eyes and had just tripped over a bench.

Davi rolled off her, waves of laughter vibrating through him. "Trystan, you can open your eyes."

"No," he said. "No way. I know you guys have to kiss and stuff, but I don't want to see it. Not my sister."

Rissa climbed to her feet and crossed to him before pulling his hand away from his eyes. "See. No kissing. Yet."

A grimace flashed across his face, and she laughed.

"You two left me at that ball," he said. "I hate these things."

Rissa smirked. "I'm sorry we left you with the ice queen." She laughed at their old nickname for Alixa.

"She still refuses to set a wedding date?" Davi asked.

Trystan sighed. "She won't talk to me about it. Until today she's been too sick and irritable to leave her rooms. She says it's all my fault she's sick, whatever that means."

Rissa bit back a smile. "You are adorably oblivious, brother."

Davi and Trystan exchanged a confused look.

"Ri," Davi said gently. "What's wrong with Alixa?"

"Other than the fact that she's engaged to Trystan?" She toyed with them. "It's not my place to tell you if you aren't smart enough to figure it out."

"Come on, Rissa." Trystan met her gaze pleadingly. "Help me out. Alixa is… difficult."

"She's not difficult, she's pregnant." Rissa slapped a hand over her mouth.

Trystan stumbled back. "Preg-" He shook his head. "But… we… she can't be pregnant."

"Do I need to explain how these things work?" Rissa asked.

Davi grinned. "Seems like Trystan knows very well how they work."

Rissa smacked his arm before pinning her brother with an unforgiving stare. "If you tell her you know before she's ready to tell you herself… she won't be the only lady around here who wants to kick you right where it hurts most."

"I'm going to make that woman queen," Trystan said as if affirming himself. Awe coated his words. "And I'm going to be a…father?"

"Yes you are." Davi laughed.

Rissa met Davi's eye in silent communication. It was time. He nodded. Trystan's life was changing just as theirs was.

"Brother," she started. "Davi and I have made a decision. We can't stay in the palace. Not anymore."

Trystan glanced from Rissa to Davi, still not quite recovered from his news. "You're going to Sona, aren't you?"

Rissa nodded. "It was untouched by the war, but many of the refugees have decided to stay there. Lady Destan says she could use our help. It's a fresh start for us and we're needed."

Trystan swung an arm over her shoulders and pulled her to him. "I understand."

"You do?" His shirt muffled her words.

"I do."

Davi blew out a breath. "Thank the earth. I was worried you'd give me some lecture about being your second."

Trystan reached out with his free hand and clamped it on Davi's shoulder. "Your duty is no longer to me, Dav. Wren can handle being my second for now since he's not returning to Isenore. But you..." He looked to Rissa. "It's time you had something other than duty."

Davi placed his hand over Trystan's.

The last time they were in that place, Rissa had thought it couldn't be just the three of them forever.

Now, as she stood wedged between them, she knew she'd been wrong.

If this war taught them one thing it was no matter where they were, who they were, what they did they'd always find each other.

The Tri-Gard's power lay in their connection by magic.

The Renauld's power lay in their connection by love.

And Rissa didn't know which held more strength.

ABOUT M. LYNN

M. Lynn has a brain that won't seem to quiet down, forcing her into many different genres to suit her various sides. Under the name Michelle Lynn, she writes romance and dystopian as well as upcoming fantasies. Running on Diet Coke and toddler hugs, she sleeps little - not due to overworking or important tasks - but only because she refuses to come back from the worlds in the books she reads. Reading, writing, aunting … repeat.

See more from M. Lynn
www.michellelynnauthor.com

ALSO BY M. LYNN

FANTASY AND FAIRYTALES

Golden Curse

Golden Chains

Golden Crown

Glass Kingdom

Glass Princess

Noble Thief

Cursed Beauty

THE HIDDEN WARRIOR

Dragon Rising

Dragon Rebellion

QUEENS OF THE FAE

Fae's Deception

Fae's Defiance

Fae's Destruction

Fae's Prisoner

Fae's Power

Fae's Promise

LEGACY OF LIGHT

A War for Magic

A War for Truth

A War for Love

ABOUT MICHELLE BRYAN

Michelle Bryan lives in Nova Scotia, Canada, with her three favorite guys; her husband, her son and her crazy fur baby. Besides her family, her other passions in life consist of chocolate, coffee and writing. When she is not busy being a chocolate store manager or spending the day at her computer, she can be found with her nose stuck in any sort of apocalypse book.

See more from Michelle Bryan
https://www.michellebryanauthor.com

ALSO BY MICHELLE BRYAN

THE CRIMSON LEGACY TRILOGY

Crimson Legacy

Scarlet Oath

Blood Destiny

The Waystation - a Crimson Legacy novella

THE BIXBY SERIES

Grand Escape (Strain of Resistance Prequel)

Strain of Resistance

Strain of Defiance

Strain of Vengeance

THE LEGACY OF LIGHT SERIES

A War For Magic

A War For Truth

A War For Love

POWER OF FAE SERIES

The Lost Link

The Lost Magic

The Lost Prince

STANDALONE

Clash of Queens

www.ingramcontent.com/pod-product-compliance
Lightning Source LLC
Chambersburg PA
CBHW030518310726
48979CB00010B/1716/J
9781970052831